WITHDRAWN

D1016688

THE LAST WEYNFELDT

MARTIN SUTER

TRANSLATED BY
STEPH MORRIS

NEW VESSEL PRESS
NEW YORK

THE LAST WEYNFELDT

New Vessel Press

www.newvesselpress.com

First published in German in 2008 as *Der letzte Weynfeldt*
Copyright © 2008 Diogenes Verlag AG Zürich
Translation Copyright © 2016 Stephen Morris

Inside cover image, *Femme nue devant une salamandre*,
by Félix Vallotton, 1900, PD-US.

The translation of this work was supported by the
Swiss Arts Council Pro Helvetia.

swiss arts council
prohelvetia

Library of Congress Cataloging-in-Publication Data
Suter, Martin
[Der letzte Weynfeldt. English]
The Last Weynfeldt/ Martin Suter; translation by Steph Morris.
p. cm.
ISBN 978-1-939931-27-6
Library of Congress Control Number 2015935266
    I. Switzerland — Fiction

THE LAST WEYNFELDT

1

DON'T DO IT, HE WANTED TO SAY. HE COULDN'T.

Adrian Weynfeldt fixed his gaze on the woman's pale, freckled fists clamped to the wrought-iron balustrade, knuckles glowing white. He didn't want to risk looking her in the eyes; she had chosen him as her witness, and he hoped that jumping without eye contact would be too impersonal for her.

Her bare feet poked through the gap between the balustrade and the balcony. Every toenail was painted a different color. He had noticed it last night. Red, yellow, green, blue and violet on the right foot; the same colors in reverse on the left, meaning that the two middle nails both gleamed green.

She hadn't extended the motif to her fingernails. They were lacquered with clear varnish, painted white where they protruded beyond the fingertip. They weren't actually visible this second, but he remembered them. Weynfeldt was a visual person.

The knuckles turned from white back to pink; she had loosened her grip. "It's only thirty feet," he said quickly. "You might survive, but it wouldn't be much fun."

The knuckles went whiter again. Weynfeldt shifted his left foot forward, level with his right, then inched the right a half step farther.

"Stay right where you are!" the woman said.

What was her name? Gabriela? He couldn't remember; he had no memory for names. "Sure. But if I stay where I am, so must you."

She didn't say anything, but her knuckles remained white.

The lights were usually on all day in the office building across the street, with its neoclassical façade. Today was Sunday, still early in the morning. There were no people on the street; the streetcars which normally went by were few and far between, and only occasionally could a car be heard. Weynfeldt shuddered at the thought of the scene taking place on a weekday. The woman was wearing a black bra and matching black panties. At least he hoped she was still wearing the panties; the green canvas sheet which hung from the balustrade to provide privacy now obscured his view of her below the waist. And when he woke she had already been standing outside.

He wasn't sure what had woken him—not a noise, perhaps the unfamiliar perfume. He had lain there a while, eyes closed, trying to remember her name; her face he could see.

A little leaner maybe, less determined, more disillusioned. But the same pale, freckled skin, the same slightly slanted green eyes, the same red hair and, above all, the same mouth, the upper lip almost the same shape as the lower.

It was the face he'd been trying both to forget and to remember for years.

Adrian Weynfeldt had spent this Saturday night as he

spent every Saturday night: in the company of his older friends. He had two circles. One was made up of people fifteen or more years younger than him. Among them he was seen as an exotic original, someone you could confide in, but also make fun of sometimes, who would discreetly pay the check in a restaurant, and help out occasionally when you had financial difficulties. They treated him with studied nonchalance as one of their own, but secretly basked in the glow of his name and his money. In their company he could visit clubs and bars he would have felt too old for otherwise.

His other group of friends was composed of people who had known his parents, or at least moved in their circles. They were all over sixty, some over seventy; a couple had already reached eighty. And yet they all belonged to his generation. Adrian Weynfeldt was born late to a couple who had remained childless for many years. His mother was forty-four when he came into the world; she had died nearly five years ago, shortly before reaching ninety-five, when Weynfeldt was fifty.

Adrian Weynfeldt had no friends his own age.

Last night he had been with his elderly friends, in the Alte Färberei, a traditional restaurant in a guildhall in the old town, only ten minutes by foot from his apartment. Dr. Widler had been there, his mother's doctor, increasingly listless in recent months, several sizes thinner and threatening to vanish inside his tailored suits— his wife Mereth all the more lively, her makeup, hair, and clothes impeccable as ever. And as ever, she took delight in contrasting her china-doll image with colorful language and vulgar remarks.

Remo Kalt joined them, Weynfeldt's recently widowed cousin on his mother's side, in his mid-seventies, wearing a black three-piece suit with a gold pocket-watch and a neat Thomas Mann moustache, as if he'd come from a portrait sitting with Ferdinand Hodler. Remo Kalt was an asset manager; he had looked after Weynfeldt's parents' capital and continued to manage it for their son. Adrian could easily have taken this over, but hadn't had the heart to deprive Kalt of his last remaining client. There wasn't much you could get wrong; these were not immense assets, though certainly solid, and conservatively invested for the long term.

They had ordered the *Berner Platte*, a shared meat dish featured on the menu throughout the winter. Dr. Widler had hardly touched a thing. His wife, a woman who had moved from willowy via slender to gaunt over the years, had taken two servings of everything – bacon, tongue, blood sausage, smoked ham. Kalt had kept pace. Weynfeldt had eaten like a man still vaguely concerned about his figure.

The evening was pleasant yet forced. Forced because Mereth Widler's provocative remarks had long begun to wear thin, and because everyone around the table knew this was one of the last times her husband would sit at it.

The Widlers left early, Weynfeldt drank one more for the road with Remo Kalt, and when shortly afterward they ran out of conversation, they ordered Kalt a taxi.

Weynfeldt waited with him at the entrance. The night was much too mild for February; it felt like spring. The sky was clear, and the moon rising high over the old town's steep roofs was almost full. The street was empty except for an elderly woman with an energetic spitz on a leash. They watched in silence: powerless, she let her dog walk her, stopping every time he wanted to sniff something, rushing to catch up when he wanted to move on, change direction, or cross the road.

At last headlight beams shone around the corner of the road, followed by a slowly-approaching taxi which stopped in front of them. They parted with a formal handshake, and Weynfeldt watched the taxi drive away, its sign switched off now, its brake lights red as it halted at the junction with the main road.

His route home included a stretch of the river and La Rivière, a bar he found it hard to pass at this time of night; it was nearly eleven p.m. He went in for a drink, as he so often did on the Saturday nights he spent with his elderly friends.

Two or three years ago La Rivière had been a run-down dessert café. Then it was taken over by one of the city's many gastronomic entrepreneurs, who had turned it into an American-style cocktail bar. Two barkeepers in eggshell-colored dinner jackets mixed martinis, manhattans, daiquiris and margaritas, served in sleek glasses. On Saturday nights a trio played smooth jazz classics at a subdued volume.

It was still half empty, but that would change in the next fifteen minutes as the cinemas emptied. Weynfeldt sat in his usual place at the bar: the first bar stool from the wall. From there he could observe what was going on, and never had to deal with more than one neighbor. The barman knew him and brought him a martini. Weynfeldt would probably just eat the olive; he was a very moderate drinker.

Nor did he indulge in any other excesses. When he dropped by a bar on the way home, he wasn't hunting for sex, warmth, a little company, like most single men. He did not suffer from loneliness. Quite the opposite: he liked solitude. When he did sometimes go in search of company, it was in a conscious effort to moderate his loner tendencies.

As for sexual needs, ever since a particular episode— or blow—earlier in his life, they had played an ever more insignificant role in Adrian Weynfeldt's life.

And so the course of events that evening was highly untypical.

No sooner had the barman served him his martini than a woman entered the bar, put her coat and handbag on the bar stool beside Weynfeldt, sat on the next one over and ordered a gin fizz. She was wearing a green silk Chinese blouse, white arms extending from its short, close sleeves, a tight black skirt and high heels a similar shade of green to the blouse. Her long red hair was tied up, secured with an imitation tortoiseshell clasp to free her neck, which the blouse's high collar circled loosely.

She had not yet looked at him, but when the barman placed her drink in front of her, she took the glass and raised it to Weynfeldt briefly. She didn't wait for him to raise his glass and return the gesture. But once she had taken a drink, half the cocktail in one gulp, she turned to him and smiled.

It was a smile Weynfeldt knew.

He was so startled he put the glass to his lips and poured the contents down his throat. The woman who had smiled at him resembled Daphne so closely it seemed impossible that instead of speaking English—Daphne's melodic Welsh-inflected English—she now greeted him with the highly Swiss *Pröschtli*, no trace of an English accent. Now she had spoken, the spell was broken, and he was no longer afraid he was seeing Daphne's ghost. Above all because the gin fizz was clearly not her first alcoholic drink of the evening and she spoke with a slight drawl. Daphne hadn't drunk at all.

"Your olive," she said. "If you don't want it, I'll take it off your hands."

Weynfeldt passed his empty glass to her. She fished the cocktail pick out and put the olive in her mouth. While she ate, she appraised him blatantly, spitting the stone into her palm and dropping it in Weynfeldt's empty glass. Then she finished her drink. "Lorena," she said.

"Adrian Weynfeldt," he replied. He was not someone who started with first names at a first meeting.

Lorena reached into her handbag, a well-worn, unbranded black leather number, and retrieved a battered wallet. She placed it on the bar, counted her money, half out loud, put the money back in her wallet, and her wallet back in her handbag. "What does a gin fizz cost?" she asked the barman.

"Eighteen francs," he replied.

"Then I've got enough for three."

"If you have no objection," Weynfeldt said, "then I can take care of the drinks."

"No objection, but I still don't want to drink more than I could pay for myself. An old single girls' rule."

"Very sensible."

"If it's sensible I'll have to think twice. 'Sensible' makes you look older. Will you order me another?"

Weynfeldt ordered a gin fizz.

"And a martini for the gentleman."

The barman looked to Weynfeldt. He shrugged his shoulders and nodded.

"You don't have to drink it," Lorena said. "It's okay for men to be sensible."

"It doesn't make us look older?"

"You're already old."

Weynfeldt kept Lorena company for four gin fizzes, his martini remaining untouched at his elbow. When she asked for a fifth, he insisted on accompanying her home, and ordered a taxi.

"Where are we going?" the driver asked Weynfeldt.

"Where are we going?" Weynfeldt asked Lorena.

"How should I know?" she replied.

"You don't know where you live?"

"I don't know where you live," she said, her eyelids drooping.

And so for the first time in more years than he could remember, Adrian Weynfeldt returned home after midnight in female company. The security people would be amused when they came to watch the videos.

He opened the heavy door to the building, led Lorena in, and closed it behind him, keeping an eye on his guest, who seemed in danger of losing her balance at any moment. He took his magnetic ID card out of his wallet, pushed it into the slot next to the inner security door, led Lorena to the elevator, controlled by the same card, and rode to the third floor.

Weynfeldt's apartment was in a nineteenth-century building in the center of Zurich's financial district. He had inherited the building from his parents. While they were still alive a bank had taken out a lease on the ground floor, using three of the remaining four floors for their offices. The bank's security measures were sometimes tiresome, but were ultimately in Weynfeldt's interest as his apartment held a valuable collection of late nineteenth- and early twentieth-century Swiss art.

He ignored the bank's repeated advances, luring him with suggestions of apartments in quieter districts so they could take over his floor too. Apart from his time at boarding school and his year in London, he had lived his entire life in this space. As a child he had slept in a room close to his parents; as he grew older he had moved farther toward the periphery of the apartment, which extended over five thousand square feet. While he was at university the servants' quarters were converted into a separate apartment for him, and the housekeeper moved into one of the three guest rooms. Another guest room was soon occupied by the nurses looking after Weynfeldt's father, who was homebound by the age of seventy-five.

His mother survived his father by nearly twenty years, which she also spent in the apartment, receiving round-the-clock care herself for the last four. Soon after her death Weynfeldt commissioned an architect from his circle of younger friends to refurbish the rooms from scratch. The old-fashioned bathrooms were transformed into superbly designed facilities, with sandblasted glass, darkened chrome and gray granite; the creaking walnut parquet was replaced with light oak; the walls and plasterwork were painted white or gray and the whole apartment was freed of the mustiness accumulated over the last hundred years.

Aside from a few special pieces, Weynfeldt put the furniture in storage and filled the rooms with his growing collection of 1920s-50s Swiss designer furniture.

This was the apartment into which he ushered the somewhat tipsy Lorena, who dropped her coat and handbag on the polished floor of the vestibule and said, "Wow!"

She said it a few more times during their tour of the rooms. "Wow! Like a museum." And later, "Wow! You have all this to yourself?"

The inspection seemed to sober her up a little. In Weynfeldt's study, a large room with a floor-to-ceiling window opening onto the rear courtyard, also added during the refurbishment, she asked, "and here?"

"Here is where I work."

"What do you do?"

"I work for Murphy's. I'm an expert in Swiss art."

"What does that involve then?"

"Writing expert's reports, supervising auctions, producing catalogues, that sort of thing."

"Sounds boring."

"No, it's not."

"That's why you have all this art?"

"The other way round. The job is because of all the art."

"Is there anything to drink in this palace?"

"Only nonalcoholic."

"I don't believe you."

"What would you like then?"

"Whatever you're having."

"Lemon verbena tea, it is."

When he came back with the tray she had left the study. And wasn't in any of the sitting rooms. He finally found her in his bedroom. She was lying in her panties and bra on his bed, apparently asleep.

Weynfeldt went into the bathroom, took a shower and put on clean pajamas. As he did every night. He owned fourteen pairs of pajamas, all tailored by his shirtmaker, all with monograms: six light-blue ones for the even days, six blue-and-white striped for the odd days and two for Sundays—one of the small quirks he allowed himself, providing his life with a little luxury and a little regularity. He believed that regularity prolonged life.

There was also the opposing theory: regularity makes each day indistinguishable, and the more events and habits are repeated, the more the days resemble each other and the years too. Till your whole life feels like one single year.

Weynfeldt didn't believe this. If you do the same things more often, go to the same places and meet the same people, the differences become subtler each time. And if the differences are subtler then time passes unnoticed. Someone you see every month instead of every year never appears to age. And you never appear to age to them.

Repetition slows down the passage of time. Weynfeldt was absolutely convinced of this. Change might make life more eventful, but it undoubtedly made it shorter too.

He returned to his bedroom. Lorena was lying in the same position, on top of the duvet. He looked at her. She was very slim, a delicate build, almost too thin. Above her groin to the right was a small tattoo, perhaps a Chinese character. Her belly button was pierced, and it sparkled—a cut stone, glittering as Weynfeldt walked to the wardrobe to fetch another duvet. He lay down next to Lorena and covered them both.

"What about fucking?" she asked, drowsy.

"Tomorrow," he said. "If you still want to."

"Okay."

He turned the bedside lamp off.

She reached her hand out and let it fall on his chest, flat and lifeless. Her breathing soon became softer and regular.

Well done, Adrian, Weynfeldt thought, as he fell asleep.

Keep them talking. That was how they did it in the films Weynfeldt had seen, when police officers tried to stop people committing suicide. Or when mediators talked to kidnappers. Distracting them from carrying out their plan was half the battle. But he couldn't think of anything to say. Like those dreams when you need to run but can't move from the spot, he stood there, facing a woman about to kill herself, and said nothing.

Like the time nearly thirty years ago when Daphne had said, "I'm leaving now." He hadn't even been able to say *Please don't go*, or *No!* Not even the one syllable, *No*. And she'd wanted him to say something; he'd sensed that. She had stood there with her suitcase and given him the chance to stop her.

Daphne was an exchange student at his university. He'd met her at an art history seminar. Everyone had fallen for her; why she'd picked him he would never know. When she returned to England he went with her, defying his parents' objections—his father despairing, his mother enraged. They rented a small apartment in Chelsea and spent a year there, a year which grew happier in Weynfeldt's memory with every year that followed.

He had never really understood why it ended. An argument, a slight tear in the fabric, a case of unfounded jealousy; he couldn't reconstruct it, no matter how hard he tried. But he knew they'd still be together today if he'd managed to utter one single syllable.

He'd had to watch, speechless and immobile, as she left. Not resolute or angry, but despondent and hesitant. As if she were waiting till the last moment for him to stop her.

She had said she would have her things picked up in a few days. When they were still there a week later he started to get his hopes up. After ten days he called her parents. They told him that two days after she left him, she had been in a car crash. She had died on the spot.

Adrian saw the fists gripping the balustrade loosen their grip, the knuckles returning to the shade of the surrounding hands. *Don't do it*, he wanted to say, *Please,*

please don't do it. Instead he just stood there, sensed the indifference his face conveyed, as unable to control this as his speechlessness. It was as if the paralysis which had gripped his tongue had spread to his entire face. As if the skin and muscles had gone limp and taken on an expression of horribly blasé indifference.

"You don't give a fuck if I jump or not, do you?" she said.

Weynfeldt succeeded in raising his eyes and looking her in the face. Even now, in the unambiguous gray light of a Sunday morning, the similarity to Daphne was startling. This face held traces of resignation and lost illusions he had never seen in Daphne's, not even on the day it all ended. And yet it was as if they had known each other for thirty years.

"You don't give a fuck," she repeated.

Now he managed to shake his head.

"It'll be messy and bad for your reputation. And all the formalities with the police will be a drag of course. But other than that ..." she released one hand from the balustrade and raised it in a gesture of apathy.

He stood there helpless. Like a stuffed dummy, his mother would have said. Then he shook his head once more.

She let her hand fall, but didn't return it to the balustrade; she stretched it out behind her, and turned her face that way, as well, looking to the street below, leaning back, holding on with just one hand, like a trapeze artist receiving her applause. "Give me one reason not to let go. Just one reason."

He felt his eyes fill with tears, his numbed face creasing up. A noisy sob burst from his chest.

The woman turned back in surprise and looked at this man in his white pajamas, crying. Then she climbed back onto the balcony, led Adrian back to bed, put her arm around him, and burst into tears herself.

"Haven't you ever felt like that? That there's no point in it all? You don't know how you're going to get through the next day? You can't think of a single thing that doesn't depress you? You can't think of a single reason to carry on living, but lots of reasons to be dead? Have you really never had that?"

They were sitting in bed, the pillows shoved between their backs and the walls, a tray placed on the duvet, with reheated croissants, barely touched, soft glossy yellow butter, honey, and two empty cups with chocolate left around their rims, exhausted like a couple who have just had a big, dramatic argument that shook their relationship to its foundations.

Weynfeldt reflected. There were certainly days when he felt pretty gloomy, dwelt on dark thoughts and didn't feel like doing a thing. But his only response was to end the day early. Not his life. "Karl Lagerfeld once said, 'I try to categorize anything I experience which might be called depression as a bad mood.' Sounds good to me."

"If I had a life like Karl Lagerfeld or you I might be more attached to it!"

"What kind of life do you have then?"

"A shit life."

"Every life is worth living."

"What a load of crap."

"A few years ago I went traveling through Central America. In a village somewhere—I've forgotten the name—the car broke down, something to do with the carburetor. It was pouring rain. A small, muddy track led off the highway, leading to a couple of huts made out of rough planks and corrugated iron. While my driver was fiddling around under the hood I waited in the car. I had the window half open—it was hot and sticky. A couple passed by, very young, almost children really. The man walked ahead, carrying a new-born baby in a cloth. The woman followed, pale, tired but smiling. They turned down the track leading to the huts. Their shoes sank into the mud. Then I heard her say, 'Now our happiness is complete.'"

Lorena said nothing. When he looked at her, after a while, there were tears in her eyes again. He pulled three tissues out of the box and passed them to her.

When she had blown her nose, she said, "Stories like that are no comfort at all. Stories like that are the last straw." She got up, walked into the bathroom and stayed there a long time. He heard the toilet and the shower. When she emerged, she was wearing one of his dressing gowns, with the monogram A.S.W. It reached the floor, and she had rolled the sleeves up. "I have to go now."

"I'll come downstairs with you." He went into the bathroom, from there to his dressing room. When he returned to the bedroom, fifteen minutes later, she had gone and the bed was made. She was waiting in the vestibule, sitting in a tubular steel chair, her coat already on. She looked at him quizzically. "You put a tie on just to take the elevator?"

They said nothing on the way down. He opened the double security doors for her, then the heavy front door to the street. They stood for a moment on the sidewalk, slightly embarrassed. Weynfeldt took out his wallet and gave her his card. "In case."

"In case of what?"

"In case of whatever."

She looked at the card. "Aha, You have a PhD I see," she said, and put it in her handbag. "I'm afraid I don't have a card myself."

Weynfeldt wanted to ask for her telephone number, but he let it go.

She looked up at the gray sky. "The weather certainly wasn't worth staying alive for."

"Anything else?"

"What else then?"

He shrugged his shoulders. "There's always something worth staying alive for."

She stared at him intently. "Can you guarantee me that?"

"Guaranteed."

She hugged him with her free arm and gave him a kiss on the cheek. Then she smiled at him. "One day I'll do it."

"No," he said, "don't do it." Now he had managed to say the words.

"Lorena. You forgot my name: *Don't do it, Lorena.*"

She walked down the street. He watched, but she didn't look back.

2

ADRIAN WEYNFELDT COULD SEE THE QUAY FROM HIS office window, the jetties and the white passenger boats, the streetcars, most of them bedecked with flags for some reason, the backed up columns of traffic, and the continual stream of hurried pedestrians.

It was shortly before five; the rush hour had begun, but the insulated windows kept the street sounds out; the lively scene was like a TV image on mute. He had often wished he could work with the window open, but Murphy's was equipped with an air conditioning system which maintained room temperature and humidity at constant levels all year round to safeguard the valuable paintings and works of art held there.

On a day like today, however, Weynfeldt was more than happy to keep the window closed. It was neither warm nor cold, damp nor dry, clear nor cloudy: a depressingly average day. He wished something unusual would happen to make it memorable.

He had worked all day on the fall auction catalogue, *Swiss Art*, writing descriptions of the pieces, listing their provenance and exhibition history, researching the secondary literature and valuing the works. There was still time till the copy deadline, but he needed this time. He wasn't satisfied. The selection was too homogenous. He needed just one lot which would attract attention and perhaps fetch a record price. The best piece was a Hodler, a landscape, oil on canvas, showing a country road with telegraph poles. He had valued it at one hundred and fifty to two hundred thousand francs, and hoped for a hammer price of around three hundred thousand. Then he had the sleeping shepherdess by Segantini, a watercolor valued at sixty-eighty thousand. In this price range there was also the mountain landscape by Calame, a village idyll by Benjamin Vautier and some roses by Augusto Giacometti. After that came the oil paintings by less familiar names: Castan, Vallet, Fröhlicher, Zünd, Barraud. The remainder consisted of studies by the big names, Anker, Hodler, Vallotton, Amiet, Segantini, Giacometti and Pellegrini, drawings and watercolors at prices in the one and two thousand category. What he lacked was works in upper middle range, between one and two hundred thousand francs, and one or two "conversation pieces," as his assistant, Véronique, would put it: pictures and stories they could feed the press.

Véronique was sitting in the outer office, two computer screens in front of her; a square, black take-out box of Thai food beside her. Ever since the Thai place in the next block had opened she was constantly battling the temptation to pop down and get something. She went in secret when she could, hoping Weynfeldt wouldn't notice her absence. Not because he would object—he was an easygoing boss. But like all addicts, she didn't want to admit her addiction to herself.

Véronique was in her mid-thirties, with a round, heavily made-up, wrinkle-free face, framed by a blond bob, perhaps intended to make her face look longer and leaner. Her body was big and appeared shapeless thanks to the loose clothing she wore during this phase. Weynfeldt had experienced all her phases during the years they worked together; Véronique was a yo-yo woman. She starved herself as excessively as she ate. She was capable of passing through every BMI classification, from underweight to overweight, in a single year. The latter was more conducive to a good working atmosphere in Weynfeldt's opinion, but of course he would never say something like that out loud.

He had been embarrassed himself when he caught her returning earlier with her Thai snacks. He had come through his door to the outer office as she came through the main door. Her taste buds had been bored, she said, as she always said when an explanation couldn't be avoided. Weynfeldt didn't react, just took the Segantini catalogue from her immaculately tidy desk—his own was submerged in hopeless chaos—and retreated discreetly. He took in the aroma of ginger, coriander and lemongrass as he closed the door behind him and gave thanks for the opening of the Thai takeaway; the nearest food outlet before that had been a sausage grill.

Weynfeldt would have been lost without Véronique. He was a recognized specialist in Swiss art of the nineteenth and early twentieth centuries; he was frequently asked to write expert reports, and even the rival auction houses preferred to have important works in this field valued by him. When it came to the administration, organization and management side of his job, however, he was clueless. He was by nature an unsystematic and impractical person.

He had never learned to handle computers for instance. At first he hadn't wanted to; they hadn't suited his image of himself. Later, when he did want to learn, he had failed. And he was otherwise a quick learner. He had passed his degree with top marks, his PhD with summa cum laude. He spoke French, English, Spanish and Italian fluently—almost too authentically as far as some were concerned, and was currently learning Russian, which he didn't find difficult even at fifty-four. But he had never been able to make friends with computers.

This was the reason Véronique had two screens on her desk. Computers were an indispensable part of Weynfeldt's job. It was unimaginable that a Murphy's expert could not be contacted via e-mail, didn't use search engines for his research or keep up to date with current prices and trends using the various art-market websites. Véronique dealt with all of that. She printed out his mail and typed up the answers he wrote by hand at the bottom of each message. Very few people suspected that Weynfeldt was useless with computers.

Cell phones were yet to enter his life either. Each time Véronique tried to help him to make friends with them, he proved to be all thumbs. If she ever suspected him of deliberately feigning clumsiness to retain some vestige of freedom, she never let it show. Weynfeldt simply wasn't available when he was out and about; but he called Véronique at regular intervals, from the increasingly rare telephone booths or from restaurants, to keep himself in the picture. He did at least have an answering machine at home. He didn't know how it worked, but Frau Hauser, who managed his enormous apartment, did.

She had been his mother's housekeeper and was approaching eighty—but still fighting fit. Weynfeldt had only recently been able to persuade her to employ assistants to help with the cleaning and to take his washing to the laundry. Since then he met women of various nationalities and colors in his apartment, who were rarely able to maintain Frau Hauser's high standards for long and were swiftly and unceremoniously replaced—much to the annoyance of the bank's security department which was forced to put each new employee through the bank's complex security clearance procedure.

Frau Hauser was a very small, gaunt figure. Ever since Weynfeldt could remember, her hair had been white with a purple rinse. She entered the apartment every working day at seven a.m. on the dot, and left it at five p.m.—unless Weynfeldt was entertaining, in which case she served refreshments she had prepared herself, or, in the case of large-scale invitations, commanded the brigades of catering staff from the sidelines. She had taken over a former servants' room adjacent to the utility rooms, where she withdrew for short breaks or, if it got late, sometimes spent the night. She had a habit of complaining half out loud to herself, not with words, but by sighing, murmuring, moaning and the occasional "aha, aha, aha," as if something she had long predicted had finally transpired. Weynfeldt only ever heard this; he never knew what precisely had aroused Frau Hauser's displeasure since he avoided being in the same room as her, but he assumed each time that it related to his untidiness. No day passed without her mentioning his mother to him—what she had always said, always done, or was lucky not to be experiencing now.

He found it easier to get on with Véronique. Not only because she never referred to his mother, although she had known her personally; she never gave Adrian the feeling his disorganization and inability to deal with practical matters bothered her. Weynfeldt and Veronique respected each other enough to overlook each other's shortcomings.

Weynfeldt was seated on an office chair from his own collection, a comfortable leather armchair on a chrome-plated tubular steel base designed by Robert Haussmann in 1957. He leafed through the Segantini catalogue, unable to remember what he had been looking for. He paused when he came to *Sul balcone*. The painting showed a young girl in an indigo blouse and a long skirt. Her right hand on her hip, she leaned against the wooden balustrade of a balcony, her back to the wind-swept mountain village with its church tower, and the milky, translucent sky. She wore a white bonnet, her head bowed, thoughtful, gazing at nothing in particular. She was standing as Lorena had stood, he reflected, but on the other side of the balustrade.

Since that strange encounter it had not taken much to remind Weynfeldt of Lorena; much vaguer connections were enough: a female portrait without the slightest similarity, sometimes just an object, something Japanese because of her blouse, or a piece of furniture by Werner Max Hofer because she had sat on one of his chairs while she waited for him. Sometimes it took even less: similar weather to that Sunday morning, croissants, one of his white Sunday pajamas. And increasingly it took nothing at all to call up the image of Lorena—of Lorena or of Daphne.

That dramatic Sunday morning was now over two weeks ago. He should have asked Lorena for her phone number. Her address, at least.

He had made four extra visits to La Rivière since then, breaking his normal rhythm, staying each time for two martinis which he consumed according to the same ritual. For the best part of an hour the glass stood at his elbow untouched, then he fished the olive out with the cocktail pick, ate it slowly and placed the stone on the little saucer the barkeeper provided with every drink. That was his sign that the barkeeper could clear the glass, still full, and replace it with a fresh drink. Once, and once only, had the barman attempted to serve him a martini with two olives. Weynfeldt had placed one of them straight on the saucer without comment.

He had not been able to muster the courage to ask the barkeeper for news of Lorena. But he undoubtedly realized why Weynfeldt was suddenly here so often. If he knew anything he would have said.

The telephone rang, and Weynfeldt forced himself to let it ring twice, three times. If it was Lorena she shouldn't think he was sitting by the phone waiting for her to call.

But it wasn't Lorena. It was Klaus Baier, one of his parent's peers' children nearly a generation older than Weynfeldt. Baier's father had run a textile firm which did business with Weynfeldt & Co. The two fathers had remained friends long after both companies were taken over by healthier competitors. They had both been keen hunters, inviting each other to their respective hunting grounds, and traveling to East Africa on safari together in the 1950s.

The two sons had never had much contact. Initially because of the age difference, later because they had no mutual interests. While Adrian was focused on his passion, art, Klaus was interested only in money. Following his father's untimely death in 1962, Klaus Baier began making risky attempts to boost his inheritance. He became a daring speculator, someone with a good nose, who frequently gambled his entire wealth, and on more than one occasion lost everything except his assets of last resort.

These reserves included a few valuable pictures, the remains of the respectable collection of Swiss art his father had bequeathed him. A seascape in oil and two watercolors by Ferdinand Hodler, a portrait of a woman by Segantini, two floral still lives by Augusto Giacometti and a notable nude by Félix Vallotton.

This modest collection was later to bring them back into contact. Shortly after Adrian had completed his doctorate, Klaus called and asked him to value his pictures. It was the first job of Adrian's career and he went to great effort to come up with plausible figures. Like many people who speculate with money on a large scale, Klaus Baier was stingy when it came to small scale transactions, and Weynfeldt's payment was simply dinner. Adrian didn't care. Even then he was financially secure, and in the course of his research he had come into contact with Murphy's Swiss art expert at the time, who subsequently engaged Adrian as his assistant for a symbolic salary.

Baier and Weynfeldt had met for occasional lunches or dinners at irregular intervals ever since, the initiative usually coming from Baier, hoping to avail himself of a free valuation. He would ask Adrian the current market value of his pictures; if the information was favorable he would pay the check, if not he let Weynfeldt pay.

Baier's most secure asset was the small Hodler seascape. The artist's market value had risen steadily over the years with little fluctuation. The Augusto Giacometti was also a blue chip, which could safely be realized at any time. The riskiest item to speculate on was the Vallotton however. Although the artist's prices had seesawed over the years, an image such as *Femme nue devant une salamandre* was capable of achieving a sensational price, independent of the artist's current rating. *Nude Facing a Stove* was extremely well known, a bestseller as a poster, yet shrouded in mystery: no one knew who owned it. In all the monographs and exhibition catalogues—and it was frequently exhibited; this enhanced its value—its status was described simply as "private collection." If it suddenly came on the market it would cause a sensation. Adrian Weynfeldt consistently valued it at a realistic figure, but always added, "Under the hammer it could easily fetch double that."

Weynfeldt had soon grasped that Baier's interest in the value of his collection was purely hypothetical. He never dreamed for a second of selling a single piece. He just liked to know how much money he wasn't liquidizing.

So Weynfeldt was rendered speechless for a second when Baier asked him, "Would my Vallotton fit in your current auction, Adrian?"

After a short pause he answered, "Yes, perfectly."

3

His chair of choice was an armchair, its seat, back and arms upholstered with a rather sorry tapestry. The other couches and easy chairs in his living room were comfier, but all too low. Thanks to his arthritic leg he was unable to get out of them without assistance.

He had stationed a glass of port on the flattened lion's head decorating the left arm. On the right was a crystal ashtray, clean except for the inch-long cylinder of ash, still intact, from the Churchill he had clamped between his lips, his eyes screwed up. He had long-distance glasses on his nose, short-distance ones on his forehead.

Cigar smoke hung in the upper half of the room, immobile, caught by the beams from the two spotlights pointing at the picture on the easel. The Count Basie Big Band swung, barely audible, from an aging stereo system.

The picture showed a naked woman, sitting on a yellow kilim rug in front of a fireplace filled by a *salamandre*, a cast-iron stove with a glass door, through which a glowing fire could be seen. The woman had her back to the viewer. The last layer she had shed, a pale lilac undergarment, lay draped around her on the rug; her dress and petticoat, yellow and mauve, were flung carelessly a little farther away. Her was head slightly tilted, perhaps contemplative, perhaps submissive; her reddish-brown hair pinned up, her waist narrow, hips broad, buttocks and thighs ample. Above the mantelpiece part of a mirror could be seen, reflecting a thin strip of the room. A red armchair protruded into the picture from the right; to the left of the fireplace the door to a recessed cupboard stood half-open.

Klaus Baier had grown up with this picture. It hung in his father's study till his death, a room which smelled like this one—of stale air and fresh cigar smoke.

As a small boy he hadn't given much thought to the woman sitting in front of the stove. She had obviously taken her clothes off because the fire had made the room so warm. But later he began to wonder what the woman gazing so intently into the flames actually looked like. When his father was out he sometimes sneaked into the study and sat in front of the picture, hoping the woman would look over her shoulder. Just quickly, just once. Later, after he realized that women in paintings never turn their heads, he still slipped into the room and imagined what the woman actually looked like from the front. He was jealous of the painter, who was sure to have seen her from the other side. During puberty the woman in front of the *salamandre* featured in most of his sexual fantasies. And all of his three wives (the last had divorced him six years ago) were slender from the waist up, broad from the waist down.

It was more the woman than the painting which had accompanied Klaus Baier his entire life. And now, as an old man, it was her above all he found so hard to part with.

When it came to the small seascape by Ferdinand Hodler it had been easy. The painting hadn't meant much to him, aside from the six hundred thousand franc estimated price and "at least a million under the hammer" which Weynfeldt had said he could have expected. It was painful only in so far as he couldn't put the work up for auction, for business and family reasons; he didn't want to create the impression he had cash-flow problems, and it was better if his two children, from the first and second marriages, didn't find out about the sale. He was forced to make a discreet private deal, and to accept the price of five hundred and forty-two thousand dollars offered by a collector from Detroit. He was truly up the creek.

He'd had a reproduction made—a facsimile on canvas in the original frame, entirely convincing to the casual observer—but not for sentimental reasons, simply to avoid questions being asked on the rare occasions his heirs visited.

Much the same had happened, during other crises, to the Segantini, the Hodler watercolors, the two Augusto Giacomettis and the other remnants of his father's collection. All discreet emergency sales below their potential auction value. And top quality reproductions of all of them hung in the familiar spots around the house.

He couldn't sell off his Vallotton so cheaply however. Weynfeldt's last estimate had been between 1.2 and 1.4 million francs. If the work fulfilled its full potential at auction it could fetch two or three times that. There was no question of a private sale this time. He would auction the painting officially, very officially, heirs notwithstanding. He needed the cash more urgently than ever.

Klaus Baier had lost a substantial sum on the stock market, yet again. But while he had previously used the discreet sale of paintings to aid his recovery from financial indisposition, to bridge a brief insolvency or to raise the funds for particularly promising speculations, now he needed the money to survive.

His financial situation was grim. The house he lived in had long belonged to the bank. If he wanted to satisfy all his creditors and avoid personal bankruptcy, he would be left with somewhere between one and two hundred thousand francs. In the old days that would probably have been enough to get him back on his feet again. But he just didn't have the energy this time. Nor the optimism. For the first time in his life he felt old.

Seventy-eight had been a number till now. Although he knew that, among other things, it represented the number of years he had been alive in the world, it never had anything to do with the way he felt. He knew lots of people with that number of years behind them, and they all seemed old to him, yet the number had no significance to him personally. The old man he sometimes saw in the mirror, when it couldn't be avoided, had nothing to do with him.

But a ridiculous flu last winter had flattened him. For almost a month he was bedridden, with recurring bouts of fever, shivering fits and aching limbs which had made his body, already far from agile, leaden and oversensitive. He lay in bed, in a foul mood, testing Frau Almeida's patience so far she threatened in all seriousness to hand in her notice. There were nights when he was convinced he would never stand on his feet again, when he reflected on his life and realized it wouldn't make much difference to him if it was over.

To his own surprise he recovered. But he wasn't the same person. He had lost his enthusiasm. And annoyingly, along with it, his money. The little he still had was nowhere near enough for him to spend his twilight years in the manner he had planned.

A few years ago Baier had registered with the Residenza Crepuscolo, a palazzo on the shores of Lake Como that had been converted into a luxurious old age home. There he had the option on a spacious two-room apartment with a view of the lake. Now of all times, when he could no longer afford it, it had become free, for the reason places in old people's homes typically do become free. Including full board and all costs, it would cost around a hundred thousand francs a year. That meant that he had enough money for a year at most. He was under no illusions about his life expectancy—high blood pressure, irregular heartbeat, prostate problems, type 2 diabetes, arthritis and a taste for unhealthy living—but he gave himself more than a year. Around ten, in fact.

His twilight years in the Residenza Crepuscolo between now and his eighty-eighth birthday would cost between 1.5 and 2 million francs, allowing for a little travel, some unhealthy living, and the resulting rise in the costs of care. Pretty much the figure he hoped to make from the Vallotton after tax.

A short coughing fit forced Baier to remove the Havana from his mouth to the ashtray. He suppressed the coughs with the practiced ease of someone who had smoked for most of his life and coughed for at least half of it. Then he took a large sip of port. Not his favorite drink, simply his favorite compromise between something advisable and something stronger.

Count Basie played "This Could Be the Start of Something Big." Baier heaved himself up with the help of the chair's arms and grasped the ivory-topped walking stick leaning against the next chair. He hobbled over to the easel, swapped the long-distance glasses for the short-distance ones and studied the work close up.

There were few things more familiar to him than this painting. The woman's hair, which his father had called "chestnut brown," pinned up and parted down the middle into two coifs. The curve of her right cheek, noticeably redder than the rest of her skin, suggesting a young, oval face. Her right arm, pressed tightly to her body, suggesting that, despite the fire, she was in fact chilly and had folded her arms against her chest. The lilac petticoat, which on closer inspection appeared to have been painted afterward to avoid dealing with certain questions of anatomy and perspective. Where were her calves? Her heels? If she was sitting on them, why couldn't you see that from the shape of her buttocks? The unexplained reflection on the shiny wooden mantelpiece just at the point where the reddish brown of the hair needed to stand out from the brown of the wood. The contrast between the upper half of a three-paneled screen reflected in the mirror, painted in broad strokes, and the more realistically painted silver cachepot on the mantelpiece. The piles of vaguely defined objects which could be discerned in the shadows of the open cupboard. Table linen? Sketchbooks? Boxes of painting utensils?

Baier touched the picture with his fingertips. He knew every patch of paint, every brushstroke, he knew how its surface felt and he would have been able to identify the painting by its smell. Which, given the speed at which his eyesight was deteriorating, he might soon be forced to do.

His Neuchâtel clock struck seven. In precisely five minutes he would hear the doorbell ring, followed by Frau Almeida's voice as she greeted Adrian Weynfeldt. Weynfeldt was a punctual man, as his father had been before him. Weynfeldt senior had called this "kingly courtesy" and had instilled it in his son, raising him along with his wife to believe that, if not a king, he was very much a Weynfeldt. Which was nearly the same thing.

At home Baier's father had often joked about the snobbish standards the Weynfeldts upheld. The awareness of being something special had been passed down to poor Adrian so forcefully it was part of his flesh and bones, making him use excessive politeness to dispel any suspicion of superciliousness.

For a long time it had looked like Weynfeldt senior would be the last Weynfeldt. Till his wife, approaching forty-four, bore the late arrival Adrian, a triumph of gynecology and genealogy.

Baier remembered Adrian as a little boy. The Weynfeldts were great hosts, always giving lavish dinners and receptions, and at every event he was paraded around like a trophy. A shy child with a disproportionately large head and—even then—tailored suits. In summer in shorts; in winter in knickerbockers.

The child had disappeared from his radar, and he first took notice of him again at Luise Weynfeldt's seventieth birthday party. Although really it was Adrian's guest Baier took notice of: a red-haired, green-eyed, pale-skinned English girl with the old-fashioned name Daphne, the important girlfriend for whom Adrian Weynfeldt had actually left home and moved to London. Baier wouldn't have kicked her out of bed either, as he observed later in the proceedings, after the birthday banquet in the Lisière, the pleasure palace on the outskirts of the city which Sebastian Weynfeldt had booked for the occasion.

Now Adrian was the last Weynfeldt. His father was not granted time to see his son ensure the continuation of the family line. His mother was denied this too, although she clung to life for nearly twenty further years after her husband's death. Baier sometimes suspected Adrian had refrained from marrying or procreating to get back at his parents for something they had done to him—whatever that might be.

Or perhaps he was gay. It wouldn't be surprising for a bachelor who lived with his mother till her death at ninety-four, surrounded himself with beautiful things and took such care of his appearance, despite the serious affair with the English art student. That sort of thing featured in every homosexual biography.

Baier couldn't care less. Adrian was good company, well mannered, helpful and useful. The latter above all, now.

He took the painting down from the easel. Without his stick, his teeth clenched, he carried it across the room and compared it to the one hanging above the bureau.

Perfect. Every detail correct. Even the smell.

He slid the painting into the narrow space between the bureau and the wall. At that moment he heard the doorbell and Frau Almeida's voice as she greeted Adrian.

4

Frau Almeida, Baier's Portuguese housekeeper, opened the door before Weynfeldt's finger had left the doorbell.

"Boa tarde," Adrian said, *"como esta?"*

"Tudo bem, obrigada," Frau Almeida said and, knowing that was all the Portuguese Weynfeldt knew, added, "He's waiting for you in the salon."

Fernanda Almeida had taken over Baier's housekeeping after his last divorce. She was a tall, slender woman, and lived with her husband and their nine-year-old twins in the little servants' apartment in Baier's villa. Her husband worked shifts in a canning factory and made a little on the side as Baier's janitor, running errands and working in the garden, much too small for the huge building. Baier's villa was hemmed in by other villas, all indistinguishable, all with gardens much too small, with a view of the city and the lake obscured by overgrown firs and pines it was now illegal to fell.

Frau Almeida took his Burberry and the gift-wrapped bottle of port he'd brought. Weynfeldt followed her to the cloakroom while she hung up his coat, and out of habit checked his appearance in the mirror.

Although his face was not sharply chiseled his skin was still very smooth for his age, and he had a straight, even nose with a broad bridge, a "Weynfeldt beak" as his mother called it, blue-gray eyes, generous lips, chin neither protruding nor receding, with a dimple tricky to shave and thick, brown hair streaked with gray. He had it trimmed every fortnight, his neck and the area behind his ears shaved every Tuesday. He wore his hair parted, shorter on the left, longer on the right and combed to the side. From midday onward, as it began to lose the elasticity from its daily, morning wash and the long part increasingly began to fall over his forehead, he would smooth it back to its proper place in an unconscious gesture, like something precious.

This haircut gave Adrian Weynfeldt a slightly 1940s look, which he knew full well, and liked to emphasize through the cut of his suits.

He straightened his necktie and the handkerchief in his breast pocket, smoothed his hair away from his forehead and let Frau Almeida show him into the living room.

Klaus Baier sat in the midst of his dimly lit salon in his high-backed, upright armchair. He waved Weynfeldt toward him. Adrian walked over and shook Baier's hard, bony hand, which somehow didn't fit the old man's rotund body and bloated face. It was at least a year since he'd last seen Baier, and now for the first time he really looked like an old man.

"Excuse me if I don't get up," Baier said, and pointed to a chair next to him. "Sit down."

Adrian perched on the edge of the golden-yellow 1960s plush armchair, sitting up straight and holding on to the arm so his eye-level wasn't too much lower than Baier's.

MARTIN SUTER

"Port or a proper drink?"

"Port is fine."

"Pity, I was hoping you would give me an excuse for a proper drink."

"I brought a good port."

"Thanks, but I've got a very acceptable *Bas-Armagnac hors d'age* open. You have something to celebrate. And I need a little consolation."

Frau Almeida, who had been waiting at the door till the drinking requirements were clear, now walked over to the bookcase and folded down the flap, opening up the little bar. A light went on, illuminating its mirrored interior, full of bottles and glasses. The two men waited till she had poured their drinks.

Weynfeldt was about to raise his glass, but before he had the chance Baier put his to his lips and took a big gulp, held it in his mouth awhile, then pointed to the painting above the bureau. "There it is. Why don't you bring it over and put it on the easel here."

Adrian did as Baier said. Took the painting down from its two hooks, held it in front of him with outstretched arms till this was too much—it measured three feet by four feet after all, with a heavy, ornate, golden frame— and placed it on the easel. He stood to one side, so he wasn't blocking Baier's view, and took a good look at the work.

"And?" Baier asked after a while.

"You know what I think about this painting. It's amazing."

"In francs please."

"Between seven-hundred thousand and a million."

"You said that last time. And since then *En prom-enade* went for 2.3 million. A tiny picture, not half as big as this."

"Auction dynamics. Two collectors were spurring each other on."

"That kind of thing can be engineered; you've said so yourself. You know the Vallotton collectors. Contact a few of them and pit them against each other."

Baier was right. Weynfeldt knew a few collectors who normally bid over the telephone. And he was the one in charge of the phone lines. It was true that he could influence proceedings. He could advise telephone bidders not to go any higher, but he could also do the opposite. He thought for a second. Valuations were tricky. Too high and the house risked being stuck with the lot; too low and the discrepancy between estimate and hammer price could be so great it would damage Weynfeldt's reputation as an expert.

"I'm not going under a million," Baier announced. "Between 1 and 1.5? How about that?"

Weynfeldt hesitated. "Between 1 and 1.3."

"Take it," Baier spluttered. "Now, at once."

This would not have been the first time Weynfeldt had temporarily stored a painting at home. A quick call to the insurance department in London was enough. They were flexible there, and Weynfeldt's apartment was easily as secure as Murphy's storerooms, given that he shared the building with a bank.

"Sure," he said, and walked toward the easel.

"No, stop! Leave it with me till tomorrow. One last night, to take my leave."

Next morning Weynfeldt was driven to Baier's villa in one of Murphy's delivery vans, where he packed the painting carefully in Bubble Wrap and corrugated cardboard, signed the receipt and took it away.

On the way to his office a vague instinct told him not to take the painting to Murphy's but first to his apartment. He was surprised at himself, as he never normally followed his instincts.

5

THE PLEATED, MOTHER-OF-PEARL SILK TOP WAS HELD together with a gathered ribbon of the same fabric. It was attached with a slender strap above the right breast, then wound its way over to the left shoulder where it formed a rosette. The top reached down just above the navel, exposing a swathe of stomach, then descended asymmetrically, tapering away above the left thigh. The turquoise silk wraparound skirt was attached using one single, white button at the hip, pleated in front of the left thigh. It opened and closed like an inverted fan as you walked. The whole outfit looked like it could be shed in an instant.

"Everything okay, madam?" The sales assistant called into the cubicle.

Lorena opened the door, came out and took few feline steps—one foot in front of the other—toward the huge floor-to-ceiling mirror. She knew how to walk in designer clothes; she had, after all, worked as a model. Not at the big fashion shows in Paris, Rome, London or New York—at five foot four inches she was too short— but she had modeled regularly for shows in boutiques and once had a permanent job as in-house model for a Swiss label for a while. For three seasons she'd done catalogues for a mail-order company too. She tried to forget those days spent in alternately sweltering or freezing studios in some provincial town. The commercial photographer acted like a star, and her colleagues fought for a few meager privileges by sharing sagging beds and shabby hotel rooms with him or his assistant or the company' advertising manager. Lorena had kept out of all this, with the result that after three catalogues she was no longer part of the team.

The three editions were also enough to do lasting damage to her modeling career, however. The agencies that recognized her face from the frumpy catalogues stopped giving her work. It made no difference that she had one of the most professional comp cards on the scene. It was designed by an award-winning art director she had been together with for a while—not least for that reason.

It was a few years since her modeling career had ended, but she still knew how to pose in an Issey Miyake number in front of a full-length mirror in one of the city's most exclusive boutiques so that the sales staff would take her for a highly promising customer. The saleswoman serving her said, "You're the first person we've had in here who can wear that." And the shaven-headed salesman with the Comme des Garçons look standing on the spiral staircase leading up to the men's department gave her a smile of respect.

Lorena sauntered over to the racks inset between the matte black shelves and began sifting through the clothes nonchalantly. Now and again she took a hanger from the rack, inspected the item and either returned it or placed it over the back of a nearby leather armchair on her short list.

She came to a Prada dress in iridescent violet and black silk and held it in her hand a little longer. She draped it against herself, drew it in around her waist and stood in front of a mirror. She hesitated, then shook her head, appearing to have reached a decision, and hung it back. She continued shifting the hangers from right to left.

She paused again at another Prada dress, black silk, simple and close fitting. She took it out and pressed to her body. It had a round neckline, fastened with a button, and an open slit extending down between the breasts to the middle of the body. The sleeves ended above the elbows, the hem below the knee. She hesitated, looked back through the hangers till she found the violet dress, retrieved it, held both dresses up next to each other, hung them both back, picked up the short list pile from the chair, had second thoughts, took the violet Prada dress back out, placed it on top of her pile and took the lot into the cubicle.

She drew the curtain and hung the violet Prada number on a hook. The black one lay beneath it. She had swiped it from the rack under the cover of the violet one. Now she folded it and rolled it up into a compact silk parcel which she stowed at the bottom of her handbag. Then she lowered the empty hanger into the wastepaper basket, hung the other dresses on the hooks, slipped into the violet Prada, did the zipper up as far as she could and opened the curtain. The saleswoman was standing just a few feet from the cubicle.

"Could you assist me with the zipper?" Lorena asked, without leaving the cubicle, instead waiting for the saleswoman to come to her. She turned round so she could do up the dress.

It had a stand-up collar, long sleeves gathered at the forearms and a generous wedge-shaped kick-pleat beginning at its broad leather belt and ending below the knee.

Lorena scrutinized her appearance in the mirror at length, giving the sales assistant lots of time to look inside the cubicle. "A little formless, somehow," she decided in the end.

Over the next quarter of an hour Lorena appeared in a slightly hippy Christian Lacroix number made of various large-scale-flower-print silks, in a steel-blue ankle-length Issey Miyake outfit, a linen blouse with a high collar and an outsized frill by Emanuel Ungaro, in a black-and-white horizontal-striped *deux pièce* with a huge black bow by Sonia Rykiel and a short, high-necked dress by Karl Lagerfeld with broad, angular shoulders and a zipper running from the collar to the hemline.

She sashayed toward the floor-to-ceiling mirror each time and observed herself over her shoulder from behind as if on a catwalk, getting a little attention from the handful of other customers and the bored staff.

Before removing the Lagerfeld piece, she called the saleswoman over into the cubicle. "Would you be an angel," she said, a shade condescending, "and put *this*, *this* and, *this* to one side." She handed her the three outfits. "I'd like to show them to my boyfriend tomorrow. That'll be fine, won't it?"

The saleswoman nodded.

"You can take the other things away, thank you."

Lorena removed the Lagerfeld and put her own things back on: a raspberry-colored DKNY getup with a short skirt, coupled with opaque black pantyhose. She had stolen it last year from a boutique in Basel when she'd been working as a trade-fair hostess.

She took her handbag, left the cubicle, smiled at the saleswoman and tripped toward the door.

There she was met by a slender woman with a bob. Probably in her late fifties, impeccably made-up, she wore an outfit that looked very Jil Sander. She smiled at Lorena. "My name is Melanie Gabel. I'm the proprietor."

"Pleased to meet you," Lorena smiled back.

"Would you mind terribly opening your handbag?"

6

Late morning one end-of-the-month Thursday, hardly the busiest time in the men's department of a boutique like Spotlight: Pedroni was bored, and grateful for the show the little redhead was putting on downstairs. He stood on the spiral staircase and watched as she emerged from the cubicle time and time again like a star on the stage at Caesar's Palace. She was good. His guess was that she had neither a credit card nor enough cash even to pay for a handkerchief from Spotlight, but that moron Manon was attending to her, and obviously thought she'd gotten a big fish on the end of her line.

Theo L. Pedroni was no newcomer to the business. He would soon turn thirty-nine, his last birthday with a three on the left, and had spent over half these years in the fashion industry, first as a sales intern in a big department store, then in various boutiques, two of them his own. Not concurrently, and only briefly, but still his. Both times he had filed for bankruptcy, in one case fraudulently, according to the court, which had made his return to employment difficult and forced him to relocate.

Pedroni had always viewed working in sales as a temporary situation, and always had some big project on the side intended to solve his money problems once and for all. Most of these diversification experiments had taken place in his home territory, fashion. He had entered the accessories business several times. He'd begun with small production runs, producing belts, watch straps, cigarette lighter pouches and—with particular zeal—cell phone pouches. He had taken care of the production, sales and marketing side each time. For the creative side he had collaborated with students from the school of art and design and with a young copywriter. He had ceased collaboration with the latter in 1989 after he suggested printing T-shirts with the slogan "Save the Wall!"

Later he began free-form diversification, as he put it. He was more interested in the money than the product anyway. As Charlie Sheen's character in *Wall Street* said, "I buy and sell money." During the period when illegal clubs were sprouting up all over the city like mushrooms, he was one of the cofounders of Schmelzpunkt, which was a huge success at first, and survived three raids unscathed. During the fourth the cops found several grams of coke, which Pedroni was convinced had been planted by one of the men behind Nachtzug, a competitor. He had been seen at Schmelzpunkt the same evening.

In any case, Pedroni's involvement with the club scene brought him into contact with people who knew where to get coke. That was the start of the most lucrative phase of his career. His day job then, at one of the most fashionable boutiques of the time, fit perfectly with this new side gig. The customers at New Label were mainly from the fashion and banking worlds and the majority were also private customers of his. In no time

Pedroni was able to move to a better apartment and buy an almost new Porsche Carrera with a reliable history.

This phase of his career was accompanied by social, not just financial, ascent. He was suddenly treated as more than just a salesman by these people; he was one of them. He had something they needed urgently; they could get it from him conveniently and discreetly, and they shared a secret with him.

By the time Pedroni was busted, his turnover had exceeded two million francs—the courts found evidence for at least half this sum—and he had made more than four hundred thousand francs profit. He only received four years jail time, however, first because he admitted to the offenses, second because he was highly cooperative and compromised a few illustrious figures in the banking and finance world. Including his time spent in custody, he served around two years of the sentence, and soon found another job in a boutique. There were various people in the fashion business keen to secure his discretion.

His income was modest, however, and his days were typically spent hanging around the men's department wearing a shiny gold Comme des Garçons suit with baggy trousers and a jacket with three buttons—the proprietor declaring the top one must be done up—and, if he was lucky, getting to watch a redhead pretending to be a big spender.

Suddenly he realized what she was up to. She was going to steal something. She was trying to behave so conspicuously no one would dream she intended to steal something. Her plan was to distract her audience like a magician, then make something disappear: hocus-pocus!

Perhaps she had already done it, and no one had noticed.

Now she was looking through the Prada rack, occasionally taking a dress out, hanging it back up, or throwing it carelessly over the back of a nearby chair, which normally provided waiting menfolk the chance to sit down.

She took the iridescent violet and black one out and held it up in front of herself.

Too sack-like, girl, a waste of your narrow hips. And too violet for your hair color.

She seemed to agree, and hung it back.

She took the simple black one out. Yes, that's the one. That's your style, girl.

She went back to the violet one, took it out again and compared it to the black one.

The black one, the black one. No question: the black one.

But then she put them both back.

Then she changed her mind again. She took the violet one back off the rack, put it with the others over the back of the chair and took the whole pile into the cubicle.

Had she taken only the violet one? Hadn't he seen a flash of something black behind it, just for a second?

He laughed to himself. Hocus-pocus. That was her magic trick. The black Prada has vanished into thin air. And no one noticed. Almost no one. Respect!

Pedroni walked up the rest of the stairs to the men's department and positioned himself in a spot where he could still see the changing rooms.

Manon slid up to the changing room. Did she have an inkling?

MARTIN SUTER

Now the curtain was thrown open and the redhead waved Manon into the cubicle itself, had her assisting with the zipper. Did his eyes deceive him, or was this chick really so cold-blooded, she was giving Manon the opportunity to look inside?

It was approaching twelve now. The first lunchtime customers were coming in. Pedroni had to serve one of them. He had fewer chances to glance downstairs. The redhead was still modeling one outfit after the other.

As he accompanied a customer to the exit—obviously he hadn't bought anything—Manon emerged from the cubicle with an armful of clothes. She placed three items to one side on the counter, and hung the others back on the rails.

Clever. The redhead had reserved three items and returned the rest. In a few minutes she would leave the changing room she had let the sales assistant empty personally.

And here she came. In a DKNY outfit from last season, with a Prada handbag too small to fit a dress in. Unless there was barely anything else in it.

She passed the counter in an over-the-top mannequin walk, gave Manon a rather patronizing smile and headed for the exit.

Now he saw that Frau Gabel was standing at the exit.

It would have to be a very special kind of customer for the boss to consider coming to the door to say goodbye in person. The redhead certainly didn't belong to this category.

He wouldn't be surprised if Frau Gabel asked her to open her handbag.

7

"WHEN THEY BAN SMOKING IN RESTAURANTS I'LL CLOSE down," Nunzio Agustoni always claimed. This was said in an exaggerated Italian accent that was an essential part of the Trattoria Agustoni's style, along with the squat Chianti bottles used as candleholders, and the white paper tablecloths from a roll, changed after each sitting. When it seemed the issue was refusing to go away, Agustoni installed a non-smoking table—between the coat stand and the entrance to the toilets—and made fun of any guests who actually sat there, with gestures and grimaces to the regulars.

Agustoni's had been there for over forty years, and throughout this time the menu had remained unchanged. It served the Italian standards—*antipasti, vitello tonnato*, homemade pasta, *manzo, ossobucco, picata Milanese, bistecca fiorentina*, pizza, *saltimbocca*, tiramisu, *zabaione* and mascarpone—at a consistent quality. The prices had been adjusted to fit the changing clientele, which had shifted over the years from workers, students and artists to a business, theatre and gallery-opening crowd who felt like eating somewhere frequented by workers, students and artists.

Adrian Weynfeldt ate there every Thursday lunchtime with a few friends. Always at the same table, always the same thing: *insalata mista* and *scaloppini al limone* with risotto. He washed it down with San Pellegrino and a little Brunello di Montalcino, because the house wine, which everyone else drank, gave him a headache.

Like most Thursdays, Weynfeldt was the first person at the table, laid for ten, five on each side. He sat at his usual seat, the last on the left, at the end. He would have been embarrassed to claim one of the center seats. It would have looked like he was playing the host. Of course he always paid the check, but not as the host; simply as the one with the most money at his disposal. Weynfeldt joined his own Thursday lunch club like a guest he and everyone else was generous enough to tolerate.

In his circle of younger friends he often found his financial situation embarrassing. He had absolutely no problem playing paymaster, but he worried it could be interpreted as showy or condescending. So he showed his generosity very discreetly. For years he had visited the bathroom toward the end of the meal, intercepting the waiter on the way back and dealing with the bill swiftly and without checking it. In this way no one would be put in the awkward situation of having to thank him. Weynfeldt's idea of good manners included making it easy for his friends to profit from him.

The surrounding tables began to fill up; now he was the only one sitting alone. Sometimes Weynfeldt suspected his friends always came late because no one wanted to be the first, and to have to sit next to him.

He didn't think they didn't like him. He didn't have an inferiority complex; it seemed more likely that his friends didn't want to give each other the impression they were sucking up to him because they wanted something from him.

Not that none of them ever wanted anything from him, of course. But such matters were not brought to the Thursday lunch club. In that situation they would arrange to meet discreetly at another establishment, or in Weynfeldt's apartment.

This time is was Hausmann who arrived first: Claudio Hausmann, filmmaker. Weynfeldt could see he would have preferred to turn right around when he saw him alone at the table; he averted his gaze, pretended not to have seen him, to give him the chance to disappear again and wait for the others outside Agustoni's. To save him from having to talk about *Working Title: Hemingway's Suitcase.*

Working Title: Hemingway's Suitcase was a film project Claudio Hausmann was developing. Hemingway had spent four months of 1922 in the Pension de la Forêt in Chamby sur Montreux, a cheap guesthouse. Hadley Richardson came to visit, his first wife, bringing a suitcase containing his complete unpublished fiction, which she lost on the way.

Hausmann had been given the brush-off by all the film funding bodies and had eventually persuaded Weynfeldt to fund the script development. Hausmann was an auteur, which meant that Weynfeldt's private script funding was transferred straight to his account. So far there had been a short synopsis and—after a further transfer—a more detailed treatment, which the film funding bodies had not deemed worthy of support. Adrian was not in a position to say whether they were right or not; film was not his field. And his suggestion of placing more emphasis on the fate of the suitcase, and less on the incident's effect on Hemingway's first marriage, was rejected by Hausmann as "too Hollywood."

The project had now grown to include the document "Four Sample Scenes" along with several folders of research Hausmann had done, and continued to do, on location in Paris and Montreux, also at Weynfeldt's expense.

Weynfeldt would never dream of alluding to the fact that his script development funding had represented Claudio Hausmann's sole source of income for nearly two years. In fact he avoided the subject of *Working Title: Hemingway's Suitcase* altogether where possible. It was Hausmann who was sometimes forced to broach it. Four weeks ago it was with the promise, unprompted, that he would have a first draft finished within three weeks. Weynfeldt had never got to see the initial two or three unfinished versions. Hausmann claimed they would have given a false impression.

Weynfeldt reached for his wineglass and took a sip, making a concerted effort to avert his gaze so Hausmann had more time.

Then a woman's voice said, "Been here long?"

So Hausmann had sent Alice Waldner on ahead, the sculptor. Weynfeldt got up, buttoned up his jacket, shook Alice's tiny hand, blackened as ever, and greeted her with three kisses, on alternate cheeks. He waited till she had sat down opposite him, sat back down himself and waved the waiter over.

He asked what she wanted to drink, although he

knew it would be Punt e Mes, then ordered a Punt e Mes.

Out of all his friends from the Thursday lunch club, his relationship with Alice was the least awkward. She made sculptures of steel so huge there was no risk he would feel obliged to buy one. Her métier was art for architectural spaces; her target patrons were public bodies, banks, insurance companies and the owners of villas with huge grounds. The material costs of her works greatly exceeded its market value and unsurprisingly she rarely sold.

With Alice Waldner it seemed to be less about selling work than about the discrepancy between her appearance and her art. She was not much over five foot, delicate, frail almost, and spoke with a cute, childlike voice. Her somewhat ungainly works, made of steel girders, railroad rails, caterpillar tracks and turbine parts, were a challenge to her and the few others who got to see them. She lived in reasonable comfort from a small inheritance and the alimony her first husband paid her, a manager in German heavy industry. She made no demands of Adrian Weynfeldt, although he had been known to cover the catering costs, unasked, for her exhibition openings at the former factory which served as her studio.

No sooner had Alice received her drink, than Kaspar Casutt and Kando arrived at the table, with Hausmann in tow. Casutt had "come down from the Grison Alps," as he reminded people at every opportunity, one of the economic migrants who had descended from the mountains to the valley. He maintained his Grison dialect as assiduously as Agustoni, the restaurant's proprietor, maintained his Italianate German. He was a pretty good architect. Too good, he felt, to waste his life designing vacation homes for dentists.

And so he spent his life falling out with one architectural practice after another, mostly when they demanded things of him he couldn't reconcile with his architectural conscience. This point was reached sooner each time, leaving him forced to earn a living as an architectural draftsman. The private clients willing to work directly with him were few and far between. And he fell out with the few who did commission him—mainly introduced by Weynfeldt—over irresoluble differences of opinion on architectural rigor. His last major private commission was several years ago: the refurbishment of Weynfeldt's apartment. There had been differences of opinion here too, but they were each decided in Casutt's favor.

Kando was Hausmann's girlfriend; her parents were among the thousands of Tibetans Switzerland had taken in as refugees in 1963. Alongside Adrian Weynfeldt she was one of the few people who believed in Claudio Hausmann and *Working Title: Hemingway's Suitcase*, and together with Adrian formed the rest of his small collective of sponsors, by paying the rent on their shared apartment and covering the majority of their living expenses. Kando was a lawyer for a large bank and earned enough for two. She also avoided being seen alone with Weynfeldt at the Thursday lunch club, but this was because she had the reputation for being a tireless fund-raiser for Hausmann's projects.

With witnesses present, there was no reason not to sit next to Adrian, now standing again, buttons done up, both hands on the back of the chair next to him ready to adjust it for her.

The three sat down and continued the conversation they had been having as they entered Agustoni's. Weynfeldt took care of the drinks.

Now Karin Winter arrived, accompanied by Luc Neri. Karin, a head higher than Luc, with cropped blond hair, looked exhausted from a morning of sluggish business and the prospect of a similar afternoon. She owned an art bookstore in a bad location in the historic city center with a name she realized was unfortunate only after she had registered the company.

This company's tacit shareholder, without voting rights, was Adrian Weynfeldt, who bought every art book he personally needed there and most of what he needed for work. This wasn't simply nepotism; Karin was an undisputed expert on art publications.

Weynfeldt got up to welcome her and ushered her to a chair, which she fell into with a deep sigh.

Luc sat opposite Karin: far from constant companion, they had a volatile relationship with separate apartments and incompatible lifestyles. His fine, thinning hair looked electrically charged, and judging by his eyes, he had probably just woken up. Luc was a web designer and mostly worked at night. Anyone hiring him to create their web presence could be sure of getting the most radical design currently available, but only if they had as much patience as Karin Winter or Adrian Weynfeldt, who was so clueless about computers he found his slick weynfeldt.com a little embarrassing.

The group got louder; everyone talked over one

another and studied the menu as if it hadn't remained the same for decades.

Weynfeldt sat there in silence, in a mixture of polite interest and paternal pride. There were still three seats unclaimed, but only one more guest was expected. The two other places were for unexpected guests—an old Weynfeldt tradition which Adrian had introduced to the Thursday lunch club. The last unexpected guest had been a shy young man Karin had brought and introduced to everyone—including Luc—as "my new boyfriend." One of countless episodes in the Winter versus Neri relationship war.

The only person missing now was Rolf Strasser, professional artist. "Professional artist, as in professional circus artist, or professional bullshit artist," as he himself was wont to say. He had years of classical art education under his belt, had studied painting at the Academy of Fine Arts in Vienna, where he won an award among his fellow master students. He was a virtuoso painter of every possible technique and style, adept at copying Old Masters and an astounding photo-realist. But one of his professors in Vienna had once said, "Strasser, you are highly skilled, but unfortunately you aren't an artist."

Whenever he was drunk—often, in other words— Rolf Strasser would repeat these words, laughing and putting on a nasal Viennese accent. But there was no doubt that he had been scarred by them.

He could claim some impressive achievements: successful exhibitions, prizes, grants, reviews in the art press. But he had never found his style; a perpetual victim of his skills.

For a painfully long period he had put his entire energy into losing these skills. His work had acquired a fake dilettantism, like an adult trying to imitate children's drawings. Then he went conceptual, constructed painting machines, left puddles of paint on quiet streets and stretched canvases over the asphalt so that the cars would leave tire marks on them.

Some while ago he had returned to straight figurative painting, and was working away wildly in the hope that an individual style would emerge all by itself: a look that would make even someone uninterested in art say, "Ah, a Strasser."

When he wasn't painting he was drawing. Wherever he was, he drew on whatever came to hand. At Agustoni's it was the tablecloths. Throughout the meal he would make sketches and studies on the paper surface, document the ever changing still lives on the table, draw portraits of the others or embellish stains with ornamentations. He was like a nervous office worker who decorates everything in reach with doodles, except that he was a virtuoso. For his part Nunzio Agustino forbade his staff from trashing any paper Strasser had drawn on. When the tables were cleared, the drawings had to be carefully detached and handed to Agustino, who added them to his collection, which he was convinced would one day be worth a fortune.

Weynfeldt and Strasser were united and divided by their shared passion: their love of art. Rolf was the only one of his friends who could hold down a proper conversation about Adrian's area of expertise. But there were no Strassers in Weynfeldt's private collection. Friendship notwithstanding, art meant too much to Weynfeldt for that.

But he supported Strasser's career in other ways: by editing a catalogue raisonné, published by a press Karin Winter founded for this sole purpose, or—killing two birds with one stone—by financing a website designed by Luc Neri.

The waiter was already bringing the starters as the professional artist rolled up and grabbed the bottle of Brunello to fill his glass, before he'd even sat down. As always, he wore a suit with a shirt and tie. As a concession to his identity as an artist—if he was an artist—every item was black.

He nodded once to the whole group, ignoring Weynfeldt. No one would have realized that he had arranged to meet him that night for a tête-à-tête.

Strasser was happy to go without a first course, but not without the Chesterfield he smoked while the others ate their antipasti and salads. Soon he had a pen in his hand and had begun adding something to Agustoni's collection.

Strasser didn't participate in the conversation, which had now turned to *Working Title: Hemingway's Suitcase*. Casutt had raised the subject with the remark: "I once knew someone who was working on a novel for years. Whenever you met him he was either nearly finished, or working on a redraft. He always had to get back home in a hurry because his text was waiting, or he'd arrive late because he couldn't make the text wait. And one day it was all gone. His wife had wiped the hard disk after an argument."

"Didn't he have backup?" asked Luc, who knew about information technology.

"Apparently not."

"Then it's his fault."

"That's not the point. I reckon he had never written a line."

"And why are you telling us this?" Kando asked suspiciously.

"In relation to Claudio's project."

"*Working Title: Hemingway's Suitcase* will soon be ready to shoot," she snapped.

"That's not what I meant. I'm wondering if Hemingway had really put his entire unpublished works in the suitcase his wife lost."

Hausmann chewed on his marinated eggplant with the face of a highly musical person forced to listen to an amateur orchestra rehearsing. Karin Winter tried to involve him in the conversation. "An interesting angle, Claudio, don't you think? The lost suitcase never contained a single manuscript. Just as an idea to investigate."

Hausmann sighed. "That's not what I'm interested in. The fact that his wife believed they were in there is all that matters."

Alice Waldner, the sculptor, chimed in. "I'm sure she knew exactly what was in that suitcase. I don't think Hemingway was the kind of man who packed his own bags."

Unnoticed by the group, the waiter had approached Adrian. "A call for you, Herr Weynfeldt," he murmured.

It took a moment for Adrian to realize: the waiter was asking him to come along because someone had called him on the telephone. It could only be Véronique. She was the only person who knew where he was. She would only bother him at the Thursday lunch club in an emergency.

He was led behind the bar to a black, wall-mounted phone of the kind he hadn't seen since the cell phone era began, a rectangular device with a round dial, the numbers faded and barely legible. The receiver had been removed from the phone and hung on a hook below. Servers pushed past him carrying steaming plates. What with the racket from the kitchen and the noise from the bar, shouts in Italian as food was ordered and served, it was hard to understand the voice on the other end of the line. It wasn't Véronique. It was a soft, female voice he recognized from somewhere. "Hello darling," the woman said, sounding blasé, "could you come by Spotlight as soon as you can and clear up an awkward misunderstanding? That would be lovely of you. They seem to think I'm some kind of ... shoplifter." She laughed as she said the word "shoplifter," and when he heard the laugh he recognized the voice: Lorena!

"A shoplifter?" Now he laughed too. "Spotlight? The boutique? I'll be there in ten minutes." He replaced the receiver with a beating heart, asked Agustoni to send him the bill later and returned to the table.

There they sat, his younger friends, immersed in conversation, all approaching forty and unable to hide their fear of this frightening birthday which would mark the end of the last new lease on life.

"An urgent phone call," he explained. "I'm afraid I have to ..."

No one heard him. No one looked up.

"Well, see you next Thursday," he muttered, and walked off through the smoke, voices and aromas filling the restaurant, out onto the busy street.

It was unnaturally warm for the time of year. City center office workers took advantage of their lunch breaks for a stroll. Some of them were clearly unable to receive the gift of a premature spring without reservations. The media had recently decided that climate change was no longer the bugbear of a few scaremongering hippies, and had finally become a serious global issue.

Weynfeldt took big strides along the sidewalk, stepping into the street whenever he needed to avoid large groups meandering toward him. Spotlight wasn't far, but if he really hoped to get there in ten minutes, he would have to hurry; three had already passed.

She had called him "darling." No word for weeks, then "darling." And what was the story with the shoplifting? Had she forgotten her wallet? Was she over her credit card limit? An awkward misunderstanding? What kind of misunderstanding?

He started to cross the street at a diagonal, but was sent scurrying back to the sidewalk by the furious ring of a streetcar bell. He made an apologetic gesture to the driver and walked swiftly alongside the Number 14 as it moved off again, and waited till it had overtaken him before crossing the road, this time more carefully.

Spotlight was on an elegant shopping street. He had often walked past it, but never entered. Weynfeldt did not buy designer clothes. His designer was Diaco, the third generation of gentlemen's tailors, whose father had made Weynfeldt's father's suits.

As the boutique came into view he slowed his pace. He didn't want to arrive out of breath. The elegant lettering on the façade was adorned with long, painted shadows. Weynfeldt recalled that at night it was lit by halogen spotlights mounted on the wall and cast real shadows. The store had four large plate glass windows in which white, almost faceless plastic mannequins modeled the clothes.

Weynfeldt entered the store and looked around. Lorena stood at the cash desk alongside a well-dressed woman with a bob and a shaven headed man in an ill-fitting suit. Adrian walked toward the group.

"Thanks for coming so quickly," Lorena said, and kissed him on the lips.

8

So in the end there was some action that dreary lunchtime. Frau Gabel got tough with the redhead and ordered her to open her handbag; the redhead refused point blank. Pedroni couldn't hear exactly what was said, but you didn't need lip-reading skills to grasp what was going on. He stood on the top step of the spiral staircase to see how the situation developed. If he'd had to choose, he'd have put his money on his boss. This customer was obviously brazen, but Gabel had seen it all when it came to shoplifting. The redhead wouldn't get off lightly.

Now Frau Gabel had waved Manon over, who had been watching the drama unfold from a safe distance. Gabel said something, and Manon went off toward the Prada rack. There she began searching, presumably for the black dress. Then she went into the changing room, stayed awhile, but emerged empty-handed.

The result of the search produced nothing more than a shrug from the redhead.

Gabel gave Manon new instructions, and she walked to the cash desk, probably to make the customer think she was calling the police, which she wouldn't really do. Melanie Gabel wouldn't want police in her store, certainly not during lunchtime.

The redhead seemed to realize this, and kept her cool,

waiting to see what happened next. Gabel seemed to be at her wits' end. She looked around the store, caught sight of him and beckoned him down. Shit.

Reluctantly he descended the stairs and joined them.

"Herr Pedroni, we have a small problem. I have asked this lady to show me what is inside her handbag, but she refuses. A dress has gone missing, which she took into the changing room earlier. Please try to persuade her; perhaps you'll have more luck than me."

The redhead stared at Pedroni in derisive anticipation. Taking a fatherly tone he asked, "Why don't you want to open your handbag?"

"Because then she will think I wanted to steal the dress."

"So it is in the handbag?"

"Not because I wanted to steal it. I wanted to show it to my boyfriend."

Melanie Gabel weighed in again: "So why didn't you take the other clothes too? The ones you asked us to reserve?"

"They wouldn't all fit in my handbag."

Pedroni suppressed a smile. "So what now? Where do we go from here?"

"Do you think I need to steal dresses? My boyfriend would buy up the whole store for me if I asked him!"

"There's no need for him to do that," Melanie Gabel said sarcastically, "I'd be delighted if he simply paid for the dress you have in your handbag. Three thousand, two hundred and fifty Swiss francs. I suggest you call him right away."

The redhead scrutinized her coolly. What she did next took Pedroni's breath away: she opened her handbag. The dress, rolled up into a tiny bundle, could clearly be seen. She reached beneath it, retrieved a small wallet, searched briefly inside till she found a visiting card, which she gave to Gabel, replaced the wallet and closed the handbag. "Perhaps you'd like to call him yourself."

Melanie Gabel was speechless for a second, then took the card, read it, looked up and asked, "Adrian Weynfeldt is your boyfriend?"

"You know him?"

"I know who he is."

They walked together to the telephone behind the cash desk. Melanie Gabel dialed Weynfeldt's office number, was told that he would only be available after lunch and handed the phone to the redhead, who told Weynfeldt's assistant this was an urgent, private matter. She was given the number of a restaurant, called it, and ten minutes later there he stood, in the store.

He oozed money: his suit, shirt, shoes, all handmade. Pedroni noticed things like that. Weynfeldt was out of breath and very nervous.

The redhead greeted him with a kiss on the mouth, which seemed to surprise him. If he really was her boyfriend then it was probably early days.

Weynfeldt greeted Gabel, who treated him with the kind of respect she reserved for old money, and listened to her summary of events so far. He took no notice of Manon or Pedroni.

The way the redhead put it, it all sounded very simple. She had tried on a few things, put some aside because she wanted to show him and one in her handbag for the same reason. By the time she came to leave the shop she had forgotten about the Prada in her handbag. Simple as that.

Everyone present knew this wasn't true. But with the arrival of Adrian Weynfeldt the story became one of those kind of lies you can accept without having to believe it.

Without asking any further questions he pulled out his wallet and handed Gabel his credit card, avoiding eye contact with her.

But the redhead insisted that he see the dress. She ordered him into one of the leather armchairs, disappeared into the dressing room and reappeared in the black Prada number—slightly crumpled from being rolled to fit in a handbag.

Weynfeldt was pleased. But when the redhead then appeared in her own clothes he remained seated. "What about the other things?" he asked.

She asked for the clothes that had been reserved and modeled them for him, one after the other, with her over-the-top catwalk choreography. Weynfeldt was pleased with them too.

Without batting an eyelid, he paid the bill of nearly twelve thousand francs. Holding four large Spotlight bags he followed the redhead out of the store.

Melanie Gabel, who had accompanied them both to the door, stayed there for ages, watching them walk away. At the register, Manon filled in the alteration form: the white blouse with the starched frills by Emanuel Ungaro had to be taken in at the waist.

Pedroni glanced over her shoulder and memorized the delivery address.

9

MEN WITH SIGNET RINGS THOUGHT THEY WERE SOME-
thing special. They talked faster than other people and
had a kind of well-bred arrogance that drove Lorena
mad. Most of them wore family crests their fathers or, at
best, grandfathers had paid a heraldry expert to research
or invent. But they wore these insignia as if they were
the descendants of some ancient dynasty with the time-
honored right to have their wicked way with girls from
the lower orders, with no honorable intentions whatso-
ever. Signet ring men were spoiled: generous when they
were coming on to you, stingy once they wanted to get
rid of you.

Weynfeldt wore a signet ring. So Lorena knew what
she was getting into.

They walked side by side through the busy city center. Excitement over the false spring lay in the unnaturally warm air. They hadn't discussed where they were
heading. Lorena didn't know if she was following him
or he was following her. After they left Spotlight she
had put her arm through his, while the boutique owner
was watching, and as far the shopping bags allowed. But
then he had started awkwardly swapping sides, walking
on her right for a while, then back to the left, till it got
silly trying to link arms with him again each time. Now
they were simply walking along beside each other, like

MARTIN SUTER

two acquaintances who had met by chance.

Lorena had thanked him first of all, and he had brushed it off. Then she added, "You didn't have to buy all the other clothes, the dress would have been enough."

"I'll remember that next time."

"No need; there won't be a next time." And because he said nothing to that, she asked, "What am I going to do with all these clothes?"

"Wear them. They look good on you."

She looked at him, from the side. He was older than the signet ring men she knew. But with the same rounded contours. He had clearly just lost the latest in a series of battles against weight gain.

You could see his suit was expensive if you looked properly. But it wasn't a suit that made this as blatantly clear as the other signet ring men's suits. Weynfeldt wore it with the ease of someone who had never worn anything else. Lorena decided that he was not a typical signet ring specimen.

"Ask me," she said.

"What do you want me to ask?"

"Why I did it?"

"That's none of my business."

"It is now. Now it's cost you a load of money."

"You haven't asked me why I did it."

"Why did you do it?"

"Because you asked me to."

"Do you do everything people ask you?"

"If it's in my power."

Definitely not a typical signet ring man.

They walked through a small park. A few people

had stopped and were pointing excitedly at something beneath a beech tree. Not an abandoned, ticking suitcase; not a cobra escaped from the zoo; simply a few cheeky crocuses and hellebores sticking their noses out of the humus.

"How have you been since that day?"

"Since I was at your place?"

"Yes."

"Up and down. And you?"

Adrian Weynfeldt seemed to be thinking. He really needed to think how he had been since then. It took quite awhile till he came up with an answer. It went, "I never get really down, I guess." And a few seconds later he added, "I never feel really upbeat either."

The path led out of the park and onto a narrow sidewalk on the left hand side of a street. Weynfeldt shifted the shopping bags from his left to his right hand and placed himself on Lorena's right.

"Why do you keep switching sides?" she wanted to know.

"Normally I walk on the left of a lady. But on narrower sidewalks I walk on the side next to the traffic. It was instilled in me from birth. It throws me off if I walk on the wrong side.

Lorena laughed. "You protect women from the traffic with your body?"

"Strange, isn't it?"

"Kind of cute too." She linked arms with him. A cement mixer came toward them. Lorena drew Adrian away from the curb. "Come here, you can't take that on."

They walked through the blazing sunshine. The top

button of Adrian's two-button jacket had been done up the entire time. Now he undid it. She noticed there was a monogram on his shirt. A. S. W., like on his pajamas.

What does the S stand for?" she asked.

"Sebastian. It was my father's name."

"Like the servant in *Heidi*."

Weynfeldt laughed. "True. That hadn't occurred to me till now."

They walked on in silence. After a while he said, "Do you mind if I ask you something?"

"Whatever you want."

"Why was it me you called?"

Lorena reflected for a long time. Then she replied, "Because now, ever since that Sunday, you are responsible for my life."

10

Sperling Strasse 42 turned out to be the pink half of a small semidetached house, its other half painted saffron yellow. The neighbors had clearly been unable to agree on a single color.

Even as he rang the bell Weynfeldt knew he wouldn't like the woman who lived there. It was her fault he had been forced to leave Lorena at twenty to three, put her in a taxi, with a voucher to cover the fare, wave good-bye and hope she would turn up as promised the next evening at Châteaubriand, the tiny, overpriced gour-met restaurant where he was very safe from his younger friends, and pretty safe from the older ones.

A dog with cracked vocal chords started barking. He heard a woman trying to silence it, without success.

The door opened a chink. A small dog's head poked through, teeth bared. "Just a minute, till I've locked Susi up," the woman's voice said. The door was closed again. Weynfeldt waited.

The tiny front garden smelled of spring. Snowdrops, crocuses and pink cyclamen were flowering in the bed in front of the house. A rusty, collapsing garden table stood under a birch tree, four chairs leaned against it. You could see this hadn't been their first winter outdoors.

It was Frau Schär herself who opened the door. A plump woman who had clearly been to the hairdresser that day; her hair hadn't suffered a night's sleep yet. She was in her mid-sixties, dressed in black, widowed a few days ago.

Taking this into consideration, Véronique had agreed that instead of Frau Schär coming to the office, on this occasion Dr. Weynfeldt would visit her.

She owned a few mountain landscapes by Lugardon which she wanted valued. She was considering parting with them, hard as it would be.

Weynfeldt shook Frau Schär's small, soft hand and expressed his condolences. She smelled of a far too youthful perfume with a very dominant lily of the valley aroma.

Lunch smells hung in the air inside. Something must have been fried on a very hot flame. Weynfeldt walked past the door behind which Susi was barking frantically, into a living room. A large window filled with flowers opened onto a back garden the same size as the front, with a chalet-style structure.

Frau Schär offered him coffee. Weynfeldt declined. He didn't have much time, he said, and suggested they got straight down to business.

Four of the paintings were hanging above the sofa, two leaning against its cushions. One of these was obviously a Lugardon. It showed a perpetually snow-topped mountain range with an alpine meadow in the foreground, painted in painstaking detail, a herd of Braunvieh cattle and a cowherd snoozing with his Swiss mountain dog in the shade of a rough-hewn alpine hut. Albert Lugardon, born in 1827 to a portrait-, landscape- and history painter, was seen as the inventor of "high-alpine realism." The paintings had recently become fashionable again. Not really Weynfeldt's thing though.

Two years ago a similar landscape to the one on the sofa had fetched twenty-two thousand francs at one of Murphy's competitors' auctions. But that painting had been larger and arguably better. Frau Schär wouldn't make more than ten thousand from this.

The others were simply imitations, painted in the style of Lugardon, and this with little feeling or talent. They were all signed A. L. on the bottom right with dates from the late nineteenth century. To the best of Weynfeldt's knowledge Lugardon had never signed his work solely with his initials. Whoever painted these pictures had clearly created a loophole in case anyone came sniffing around. They were worth nothing. Not to a house such as Murphy's.

Frau Schär had been watching Weynfeldt triumphantly as he examined the paintings. Now she explained, "I don't know much about them, but whenever my husband got fed up with work he'd say, "Let's just sell our Lugardons and live off the interest."

"Our Lugardon," Weynfeldt corrected her. "That one is the only Lugardon; the others are ..." He restrained himself, and said simply, "The others are not Lugardons."

Frau Schär was speechless for a few seconds. Then she said. "You are mistaken. They have always been Lugardons."

"There were lots of people who painted in his style at the time."

"But it says A. L. Albert Lugardon. A. L."

"Lugardon always signed his works using his full name."

"You know every single one of his paintings, do you?" The rouge on her cheeks deepened as her face reddened.

"Of course not. But every one I've seen was signed Albert Lugardon. Like this one." He pointed to the genuine Lugardon.

"And what is it worth?" she asked, businesslike again.

If she hadn't forced Weynfeldt to pass up his first chance in years for an afternoon with a woman he fancied, he might have pitched higher. Instead he said, "Eight thousand francs."

Frau Schär wouldn't even let him use her phone to order a taxi. He was lucky she didn't set Susi on him. He had to walk for ages till he found a phone booth. It was times like this when he considered actually getting a cell phone.

Now he was standing in front of a phone booth, waiting for a taxi, thinking about Lorena. Did she do things like this often? Steal three-thousand-franc dresses? And why? Simply when she liked a certain dress but couldn't afford it? Out of sheer boredom? Professionally—did she steal expensive clothes and sell them?

A taxi approached. Weynfeldt took a couple of steps toward the curb. The taxi didn't slow down. Weynfeldt raised his arm to hail it. The driver pointed over his shoulder to the passenger seat, filled by a plump figure, Frau Schär. She smiled vindictively at him. Weynfeldt didn't react.

Perhaps Lorena was a kleptomaniac. Adrian wondered which explanation he preferred. He came to the astonishing conclusion that he wasn't interested. He didn't care why she stole clothes. Not only that. He didn't care *that* she did it. In fact he was pleased she had done it. Who knew when or if he would otherwise have seen her again?

During the time since their first encounter her face had fused with Daphne's in his mind. Thinking of Lorena, he had seen Daphne. And when his thoughts had turned to Daphne—which they still did after all these years—he saw Lorena before him.

But after today he was able to distinguish the two. Lorena's features were starker, as if drawn with a harder, sharper pencil. Her face was already marked by a life more excessive than Daphne would have led. A longer one too. The skin around Lorena's eyes was a shade darker and even when she wasn't smiling, at the corner of her eyes were the fine wrinkles his mother had called "crow's feet."

Weynfeldt was so lost in thought he only noticed the taxi as it pulled up alongside him. He asked to be taken to the office, and was grateful the driver said nothing. He was too polite to fend off chatty people.

"Was it worth the effort?" Véronique asked immediately.

"No."

"Six Lugardons but it wasn't worth it?"

"One Lugardon and five imitations."

"Oh, I'm sorry; the woman sounded very convincing. Next time I'll insist on photos." She gave him a searching look. When it looked like he would return to his office with no further comment she asked, "Was it okay for me to give Agustoni's number to that Lorena? She said it was very urgent and personal."

"Yes, it was fine, thanks."

He could see she was dying to know more. There weren't many women in Weynfeldt's life. When she realized no more details were forthcoming, Véronique said, "I'm just popping out; I'll be right back."

"Would you bring me something please; I haven't eaten."

"What?"

"Whatever you're having." He went into his office to continue working on the catalogue.

A short time later Véronique returned, bringing stuffed bamboo shoots with sweet plum sauce and pork dumplings. "The same as I'm having," she said, adding, with a rare touch of ironic self-reflection, "but not as much."

Rolf Strasser wanted to "discuss something in private" with him, and suggested they meet in Weynfeldt's apartment. Don't go to a big effort, he had said.

Weynfeldt never went to an effort. He left that to Frau Hauser. She would prepare what she called "a morsel"—tiny canapés with salmon, foie gras, roast beef, *viande des Grison*, lobster garnished with homegrown oat and lentil sprouts and radishes. For dessert there would be more morsels, this time sweet— *éclairs*, mille feuilles and the whole pâtisserie repertoire, all in dollhouse proportions.

Weynfeldt had asked Frau Hauser to lay the table in the Von der Mühll room, a small space with a window onto the rear courtyard devoted to the noted Lausanne architect. He had furnished it simply with a walnut ensemble consisting of two uncushioned chairs, a table, and a file cabinet for drawings. Von der Mühll had designed the minimal, right-angled ensemble back in 1924, as furnishings for an office waiting room—at a time, in other words, when Lausanne was still dominated by Parisian Art Deco. Only a handful of experts knew it still existed; even fewer that it belonged to Adrian Weynfeldt.

On the walls hung works by Paul Zoelli, geometric oils from the same period. Although he had no evidence, Weynfeldt was convinced Von der Mühll and Zoelli must have known each other.

The room was ideal for a private conversation. And alongside its aesthetic rigor, there was another advantage to the furniture: it was so uncomfortable that any conversation held sitting on it would not be drawn out. Although in this situation that wasn't an issue. This was undoubtedly about money, and when it was about money Weynfeldt generally gave in sooner rather than later.

He went to sit in his study till Strasser came. The high plate-glass window let in light from the brightly lit offices which framed four floors of the rear courtyard. In some of them teams of cleaners could be seen, vacuuming, emptying wastepaper bins, dusting telephones and wiping screens. In one office sat a lonely figure working to get ahead; in another a meeting was being held.

The dim light fell on the walls filled with bookshelves, and on easels holding pictures—Weynfeldt's own and those he had to write expert reports on.

He flicked a switch on; a spot threw a beam of light onto an easel in the center of the room. *La Salamandre* shone out, with its yellows, reds, lilacs, browns and flesh tones, as if the light emanated from the painting itself.

The picture had been here since he picked it up from Baier. He had told no one that it would be put up for auction. Not even Véronique. He wasn't sure what was holding him back; the work would give the next auction a whole new impetus. But he had strange misgivings.

La Salamandre had been reproduced millions of times to be sold as a poster, but the original had remained in private hands since it was painted. And it was a very private image. Not all art was meant to be public. Somehow Weynfeldt couldn't bring himself to disrupt the intimacy of the scene by releasing it into the public domain.

He knew this was ridiculous. But why shouldn't he have the picture to himself for a few days?

The bell rang. Weynfeldt went to the door and spoke into the intercom. It was Rolf Strasser. He asked him to wait while he came down in the elevator.

Strasser was drunk. That didn't surprise Weynfeldt; Rolf was normally drunk by this time. The question was simply which stage of drunkenness he had reached. He had undoubtedly passed through the lucid stage at Agustoni's, staying for a bottle or two of Brunello with those members of the group who had stamina, making them laugh. He had hopefully seen off the sludgy stage with a late siesta on his studio sofa. He had probably got over the headache stage with an aperitif in his local bar. The question now was whether he was still in the peaceful stage, already in the sentimental stage, or slipping into the aggressive.

Weynfeldt led him into the Von der Mühll room. Strasser sat on the hard, angular chair with a reproachful look.

"Would you like a glass of white?" Weynfeldt inquired. He had put a bottle of Twanner to cool and showed Strasser the label.

"You got beer too?" Strasser asked.

Strasser drank beer the way other people drink mineral water when they want a brief pause from alcohol. That meant that he wasn't yet in the aggressive phase. Weynfeldt went to the kitchen for beer. He could have waited till Frau Hauser brought the morsels and asked her to bring beer. But this would have represented another defeat in his long-running, losing battle to prove she wasn't indispensable.

He had only just returned with a beer and a glass for Strasser when she arrived with the first tray, and handed him the bottle opener which he had forgotten.

Strasser took a drink, wiped the froth from his mouth and asked, "How long have we known each other, Adrian?"

The sentimental stage had begun.

"When did you return from Vienna?"

Strasser emptied his glass as he reflected. "About twelve years ago."

"Well, that's how long we've known each other."

"How long or how short, depending how you look at it."

"How do you look at it? Long or short?"

Strasser poured out more beer. "I feel like we've known each other for ages. Longer than just twelve years."

"Strange how the same period of time can seem short or long depending which vantage point you see it from."

"You know what I hate? When time moves on but you stay stuck in a rut. Like me."

"You aren't stuck in a rut," Adrian protested.

"You and your fucking politeness. Of course I'm in a rut. I'm just where I was twelve years ago. What the fuck? Twelve years ago I was further ahead. Then I still had a fucking future!"

Weynfeldt could see that Strasser's mood was tipping. There was no point arguing with him. But he couldn't agree with him either. "I know what you're talking about. You begin the day and immediately realize you've begun hundreds of days like that. That it'll be like all the days before and to come. Pretty depressing, I know."

"With me it's not just a feeling. With me it's a certainty."

"With me too perhaps, but I try to treat it like a feeling."

"If I had your life, I might actually be happy that nothing changed."

Once people took this tone Weynfeldt was helpless. He didn't seek to defend his affluence, and for them to broach the subject he found tactless; there was nothing he could say to ease the awkwardness.

The fact that Rolf had brought it up was a sign to Weynfeldt that he would soon reveal the real reason for his visit. He helped him out: "Do you have any idea what you could do about it? About the stagnation, I mean, whether genuine or perceived?"

"New impulses. A clean break. New start. Brainwash. Back to square one."

Frau Hauser knocked and came straight in with further morsels. She placed the silver tray on the table and wished them *bon appétit*.

Strasser had finished the beer and now switched to white wine. "Where was I?"

"A new start."

"Yes. I have to get out of here."

This wouldn't be the first time Strasser had sworn by this remedy. There had been trips to Italy, the USA, North Africa. With Weynfeldt's support each time. Adrian didn't mention this, just nodded sympathetically.

Strasser did mention it: "Not like Italy that time, or North Africa. Then I just wanted to get away from here, anywhere. That was a mistake. I don't need to get away from here." He stuffed two salmon canapés into his mouth and swilled them down with wine. "I need to go somewhere!"

Adrian concurred. "Do you have a specific idea where?"

"Hiva Oa." He sounded irritated at having to explain, as if Weynfeldt had asked a stupid question.

Adrian risked inquiring nonetheless. "Where is that?"

"Marquesas. The largest of the Marquesas Islands. Gauguin is buried there."

"Oh yes. French Polynesia. Pretty far off the beaten track."

"Gauguin managed to make a new start there."

Weynfeldt said nothing—Gauguin was already very established by this point—except, "True."

"Gauguin said, 'To create something new, we have to go back to our origins, to humanity's childhood.'"

Weynfeldt's favorite Gauguin saying was, "Art is either plagiarism or revolution." But he held back from quoting it now. He ate Frau Hauser's morsels in silence—first the savory morsels, then the sweet morsels—and listened to Strasser's argument for a sojourn on the Marquesas. With every sentence and every glassful he became more enthusiastic, but the threatening undertone crept into Rolf's voice, which silenced any form of objection or doubt.

Weynfeldt fixed his eyes on the bridge of Strasser's nose, a trick he had learned from his father. It gave the person you were talking to the impression you were gazing profoundly into their eyes. At the same time he nodded occasionally in agreement or encouragement, depending on the tone of Strasser's voice. His thoughts returned to Lorena. He pictured himself with her in Polynesia, both of them wearing big sarongs with hibiscus-flower prints, and fragrant garlands of flowers.

At some point Strasser leaned back in expectant silence. Weynfeldt knew the moment had come to say, "Well, that certainly makes sense to me. If there's anything I can do to help realize the plan ..."

According to Strasser's research the most convenient option was a business class ticket to Papeete, because that way the return flight date could be left open, an important condition for a new start. He could book the connecting flight from Papeete to Hiva Oa when he got there. Or perhaps he would opt to take the ferry. You should arrive by boat on an island where you plan to stay awhile.

Rolf Strasser estimated the costs at around fifty thousand francs, with the option of a further twenty or thirty, depending on the time limit. As the Marquesas were so far-flung, life on the islands was expensive, and the ongoing costs here in Zurich would continue—studio, insurance, health care, pension etc. This would be a refundable loan with interest obviously; he was certain that on his return he would finally make it big.

Weynfeldt knew he could neither prevaricate excessively nor agree too swiftly; either could bring one of Strasser's tirades of hatred down on his head. He took his notebook from the inside pocket of his jacket, pulled a small silver pen out of the loop in the binding and wrote "Rolf" and "Hiva Oa" and "50,000" and "new start." Strasser regarded him distrustfully. Finally Adrian shut the little book, replaced it and said, "Sounds very sensible."

Strasser filled both of their glasses and raised his to Weynfeldt. "Hiva Oa."

"Hiva Oa," Adrian replied.

Strasser drained his glass. "Do you by any chance have some slightly comfier seating, in a room that's not too far from here?"

Weynfeldt had hoped Strasser would start taking his leave, now the business had been concluded to his satisfaction. But he clearly felt obliged to stay a little longer. Adrian led him down the corridor to the Green Salon, as his mother had called it. The name had stuck, although during the renovation he had consistently avoided the color green.

They passed his study on the way. When he'd gone to answer the door to Strasser earlier, Weynfeldt had left the door open and the spotlight on. Now *La Salamandre* glowed in the dark room as if deliberately put on show. Strasser paused, entered the room, stood in front of the painting and stayed there for a good while, saying nothing, till Adrian observed, "Vallotton. Probably going in the next auction."

"You mean this Vallotton, this one here, will be put up for auction?"

Weynfeldt put the strange question down to the level of alcohol in Strasser's blood, and said simply, "Yes."

Strasser left the room. Seen close up he looked pretty tired. "What would you value something like that at?"

"I'm really not sure, but I think we'll start at around a million."

Rolf Strasser didn't stay much longer. Soon after this he willingly let Weynfeldt put him in a taxi, with one of his vouchers to cover the fare.

People were sitting at the tables outside one of the bars in the city center, perched with their drinks on the windowsills, leaning against the wall, as if it were the middle of summer.

"And it's only February," the taxi driver said.

Strasser didn't reply. He had no desire to start yet another conversation about the weather, climate change, the Kyoto Protocol, George Bush, Al Gore, Iraq or the trend towards hybrid vehicles. He had other problems.

He fished a Chesterfield out of his pocket and went

to light it.

Without uttering a word, the driver tapped against a sign on the dashboard. It said, THANK YOU FOR NOT SMOKING.

Strasser kept the cigarette in his mouth, unlit. The bastard, he thought. What a bastard! Takes me for an idiot. *I can't bear to part from the painting. As accurate as possible, please. So I won't realize it's not my* Salamandre *anymore, the one which has been with me my whole life. My whole life! Sob, sob!*

The bastard. For eight thousand! A hundred and twenty hours work! At sixty-six francs an hour. For an artist! And then he wants to auction the copy and keep the original. He can play tricks on a dope like Weynfeldt. But not on Strasser. Not on Strasser. The bastard!

They had left the center behind them now and were driving though the quiet streets of the villa district. Strasser lit the cigarette.

The driver took his foot off the gas. "This is a no-smoking taxi."

"But I'm not a no-smoking passenger," Strasser snapped.

"I'll say it again."

"Just drive. We're nearly there."

The driver braked abruptly. "Sixteen eighty."

Strasser made no reply, simply a gesture implying he should keep driving.

"Sixteen eighty," the driver repeated, with studied calm.

"Drive on."

The driver held out his open hand to Strasser in

silence. Strasser opened the door and made to step out. But the planned haughty exit degenerated into humiliating slapstick: he had forgotten to release the seat belt.

By the time he had found the catch, the driver's hand was already on it. "Sixteen eighty."

Strasser flung him one of Weynfeldt's signed vouchers. "Put whatever price you want on it."

The driver looked at the paper. "Behaves like a rock star but can't even pay for a taxi himself." He released the seat belt; Strasser got out, slammed the door and said, "Asshole!" The taxi drove off.

The street rose steeply. The upstanding villas of the city's upper classes stood dreaming behind precise hedges and mature front gardens. Here and there a window was lit, but no one could be seen; the rooms facing the street were mainly bathrooms, kitchens and utility rooms. Up above in the attics were the maid's rooms, rarely used now.

He took a shortcut, part footpath, part steps. In white letters on a blue enamel sign, the path was named Bienensteig—"bee rise." He began panting after a few feet.

I think we'll start at around a million. Complacent rich kid! *I think! I'm not quite sure yet. Maybe we'll start a few hundred thousand higher or lower. It's not a big deal. It's only money.*

Strasser paused, bent with his hands on his thighs, gasping for breath. Perhaps he would quit smoking on the Marquesas. Jacques Brel was buried there. Lung cancer.

We'll start at a million and take it from there. Two mil-

lion, three million, many millions, whatever. But let's palm Strasser off with eight thousand. The old bastard.

Strasser began climbing again, slowly this time, controlling his breathing.

He would ask for ten percent, that was fair, he thought. Not ten percent of the hammer price, he knew his limits. But ten percent of the estimate. If it fetched two or three little million francs that was thanks to Vallotton. But the fact that this could happen at all, that it could fetch even one million, was thanks to Strasser.

The path returned to the street it was shortcutting. He recognized Baier's house from a long way off. It rose, ghostly, from its garden of conifers and acid-loving plants. Except for the diagonal row of windows marking the stairway, it was dark.

A car approached, maintaining the required speed limit, blinding Strasser briefly, till the driver noticed him and switched off his brights. It was a Bentley with an almost inaudible motor, a vision which made Strasser so mad he raised his share by a percent. One hundred and ten thousand, not one hundred, was the sum Strasser would make Baier promise him, if he didn't want to be busted.

He opened the garden gate, walked along the granite flagstones to the front door and rang the bell.

Nothing happened. He rang again, this time for longer. After the third time he heard Baier's grumpy voice over the intercom. "Yes," he said brusquely.

"Rolf Strasser. I have to talk to you."

"Do you know what time it is?"

"Do you think I've come all this way to tell you what

the time is?"

"Come back tomorrow."

"Fine. But first I'll drop by Murphy's and tell them who really painted your Vallotton."

Baier's intercom buzzed.

11

GIULIANO DIACO HAD DRAWN THE DEEP RED VELVET curtain aside. The sun threw a glaring quadrant onto the worn oriental carpet. In this merciless light they scrutinized the fabrics.

Diaco rolled a few yards of cloth from the bale and draped it over Weynfeldt's shoulder from behind. Weynfeldt looked at himself in the full-length mirror: over his right shoulder the roll of fabric, over his left the critical eyes of the diminutive tailor; Diaco could barely see over Weynfeldt's shoulder.

A veil of dust shimmered in the sun's rays. The room smelled of new cloth. Weynfeldt loved that smell. It evoked childhood memories for him. His father in a new suit. His favorite hiding place in his father's closet. The measurements and fittings for his little suits with the knickerbockers and short trousers, in this selfsame tailoring workshop.

Giuliano Diaco was the third generation of his family to run the business. His father, Alfredo Diaco, had handed it down five years ago. But he still appeared in the workshop regularly, and the older tailors still addressed him as "padrone" which in practice he remained.

Weynfeldt had been in Diaco's fabric storeroom over half an hour now, Diaco showing him one fabric after another, all merino wool, all top line plus, plus—the highest possible quality. He needed a suit for this spring they were having in the middle of winter. "Needed" was something of an exaggeration; he had a walk-in wardrobe full of suits. But he liked going to his tailor, and this weather provided a useful excuse for another visit.

"Do you know what a body scanner is?" Diaco asked.

"Something used in hi-tech medicine?"

"In just a few seconds, a body scanner can take several million measurements, which another computer then uses to cut the cloth for your suit. And someone in a sweatshop in the Czech Republic sews it for slave wages."

Weynfeldt sighed. "So that's the future of your fine craft."

"Not even the future. There's already a company in Zurich using them. They can sell you a made-to-measure suit for under a thousand francs. But they make a big profit on it."

No wonder Diaco was worried. His suits started at ten times that. "There will always be people who would miss being measured personally, the conversations with you, the time spent thinking solely about their appearance," Weynfeldt consoled him.

"They can still have all that. The proprietor pretends to be taking measurements, but the machine scans the client in the changing room without his realizing. No, no, Dottore, you can forget us tailors. We've had our time."

"Dottore" was what Giuliano Diaco's father had called him, even before Adrian had begun his dissertation. The title had been passed down a generation intact.

It was indeed possible that Diaco's days were numbered. Only Weynfeldt's older friends went there. And they were becoming ever fewer. His younger friends couldn't afford it. And the really rich people he knew, collectors for the most part, went to Caraceni in Milan or Savile Row in London.

Adrian had registered the first sign that Diaco was in trouble some while back. He had suddenly started stocking accessories. Entering the discreet premises, on the first floor of a retail building in one of the best locations, you were greeted by stands full of colorful neckties. A vitrine held leather articles—key cases, wallets and change purses, belts etc.—and another displayed products from an unknown cosmetics brand, created exclusively for Diaco.

On any other day, the prospect that Diaco's would soon cease to exist, and that yet another law firm would take over the premises, would have depressed Weynfeldt. But today his mood was not easily dented. The prospect of dinner with Lorena had made him impervious to the grim realities of everyday life.

That morning he had corrected the initial proofs of the catalogue, appalled by the quality of the printing. He had spent over an hour on the phone to the manager of the Grand Imperial Hotel, in whose ballroom their auctions were always held. The date which till now they had promised him, verbally, was suddenly unavailable due to a clash of bookings. And Véronique had bombarded him with questions after he asked her to research Vallotton's prices over the last decade on the Internet. He stonewalled in response since something still didn't feel right about *La Salamandre*. Still, there was no doubt the picture would look better on the cover than Hodler's *Landscape with Telegraph Posts*.

Some days that would all have dampened his mood. Not that he would have been bad-tempered; he was much too well bred to let his moods show. But it would have made him slower and more laconic.

Slower, yes. It had taken years for Weynfeldt to realize that his "slow-motion days," as he thought of them, the days he felt as if he'd run aground, these days were what other people called depression. He had discovered this reading a novel, as the protagonist's emotional state was described. It wouldn't have occurred to him otherwise. And he didn't have anyone he could talk to about his feelings.

But today, although it had all the makings of a slow-motion day, everything felt light and breezy.

To make sure Diaco felt the same way Adrian ordered two suits, "transitional clothes" as his mother would have called them.

He ate a light, late lunch, alone, in a self-service vegetarian restaurant, and spent the rest of the afternoon dealing with the date problem and writing an expert's report on a Lake Geneva sunrise by Ferdinand Hodler for a colleague in the New York branch.

It was early as he left the office, wishing Véronique a good evening; he wanted to go home and change before going out. He didn't always, but today he would.

Châteaubriand had only eight tables. It was more like an elegant, private apartment than a restaurant. It was furnished with antiques; dimmed Venetian glass chandeliers provided a relaxing light throughout, and a multitude of table lamps and sconces ensured an intimate atmosphere at the tables and in the niches.

It was a pleasant, cozy place; the pictures hanging on the walls were the only thing not to Weynfeldt's taste.

The restaurant didn't have a bar at which he might have waited for Lorena, and he was led directly to the place he had reserved, a four-person table laid for two, in a window-niche, barely visible from the rest of the restaurant. He knew this table from previous meals, mostly business-related, and liked it. You could talk without being disturbed or overheard, and if you ran out of things to say, you could gaze out into the prettily lit garden, or down to the glittering city below, its lights reflected in the lake.

But now he was meeting a woman here, the choice of table seemed slightly indecent. He wondered if he should ask for another, but couldn't come up with a plausible explanation, and let it be.

He was twenty minutes too early. Five of them were left from the traveling time he had allowed, the other fifteen was the amount of time he liked to be early when he was the host, in case a guest arrived before the time arranged. He ordered a glass of sherry and settled himself, preparing to sit out his fifteen minutes and then hers.

When both had passed, he ordered another sherry; the waiter kept asking if he could bring him anything. For a woman to be half an hour late was unremarkable. But Adrian still began to be nervous. He got up twice and looked around the restaurant, in the unlikely event that Lorena had arrived and was unable to find his table. Even before the unremarkable half hour was up he began envisaging scenarios. She had forgotten the name of the restaurant and couldn't call him because he was an idiot and didn't have a cell phone. She hadn't forgotten the name of the restaurant, but was stuck in a jam and couldn't call because she had forgotten her cell phone. Had forgotten to charge it. Had run out of credit. She had gotten the day wrong and was planning to come on time—but tomorrow. Or it was him! He'd gotten the day wrong!

He could have stood closer to her in Spotlight when she was telling the saleswoman the delivery address for the blouse. But that wasn't his style. If she had wanted him to have her address she would have given it to him.

When the thirty minutes were over, he started to worry. After all, Lorena was suicidal, as he knew all too horribly well.

But even in that scenario she had stood him up. Was there a more radical way to stand someone up than to take your life?

Stood up: he ordered another sherry, as that long forgotten feeling sank over him. He'd been spared it since his youth. The feeling of being abandoned was familiar to him, had made him cry for hours in bed when his parents went out for the night, while a nanny at her wits' end tried in vain to console him. It had plagued him in the various boarding schools he was sent to. And it had knocked him flat when Daphne packed her bags.

But the feeling of being stood up was different. Not

as devastating, but certainly humiliating. Whereas most abandoned people talk nonstop about their experience, people who've been stood up stay silent in shame.

Now Adrian was relieved he had reserved a table where he couldn't easily be seen by the other guests. He didn't feel like playing the stood-up man in front of a huge audience; how long should this man wait before admitting he had been stood up? And what should he do?

An hour after the time of their date Weynfeldt made a decision; he had the second place setting cleared, ate something small as a gesture and left a tip quite large enough to compensate for the money lost on the second cover.

In the taxi on the way home he realized it had become a slow-motion day after all.

12

As soon as she opened her eyes she would have to deal with reality. So she kept them closed. She was getting that champagne feeling, the feeling after the euphoria and before the headache. You could get rid of it with more champagne or Alka-Seltzer, or just ease it with lots of water, or you could sleep it off.

She wanted to sleep it off.

But now her eyes started opening on their own. In the same way they closed themselves when you were very tired, now they were doing the opposite. It took great effort for Lorena to keep them closed and look relaxed. She could force them shut, but then it would be obvious she was awake. She didn't want that.

She wished he was one of those men who was gone by the time she woke. Sometimes that was insulting, but it was often quite nice actually. You were saved from finding out what they looked like sober, in the cold light of day.

But this one here wanted more from her than he'd had so far. She didn't know exactly what, but he wanted more; she was sure of that.

He had called to arrange delivery of the Ungaro blouse, then brought it personally. Stood at the door holding a Spotlight bag in one hand, two bottles of cold champagne in the other, covered in condensation. She could hardly not invite him in.

One look at her apartment—a tiny studio with a kitchenette in the recess next to the bathroom, cardboard boxes everywhere, most of them open because she was living out of them—and he knew: "Congratulations. I was very impressed."

She washed two glasses, not exactly champagne flutes, and they drank the Veuve Clicquot, not exactly her preferred brand, while it was still cold. She didn't have ice, and her tiny fridge was already feeling the strain.

He was funny. He described exactly how she had caused the dress to disappear, and parodied her performance with Weynfeldt. He was good-looking in a conventional kind of way, with just the right dash of insolence, and she didn't have to pretend anything with him.

It wasn't hard for him to get her into bed. It was the only thing to sit on.

"I have a date in an hour," she told him first.

"With him?" he asked.

"Yes."

"Stand him up."

"I'll give him a quick call to cancel."

"I've watched him: you've got him eating out of your hand."

"That's why I need to call, to keep him interested."

"Wrong. Don't call, to keep him interested."

13

THE SKI SLOPES ABOVE THE GRAND HOTELS AND APART-
ment buildings were a muddy green, aside from a few
scraps of snow in the shaded dips. But the lake was fro-
zen, and the sky clear. A city of tents had been built
behind the grandstand, white plastic pavilions with
pointed gables, looking to Weynfeldt like a faintly oriental version of the plastic summerhouses which had
sprung up in gardens and on roof terraces in his country
in recent years.

Ever since he could remember, Adrian Weynfeldt had
been at home in the Engadin. He had spent all his winter vacations and much of his summers up here, and
had attended an international boarding school nearby
for several years as a teenager.

The landscape had always been so familiar to him,
he never perceived it as especially beautiful. It was only
when he saw it through the eyes of Giovanni Segantini that it revealed its beauty to him. His father had
owned several Segantinis. Adrian had seen the paintings hundreds of times, but he was twelve or thirteen
before he identified one of the landscapes—the view
from his hotel room on vacation. Even then it was only
after a casual remark from his father that he recognized
it. It looked so different, even though every detail was
represented.

After that he began to imagine how the things he saw would look painted—first the landscapes, then the interiors, the people and the still lives—by Segantini, later by other painters from his father's collection.

Beginning as a game, it gradually became a mania, and became Weynfeldt's way of seeing the world. When he finished high school he started art school, but soon accepted that no amount of enthusiasm could make up for a lack of talent. And so he had to content himself with being an art historian.

The image in front of him now couldn't be salvaged even by asking how Segantini would have painted it. He was seated on a plastic chair upholstered with white fake fur, under artificial palms with the usual circle around him, all offspring of his parents' friends.

Karl Stauber was senior director of an old Swiss corporation, his wife, Senta, a woman full of joie de vivre and fire in her younger days, was now a gray, nondescript old thing, hair dull and brittle from an illness her family endured with scant patience, and hushed up with great effort; Senta Stauber had been an alcoholic since she turned forty.

Charlotte Capaul was the third wife of Dr. Capaul, family practitioner to most of those present. She was a dreamy, childlike creature, in her mid-thirties and as such thirty years younger than her husband, who was unsuited to her in every other way too.

Kurt Weller, son of Max Weller, the man who had handled international transport for Weynfeldt & Co, was a dyed-in-the-wool Bavarian. He owned one of Germany's largest transport businesses and spent most of his time either in St. Moritz or on the island of Sylt. His wife, Uschi, was Munich born and bred, her skin prematurely aged from a lifetime of sun worship—all over, allegedly. A patient of various plastic surgeons, she had an extensive medical history, which she related openly and not without humor, to the present company.

The Widlers were not there, for the first time since Adrian could remember. A sign that Dr. Widler was in a very bad way.

They picked at *viande des Grisons* from a big platter and drank champagne, which the air temperature kept cold, almost too cold.

The third day of the St. Moritz White Turf races was a fixture in Weynfeldt's calendar. Even as a small boy Adrian had stood by the saddling boxes admiring the horses, and above all the jockeys and their racing colors, shiny and silky with big checkered patterns, stripes or spots. And while his parents sat with the parents of the people he was sitting with now, keeping their temperatures up with mulled wine and their spirits up with champagne, he would run around along the fence by the racetrack, waiting for the muffled drumming of the hooves.

Adrian begged his parents for riding lessons till they finally agreed. Under the vigilant eyes of his overanxious mother, he took a few lessons, but they were stopped immediately following a harmless fall onto the soft sawdust in the riding hall. He abandoned his plan for a career as a jockey and restricted his passion for equestrian sports to learning the names and colors of every stable, and the biographies of all the major jockeys.

When he was twenty he took up riding lessons again—secretly—and soon realized that not only did he lack aptitude, he had lost his childhood passion.

But he could always be found here on the third race day. For the long weekend he stayed in the same suite at the Palace Hotel his parents had always booked; he held the same conversations, bet the same moderate sums and did everything he could to structure the passage of time and thus slow it down.

But this time it all felt stale. Karl Stauber seemed to have aged years since the last time, was absentminded and confused, and kept repeating himself.

Dr. Capaul provoked his wife with inappropriate remarks about the scantily clad samba dancers who performed during the pauses between races.

Kurt Weller seemed absent and thoughtful, and his wife, Uschi, tried desperately to keep the conversation going, becoming louder and wittier.

For the first time in his life Weynfeldt wondered whether the people who thought regularity shortened your life were in fact right. It suddenly seemed no time at all since Februaries here meant snow on the roofs, woods and slopes, and before horse races on ice were given titles such as the "Gaggenau Home Appliances Grand Prix."

Weynfeldt's face had acquired some color by the time he returned to the office on Tuesday. The city was still in the middle of a false spring. Every day new buds, shoots and blossoms exposed themselves to the frost which might descend on them at random and without mercy at any moment.

No word from Lorena. Her name had not appeared on Frau Hauser's handwritten list of answering machine messages. There were none of the question marks his housekeeper placed by unidentified messages. And her name was not among Véronique's stack of notes and printed e-mails.

Instead Strasser had called several times, insisting—Véronique had underlined the word twice—that they meet. Ideally for lunch; that evening at the latest.

It was the third Tuesday of the month, and lunchtime was reserved for a regular meal in the Krone with the Etter clan, a group of aging art historians associated with Professor Etter, his tutor at university. But given his recent doubts about his theory of regularity, and that Strasser was much nicer company at midday than at night, Weynfeldt excused himself from the Etter clan and arranged to meet Strasser for lunch in Es Corb, a small Catalan restaurant which he knew Strasser liked.

He assumed that this was about Rolf's trip to the Marquesas and took his checkbook.

He was early. The air in Es Corb was still fresh; they were just closing the windows. Weynfeldt sat at a window seat for two and ordered a water, then added a *Jerez*, to reduce his vulnerability to attack; Strasser took it personally if someone failed to drink alcohol in his presence.

Es Corb was previously called Raben and had been a bar surviving mainly on its beer sales. Just under a year ago a group of young second generation Catalans had taken the place over, serving a fusion of Catalan and Swiss food.

Unusually, Strasser was almost on time, standing at the entrance while he looked defiantly round the room, before seeing Weynfeldt and making his way to his table.

"Been here long?" he asked Weynfeldt, who had stood up to greet him.

"Just arrived," he said, and shook his hand. They both sat.

Strasser began studying the menu. Weynfeldt did the same. "The *bacalao* and *saucisson* dish sounds interesting," Weynfeldt observed.

"Just to be clear," Strasser said, without looking up from the menu, "I'm paying this time."

Weynfeldt concealed his surprise and said simply, "Thanks. My turn again next time," and decided against the *bacalao*. By the time the waiter had come to take their order he had decided on the marinated tuna with onion aspic.

"I thought you were having the *bacalao*," Strasser said, irritated. "The gentleman is having the *bacalao*," he told the waiter.

The waiter looked at Weynfeldt.

"Perhaps a little heavy for lunch, don't you think?" Adrian asked.

Strasser didn't give the waiter time to answer. "It's only at night you shouldn't eat anything heavy. Please bring us two *bacalao*."

The waiter looked toward Weynfeldt again: "The portions are fairly small."

"Okay, the *bacalao*," Adrian nodded.

"You see, that's what makes me sick about you," Strasser began, once the waiter was gone, "always this patronizing attitude. You're thinking, *the poor bastard wants to pay for himself for once, I'll grant him the pleasure and order something cheap.* I've had it up to here!" He held his hand up horizontally, level with the bridge of his nose.

Weynfeldt was shocked. He had experienced Strasser's fits of rage for years, but never seen them at this time of day, in this situation. "I'm sorry, I didn't mean it like that. I really was just concerned about how heavy it was. I have to work this afternoon."

"There you go again! Do you think I don't have to work? Do you think you are the only one who works? You don't even realize how supercilious you are."

Weynfeldt sat in guilty silence. The accusation that he was condescending toward people, without intending or realizing it, was not new.

The waiter brought the wine, a small carafe of Ceps Nous. They waited silently till their glasses had been filled.

Adrian considered asking how Strasser's Polynesia plans were going, to change the subject, but changed his mind. It could be taken as an attempt to remind Strasser of his position as mendicant.

They gazed out of the window, saying nothing. Outside it was pretending to be spring, and the people passing had fallen for it. They weren't even carrying warm clothes over their shoulders and arms; they were dressed for spring, as upbeat as the misleading weather.

Strasser was the first to speak, once he had emptied his glass and refilled it. "About the Marquesas—forget it."

"Have you changed your plans?"

"Only in as far as I'm going to finance it myself."

"Ah. I see."

Strasser was not satisfied with this reaction. "I don't want to wake up in the middle of the Pacific Ocean every day and think: *All this is thanks to Adrian. Thank you, Adrian! Thank you, Adrian!*"

"You wouldn't have to. I'd have been happy."

"I know. You like it when other people are dependent on you. No sacrifice is too great."

"It wouldn't be a great sacrifice, Rolf," Adrian assured him, and immediately wished he could swallow the words.

"Thanks for rubbing my nose in it. The sum my whole life depends on is chicken feed to you. *Thank you, Adrian! Thank you, Adrian!*"

The waiter brought the food. Three slices of dark *saucisson vaudois* topped by three pieces of pale cod, garnished with spring onions and black lentils. They began to eat. Neither had much appetite.

"You have no idea how liberating it is, no longer having to be grateful to you."

"I didn't know you felt that way. Please excuse me."

"*Please excuse me, please excuse me.* Ditch the fucking politeness for a change. It's all just part of your unbearable superciliousness!"

For a while Weynfeldt said nothing. Then: "Did you arrange to meet just to pick a fight with me?"

"Damn right!" Strasser yelled. "The great changes in life can't happen without a fight. Opinions have to clash, emotions, worlds! Fight for once! Live for once!"

People at the neighboring tables were beginning

to notice them. Weynfeldt wondered how they must appear to the spectators. Most likely as a gay couple at the climax of a relationship drama.

He made the mistake of saying this to Strasser. Sometimes a joke had the effect of calming him down.

But this time Strasser was not in the mood for jokes. He stood up, drained his glass, threw his napkin onto the table, hissed "Asshole" and left the restaurant.

Weynfeldt watched through the bare window as he wound his way rapidly through the pedestrians, black tie waving in the breeze. He watched him till he was out of sight.

Being punished with abandonment was familiar from his childhood. His mother had used the threat as a deterrent. "I'm leaving now and I won't come back," was a sentence she had successfully brought him into line with, even as an adult. Only after he met Daphne did it lose its effect. But it was only when his mother was very old indeed that he first thought—didn't say, but at least thought—*so do it*.

He had no idea Rolf Strasser felt such hatred toward him. He had always thought Rolf was just a volatile person, and that because he was also a frustrated artist, this characteristic was often accentuated. He had never taken his nasty comments and coarse remarks personally. Adrian was never inclined to take things personally. Perhaps that was a mistake. Maybe many things were meant more personally than he took them.

It seemed as if the passersby had started walking more slowly. He finished the food on his plate at the same slow pace, and ordered dessert too, a combination of *crema catalana* and crème brûlée, and a two-glass carafe of the Ceps Nous, as Strasser had finished the previous one.

Weynfeldt asked for the check. It was a tall, slender woman who brought it, not the waiter. *"Boa tarde,"* he said in surprise. *"Como esta?"*

"Tudo bem, obrigada," Frau Almeida replied.

"You've started working here?"

"Three times a week at the moment, more often soon. Herr Baier is reducing my hours gradually."

"Of course. He's moving to Lake Como." Adrian paid the bill.

"Herr Strasser had to leave in a hurry," Frau Almeida observed, bringing his change.

"He had forgotten an important appointment," Weynfeldt said, and left a generous tip on the plate she brought the change on. He stood up and said good-bye.

He got halfway across the restaurant then stopped, and returned to the table. Frau Almeida was busy clearing it. "Tell me, how do you know Herr Strasser?"

"He's a professional artist, of course. He came to visit Herr Baier every day for a long time. To paint."

"Do we have a Vallotton in the auction?" Véronique asked.

It was nearly three by the time Weynfeldt got back to the office. He hadn't warned her he would be late, instead bringing a box of assorted macarons—vanilla, champagne, mocha and pistachio—from his favorite confectioners. She took them without a fuss as the compensation due to her for his lateness.

"... because someone called and asked about the Vallotton in our spring auction. I told him there wasn't one, but he insisted there was. 'Ask your boss!' he said."

"What was his name?"

"Gauguin, like the painter. He sounded drunk."

Weynfeldt smiled and shook his head. "I know him."

"And? Do we have a Vallotton?"

"If we get a Vallotton, you'll be the first to know."

He did two hours of work in his office. At five he took his leave from Véronique. The macaron box lay between the two computer screens. It was empty.

He must have pressed the wrong button. The elevator that opened its doors was the size of a whole room. He went inside and pressed floor six.

It stopped on the second floor, the doors opened and a blue-clad orderly wheeled a bed in. Weynfeldt clung to the wall. In the bed lay a man of around thirty, hollow eyed and apathetic.

"That one is normally the elevator for visitors," the orderly said, pointing behind him. The patient ignored Weynfeldt.

The doors closed and the elevator rose. At the head of the bed sat a yellow, worn teddy bear, as listless as its owner.

The elevator stopped one floor higher and the orderly pushed the bed out. The doors closed and the elevator continued. Weynfeldt wished he hadn't seen that teddy bear.

Mereth Widler was waiting for him outside Room 612. The attendant had informed her of Weynfeldt's arrival. From a distance she still looked very much the china-doll lady, but close up Adrian saw that she had freshened her lipstick for his arrival without using a mirror, hastily, with an unsteady hand. Her eyes were tired, and her hair was lopsided. But she knew that her reputation came before her and as she embraced him, muttered, "I should warn you, he looks like a bag of shit."

Dr. Widler lay in the bed as if a part of it, not its contents. His skin, his hair and his nightdress were identical in tone to the sheets surrounding him.

As Adrian entered, he turned his eyes toward him, showed a hint of a smile, raised his right hand with the thumb pointing down and let it drop onto the quilt, like an object which had nothing to do with him.

Weynfeldt lifted it up again, held it and placed it carefully back down. He handed Mereth a box of sweets, from the same confectionery as Véronique's macarons. "I wasn't sure if you …" he said, "but if not, I'm sure Mereth will …"

With his eyes, the old doctor pointed to the chrome chair next to him, upholstered with green plastic. A classic hospital visitor's chair with an adjustable back such as he'd sat on at his father's sickbed and, twenty years later, his mother's. He decided to find out who had designed them and perhaps include an example in his collection.

Weynfeldt offered the chair first to Widler's wife. Only after she had categorically rejected it, did he sit down. The room smelled of flowers and disinfectant and sickness. An IV tube fed into the crease of Widler's thin, sinewy left arm, dusted with white down. Two tiny plastic tubes were inserted into his nostrils. Further tubes emerged from under the covers. Weynfeldt knew better than to wonder where they were going or coming from.

The doctor wanted to say something. His lips began forming a letter, a syllable, perhaps a word. His whole face seemed to be trying to help his lips with this difficult task. But just as Adrian thought that now, now he would succeed, Widler raised his right hand again, with a dismissive gesture, and let it fall to the bed in the same moment.

Weynfeldt nodded as if he'd understood what the sick man had said. Then he started describing the weekend in St. Moritz, passing on the others' greetings and reporting on the races and the results, as far as his memory served him.

After a few minutes Dr. Widler fell asleep. Weynfeldt went silent and gazed at the white, shrunken face. He was not quite as old as he looked, not yet eighty. His mother had been over twenty years older than him. He remembered that when she first became his patient, she had said, "You know you're getting old when your doctors are younger than you."

Mereth indicated that he could reasonably leave now—with a grateful nod and the understanding the old show the young when they let them go and have their fun.

Weynfeldt glanced once more at Dr. Widler. He was reminded of Ferdinand Hodler's portrait series of the dying Valentine Godé-Dârel.

14

SOMETIMES ADRIAN WEYNFELDT FOUND IT EERIE TO return home. The harsh neon light in the entranceway, between the creaking oak door to the street and the noiseless sliding security door. The knowledge that his every move was recorded and saved for two months. The elevator which took him in silence past the floors closed to him, in a building he owned. The steel door which opened and released him into the paneled hallway with oak parquet. The double doors to his apartment, Art Deco motifs etched into their frosted glass panes.

On nights like these he felt as if he had been sucked through a steel tunnel into another world and time. And when he entered his apartment, he felt like the sole survivor of a distant disaster. No other human being lived in this building, or in the surrounding buildings. He was entirely alone with his collection of paintings and furniture. Witness to an extinct culture which no one would ever revive.

He opened the door with the key his father had used, and his father before him, put the lights on and was happy that the flooring was another of the issues where Casutt had overruled him. The old parquet boards, creaking at various pitches, had not been restored, replaced instead by solid-oak ship-deck planks, which he could now walk on without hearing ghostly steps behind him.

Frau Hauser had left him her usual note, written in her small, neat handwriting and attached with a magnet in the form of a yellow duck to the chrome expanse behind which the fridge, freezer, climate-controlled cabinets, roasting oven, steam oven, microwave oven and warming drawers were all concealed.

Kaspar Casutt had provided Weynfeldt with a professional kitchen. Its chrome surfaces alone occupied a large proportion of Frau Hauser's ever changing assistants' time. The consequences of Casutt discovering the duck magnet were unthinkable.

The note said, "Roast beef and mixed salad in climate cabinet; salad dressing ditto, separate; remoulade ditto; toast, ready toasted, in microwave—one minute (yellow button); no messages on answering machine; bon appétit! Hauser."

Adrian had to open several doors before he found the climate cabinet. It contained vegetables, fruit and other foodstuffs, each in different climate zones, the temperature and humidity regulated separately. He took the tray with the roast beef and salad out, poured the dressing on and mixed it with the designer salad servers also chosen by Casutt. Then he pressed the yellow button on the microwave, waited for the machine to beep, took the toast out with the bread tongs waiting nearby in ready position and placed it in the bread basket, also handily placed and lined with a napkin. This was about the extent of his culinary abilities.

He found the wine cooler immediately, however, chose a local pinot noir, and carried the tray all the way to his study, the one room aside from his bedroom where he felt alright on nights like this.

He flicked on some light switches. The room's indirect lighting came on, and a spotlight threw a beam onto the Vallotton in the center of the room.

Adrian switched the reading lamp on and turned the indirect lighting off, made some space on his desk and placed his supper on it. He put a CD on the stereo—J. J. Cale, music from his youth. He poured himself a glass of wine and started eating.

The room became a shade darker as the lights went out in a row of windows in one of the office buildings opposite. He sat in the cone of light thrown by his desk lamp, lonely as the man on the moon. A few feet away from him, Vallotton's model knelt in front of the *salamandre* stove; she too was lit by a single light source.

Why had he obscured her lower extremities? Such a virtuoso draftsman and practiced anatomist as Vallotton? Was the author of his catalogue raisonnée, Marina Ducrey, right that it was a reference to the Cycladic idols from 2000 BC? And that it preempted Man Ray's *Le Violin d'Ingres*, the phallic female torso with *f*-shaped violin holes superimposed?

J. J. Cale's soft, husky voice sang "After Midnight." Adrian fished through his salad, removing the radishes. He didn't like radishes, they made him burp. He had missed the opportunity, some time years ago, to tell Frau Hauser this. Since then he had been finding more or less imaginative ways of making radishes disappear. Sometimes he suspected Frau Hauser had known for years and was tormenting him pedagogically so he would one day pluck up the courage to tell her.

His thoughts wandered to his strange lunch with Rolf Strasser. How had Rolf's feelings built up like that, without his realizing? Were there other people who felt the same way? How little he knew about his friends. Rolf thought he was supercilious. Saw his politeness as a form of condescension. Found his generosity intolerable. Knew Baier. Had been visiting him for a long while, to paint.

What had Rolf been painting at Baier's house?

He placed a slice of roast beef on a piece of toast, now cold again, and spread remoulade on top, lost in thought.

What had Rolf Strasser been painting every day at Baier's?

Weynfeldt took a bite out of the roast beef toast and put it back on the plate, stood up and walked, chewing, to the easel with the Vallotton.

The light from the spot fell at an angle onto the painting, and picked up its matte sheen. Like almost all temperas by Vallotton it was not varnished. Many of these tempera works had a note on the reverse in Vallotton's own hand saying, "never to be varnished."

The matte sheen coating the image was the patina of time. Dust, nicotine, variations in temperature and conscientious maids' dusters had left a thin film across the surface of the painting, like a matte wax finish.

In one of the four drawers of the black sideboard by Paul Artaria, a one-off from 1930 which Weynfeldt used to store equipment, was a large magnifying glass. He fetched it out and inspected the surface of the painting.

Hardly a brushstroke could be seen. When he'd used

this technique Vallotton had worked with the largest brushes and the most homogenous color fields possible.

Adrian put his "Weynfeldt beak" to the painting. It smelled familiar and, almost imperceptibly, of something old and organic. The board, and whatever the painter had used as thickener—bone glue? Egg yolk?

The painting was signed "F. Vallotton. 1900" on the top right.

Weynfeldt knew that signature well, along with the painter's little obsession with adding a period after his surname.

In the red of the armchair protruding into the picture from the right were some mildew stains, big enough to be visible in a reproduction. Mildew stains were not conclusive proof that a picture was genuine; forgers often created them, with freeze-dried coffee powder, with a solution of rust, or simply with some thinned down raw umbra.

He went to the bookshelves, took down the second volume of Vallotton's catalogue raisonnée, and looked under 1900 till he found the picture. Marina Ducrey had allowed over half a page simply for the reproduction.

The mildew stains were there. The same number, in the same places. He ran the large magnifying glass over the reproduction. Everything was the same, including the signature.

Weynfeldt shut the book, picked up his toast and returned to the painting. His mouth full, chewing, he searched all over it; he didn't know what for. He shoved the last mouthful in and continued searching.

The period!

In three paces Weynfeldt was back at the catalogue raisonnée on his desk. He licked the traces of remoulade from his fingers—something he never did!—and rubbed them dry on the inside of his trouser pockets, then flipped through the book till the page with the painting was open in front of him again.

He took the magnifying glass, switched its little lamp on and enlarged the signature. "F. Vallotton 1900." Without a period after the surname.

Once you know a picture is forged it's easy to find proof. Weynfeldt took it out of the frame and found ten pieces of evidence immediately. The paint, for instance, was too fresh and elastic; he was able to test that on a thick patch at the edge, hidden by the frame.

The board had been primed, but Vallotton always worked with unprimed card.

The matte sheen on the surface was not the patina of time, it had been created using wax varnish. A test with a cigarette lighter in a discreet corner proved this.

In less than an hour Adrian Weynfeldt knew for certain what Rolf Strasser had been painting every day at Klaus Baier's house.

15

THIS WOULD BE LORENA'S FIRST BOOTH-BABE JOB, BUT she couldn't be choosy; February was not a busy month for trade fairs.

The agency that usually got her hostess and promotional jobs had asked if she wanted to work at the motorbike fair and she had said yes. She thought she would be offering provincial bike dealers lukewarm Prosecco, wearing a two-piece costume with a matching pillbox on her head. Then it came out that she was expected to present the exhibits: writhe around on motorbikes, in other words.

Well, she thought, even the booth-babe thing can be done with style. Even in the booth-babe world there were hierarchies and she would soon find out how they worked.

It was much like the world of modeling, where the top models got to present the top outfits. And the top motorbike at this year's fair was the Ducelli 7312. Everyone wanted to writhe around on the Ducelli.

The changing room was normally the exhibition center storeroom, by the toilets. Waiting around, among boxes of Kleenex, makeup cases and coffee cups full of soggy cigarette butts, the women teased each other about the Ducelli, like girls at dance school discussing the most handsome boy in the class.

MARTIN SUTER

From time to time men came in, without knocking, and looked at the girls. Most of these men were stocky, with an exhibitor's pass dangling on a broad, colored ribbon over their belly; cocky yet shy, reminding Lorena of nightclub guests.

The girls peered at the brand name on the men's passes and, depending on what it said, they were either friendly, or very friendly.

Lorena soon concluded she wasn't going to be the one presenting the Ducelli, so she either ignored the exhibitors or looked disparagingly at them. There were not enough chairs, and she stayed seated on her plastic stool, wrapped tight in her coat as the heating wasn't working properly in the windowless, smoky room.

So she didn't realize what was going on when one of the men, younger, more slender, better dressed and without a colored ribbon, said something to his stocky colleague and pointed to her.

It was only when the other girls' heads all turned toward her that she got it: she had just become the Ducelli girl.

A few minutes later she was sitting at a makeup table, in tight black-leather trousers; knee-length, high-heeled, pointed boots; a tight black shirt with the Ducelli logo and an unzipped biker jacket the same shade of red as the 7312, also with a logo, trying to stop the older woman who had dressed her from applying so much makeup she would be unrecognizable.

Her social standing among the other booth babes had changed in a flash. She was treated with sudden respect, and received the occasional smile, albeit affected. One

of them brought her a coffee, another offered her a cigarette and another tried to get on the right side of her
with a few friendly words. Lorena had to admit she was
enjoying it. This is what it's come to, she thought, you're
gratified to be chosen as the Ducelli girl.

It was loud in the exhibition hall. Music from different
stands clashed with sudden roars from revving motorbikes and a dull drone from an adjacent hall where the
Streetbike Freestyle Cup participants were training.
The Ducelli stood on a pedestal, its outline discern-
able beneath a red cloth. It was surrounded by visitors,
mostly dressed in casual clothes, sportswear with logos,
motorbike gear, all-weather jackets and jumpsuits.
Almost all of them had cameras around their necks, or
held minicameras and cell phones above their heads. A
man in a business suit with an Italian accent was giving
an enthusiastic speech full of technical details.

Lorena stood in the background and waited for the
agreed signal. She was genuinely nervous. She had let
her new friend, the Moto Guzzi 8V girl, persuade her
to accept a shot of vodka in her mineral water, which
wasn't difficult.

"Eccola!" the man in the suit said. A flourish of rock-
guitar riffs burst from the loudspeakers and Lorena
made her way to the pedestal. She was good at the catwalk thing, even in pointed, high-heeled boots, even a
size too small.

She probably took slightly too long to reach the edge
of the pedestal where the man was waiting for her—a
man not accustomed to waiting—and a little concluding

flourish wouldn't have gone amiss, but her performance was good. The man helped her up, placed a corner of the red cloth in her hand, took the opposite corner and… *eccola!*

Shiny and red like a well-sucked raspberry candy, the bike stood in the storm of camera flashes. Lorena stood next to it, stroked it, nestled against it, posed on it, looking now at one camera, now at another, responded to the photographers' shouts and really got into her stride.

One of the photographers was standing half on the pedestal and gave her a hand signal she didn't understand. Only when another next to her made the same one, and another behind him too, did she understand: they wanted her to move aside.

She looked toward the presenter, inquiring, and he nodded. She stepped a few paces away. Now the flash storm reached its crescendo.

Lorena stood next to the pedestal, wanting to sink into a hole in the ground. But then a chubby young man nudged her and nodded at her encouragingly. He had three cameras around his neck and two camera bags over his shoulder.

"Press. If you have time later, I'd love to take some more shots once the amateurs are out the way." He gave her his card, with a picture of a girl on a motorbike. "Felix Scheiblin, photographer," it said. And lower down, the name of the publication he worked for: *Bikes & Babes*.

When the fair closed for the day, the Ducelli team invited them for cocktails. Lorena and Miss Moto Guzzi

8V rode in a taxi to the Fairhill, a nearby trade fair hotel, with Luca, the man who had made her Ducelli girl, and Franco, his stocky colleague.

Two other Ducelli colleagues were already in the bar, also accompanied by booth babes: Miss Kawasaki ER 6F and Miss BMW.

The bar was full of exhibitors and buyers, networking and poring over leaflets, catalogues and order forms, the hand holding their glasses stretched a safe distance from their paperwork.

Luca ordered Lorena a glass of champagne. She changed the order to a Bloody Mary, the best cocktail when you haven't eaten properly all day. She could see that Luca didn't like it when his decisions were overturned.

It soon became clear that this was not an official Ducelli business event and that dinner together was not part of the plan. One of the team soon disappeared, accompanied by Miss BMW, and by the time the barman brought Lorena's second Bloody Mary, Moto Guzzi 8V and Kawasaki ER 6F had also vanished along with their companions.

Luca left briefly, returned and put his room key on the little table in front of them, his hand on Lorena's thigh—high up, at the hem of her short skirt.

Lorena's Italian was limited, and Luca didn't speak a word of German. The few words they spoke were in English. Luca pushed his right hand under her hem, with his left he pointed to the Bloody Mary, almost full, and said, "Hurry up!"

Lorena took the glass and poured it all over his suit.

His white shirt front went deep red. She stood up and looked down at him. "Fast enough?" He sat immobile in his chair, like a victim of gang warfare.

Only when she turned to go did he rouse himself. As she left he punched her, hitting her kidneys hard. The blow took her breath away, and tears rose to her eyes, but she walked out of the bar with her head held high.

"*Puttana!*" he shouted after her. "*Puttana di merda!*"

Lorena walked down the narrow sidewalk by the four-lane highway. She held her left hand to the spot where she felt the pain, in her kidneys, and continued marching straight ahead. She took no notice of the cars, some reducing their speed, some sounding their horns. She threw up twice on the side of the road. The first time she was startled by the color of her vomit, till she remembered she had been drinking Bloody Marys.

She was cold. She had had a coat with her—not a bad one, black gabardine, Donna Karan, fall 2005—but had left it hanging on the coat stand in the bar. It would have ruined her exit if she'd retrieved it.

She was somewhere in the outskirts, but didn't know exactly where. A long way out for sure. Too far to walk home. Certainly not in the state she was in.

Here goes the Ducelli girl, she thought, and gave a sob. She wasn't prudish. She had gone to bed with people in similar situations in the past. It was just that asshole's presumption which made her mad, thinking he could take whatever he wanted. Not like that, he couldn't. Not after a day like today.

Another car slowed down, put its blinker on and

stopped a little way in front. Lorena kept her eyes on the sidewalk ahead. As she passed the car, a voice asked, "Taxi?"

She stopped still and nodded. The driver reached into the back and opened the door. Lorena slumped inside and pulled the door shut.

The driver was older, with tired, friendly eyes. He looked at her in the rearview mirror. "Everything okay?" he asked, in a Slavic accent. When he saw that his passenger wasn't capable of uttering a word, he said. "I'll just drive towards the center, okay?"

Lorena nodded. She relaxed. It was warm in the taxi, and smelled the way all taxis did, of the Little Tree air freshener hanging from the mirror.

She took her wallet from her handbag and her suspicion was confirmed: she had less money on her than the sum already displayed by the meter. She had been booked for all four days of the fair, and was to be paid on the final one.

That meant she couldn't go home. She had to go to someone who would pay for the taxi and ideally help her out with some cash too. Right now that meant one of only two people: Pedroni or Weynfeldt.

She gave the driver Weynfeldt's address. She couldn't cope with a man tonight who wanted something from her.

She took a small mirror out of her handbag and sorted her face out as best she could.

"Are you sure this is the right address?" came the driver's voice. "This is a bank."

Lorena hadn't noticed they had already arrived. "Yes, this is it. Please wait a moment and I'll ring." She got out of the car and pressed the bell. There was no sound from the intercom.

She rang again. Still no reaction.

Lorena returned to the taxi and called the private number on Weynfeldt's card, holding it under the passenger light. The driver watched her with a look of resignation.

Weynfeldt's answering machine came on. Just as Lorena was about to leave a message, the heavy wooden door opened. Two men came out. One of them was Adrian Weynfeldt. The other an old man with a cane.

16

AFTER HIS DISCOVERY ADRIAN SAT FOR A LONG WHILE at his desk, ate Frau Hauser's cold supper mechanically and finished the bottle of wine.

The monstrousness of the whole thing had paralyzed him. He wasn't sure who he was more disgusted by: Baier, a very old friend of the family, who had taken advantage of his trust so shamelessly, fully aware that he would ruin Weynfeldt's good name and his reputation as an expert, or Strasser, someone he thought was a good personal friend, who had let himself be exploited and drawn into this sleazy fraud.

Weynfeldt had picked up the telephone, but couldn't decide who to call first and confront: the forger or the fraudster.

It was nearly eleven thirty before he decided—on the forger. If he was honest, it was only because the fraudster belonged to the generation you didn't disturb with a phone call after ten p.m.

Strasser didn't answer the phone, neither his landline nor his cell.

He overcame his scruples and called Baier, imagining the telephone ringing through the house, Baier clambering out of bed in pain, putting a light on, looking for his cane. Or did he have a telephone next to his bed?

After the sixth ring, he heard Baier's daytime voice

explaining he was unavailable at the moment and inviting him to leave a message after the tone.

Weynfeldt did not leave a message. He hated talking to machines. It made him nervous; he could hear himself speak and got in a muddle. He would call Baier first thing in the morning. In the morning it was the other way round: Strasser belonged to the generation you did not disturb before ten a.m.

He went to bed with a lemon verbena tea, and had almost fallen asleep when a sudden realization brought him wide awake again: you have just been deceived in the most underhand way by two people you thought were friends and you're wondering what time of day to call without disturbing them? Why? Irreparable damage due to your upbringing.

He got up, slipped into his leather slippers, pulled on his dark-blue cashmere housecoat, went into the bathroom, combed his hair, straightened the collar of his pajamas where it showed beneath the housecoat and scrutinized himself in the mirror.

The last Weynfeldt.

Adrian wandered down the long passageway, past his museum-like rooms to a door at the end of the corridor. He lifted the painting next to the door frame away from the wall—a landscape by Gustave Buchet—and took the key hanging on a nail behind it, to open the door.

It was the room in which his mother had spent her last years. Weynfeldt had excluded it from the gut renovation, the one point on which he'd insisted Casutt couldn't have his way. Everything had been left just as it was at her death, apart from the hospital bed; he had exchanged that for her walnut Biedermeier bed.

The room was furnished with a Napoléon III sofa, two armchairs and a dressing table from the same era, a bureau and a chest of drawers. Between the two windows, each flanked by heavy curtains, stood a vitrine holding her collection of Venetian glass paperweights. Adrian's only other intervention had been to place the portrait of his mother which had hung in the sitting room for years above the sofa here. It showed her in all her splendor, as Weynfeldt's father used to say, sitting on this very sofa. She had her arms folded, and her watchful eyes on Adrian, wherever he was in the room. Outside of the room too.

The painting was by Varlin. It was done in nervous yet precise strokes, which seemed to begin by chance at the edge of the image, but came together at the center to form an unmistakable, unsparing likeness of Luise Weynfeldt.

Adrian sat on the side of the bed, as he had done so often in her later years. The room smelled slightly of floor polish, and of the lavender bags Frau Hauser hung and hid all over the house to improve the air quality and combat imaginary moths.

He gazed at the picture for a long time, feeling both affection and recrimination. Then he stood up, pointed at himself and sighed: "Irreparable damage."

He went back to bed, dosed off, but was woken from a light sleep by another thought: What if he had already accepted the Vallotton officially? If he'd taken it to the storerooms and shown it to Véronique? To his boss? To the press? If he had told the other branches, in London,

Paris and New York they should contact their Vallotton collectors? The forgery would have been exposed. And even if he had managed to make it clear he had acted in good faith, the dirt would have stuck to him.

He tried to drive these thoughts away. But no sooner had he succeeded in banishing them, others entered his mind and kept him from sleeping: Dr. Widler, his mother's young doctor, old now; he might well take his last breath this night.

And Lorena. Lorena on the wrong side of the balustrade. Lorena in Spotlight. Lorena in bed. In exactly the spot he was now, tossing and turning. Lorena not at Châteaubriand. Lorena not on the answering machine. Lorena not on the telephone.

As on every other workday, by half past seven he was sitting in his breakfast room—bright, and furnished with pieces by Hans Eichenberger from the 1950s— reading the newspaper and eating the two croissants Frau Hauser had bought on her way to work from Schrader's bakery, with her homemade, runny cherry jelly, but without butter. He drank a freshly squeezed orange juice along with them, followed by a caffè latte.

Straight after his breakfast he called Baier. Frau Almeida answered and suggested he try Baier's cell phone; he was at Lake Como right now, but was expected back today. Weynfeldt tried, and Baier did indeed answer. He was upbeat, asking immediately about the weather in Zurich, because on Lake Como it was more than spring-like; on Lake Como it was summery.

Weynfeldt was able to assure him that he too had

breakfasted with the window open. Then he fell silent.

"Yes?" Baier asked finally. "What can I do for you?"

Adrian cleared his throat. "I have to talk to you about *La Salamandre*."

"What about it?"

"You know what."

Now it was Baier's turn to be silent.

"Frau Almeida says you are coming back today—when?"

"Half past five."

"Shall we say seven?" Weynfeldt was amazed at his resoluteness.

"Where?"

"My apartment."

Véronique had two phone message for him. One was from yesterday, after Weynfeldt had left the office. That man who called himself Gauguin again, wanting to know what the Vallotton was valued at; he had laughed at her when she repeated that there was no Vallotton in the auction. So was there?

The other had come ten minutes ago. A Frau Widler. Had asked if he would call back.

Weynfeldt knew what it would be about. He called, expressed his condolences and asked if there was any-thing he could do. Luckily Mereth Widler declined his offer.

"It is true, isn't it?" Véronique asked. "We don't have a Vallotton?"

"No, no, and once more no," Adrian said, able to look her in the face as he said it.

He was distracted that day, unable to concentrate. All morning he postponed the decision whether to confront Strasser or not. In the afternoon he decided it would be shrewder to wait till he had talked to Baier. He took a walk by the lake at lunchtime, where it looked like Woodstock without the rain.

He got home early. Frau Hauser and a young Asian woman he hadn't met before were busy preparing the evening meal he had ordered. He changed, got himself a beer—something he seldom drank, as it made one's breath more alcoholic than other drinks, despite being less alcoholic—and withdrew to his study.

The painting stood in the dim, subdued light like something dirty or dangerous. The skin of the kneeling nude had the same shine to it as the bodies in the photos you could borrow from older boys at boarding school, in return for money or cigarettes.

Klaus Baier arrived on time. The doorbell rang at seven and Weynfeldt took the elevator down to let him in. He found Baier waiting at the door in the company of a man holding a large portfolio with strengthened corners. At the curb stood a taxi, its door open and hazard blinkers on.

The man was the taxi driver; he handed Weynfeldt the portfolio and Baier paid him.

They rode the elevator up to the apartment, in silence, and Weynfeldt took his guest straight to his study, where he leaned the portfolio against the wall by the door. He assumed Baier had brought it to transport the forgery away after their discussion. It seemed Baier wanted to keep things brief; he unfastened the black straps and opened the gray cardboard flaps.

But the portfolio contained the genuine Vallotton.

Weynfeldt was not sure he would be prepared simply to accept the exchange and let the matter drop. But Baier took the picture out, hobbled over to an empty easel next to Strasser's Vallotton, also unframed, and placed the genuine one on it. Then he turned to Adrian like someone waiting for a compliment on some great achievement.

Weynfeldt said nothing. But he had to admit, Rolf Strasser had done an excellent job. Even now, side by side with the original, under the merciless spotlight, although his forgery didn't stand up to comparison in every respect, it certainly came off well. The original looked strangely fresher than the copy; Strasser had taken the artificial aging process too far. But the forgery really looked like a clone of the original. Even the expressive quality, essentially indefinable in any artwork, was uncannily similar to that of the original. His Viennese professor's judgment, such a blow to Strasser, was confirmed yet again: he might not be an artist, but he was certainly skilled.

"And what if I hadn't realized?" Aside from a brief greeting, these were the first words Weynfeldt spoke to Baier.

"Then no one would have realized."

"You're wrong there. The only reason I didn't realize was because it never occurred to me you would palm me off with a forgery. Think about it; I trusted you. I never thought you, an old friend of the family, would abuse my trust so shamelessly."

There was a knock, and Frau Hauser entered. She would be serving a hot meal later in the Green Salon; would the gentlemen like to take their aperitif here in the study?

Without waiting for Adrian to respond, Baier ordered a brandy and an ashtray, as if it were his house. He sat on the yellow fiberglass shell chair Weynfeldt used at his desk and took a leather case for three cigars out of his breast pocket.

"I'm sure you don't mind," he observed, bit the tip off a Havana and began ceremoniously to ignite it.

Weynfeldt certainly did mind. He hated it when his study stank of stale cigar smoke. But he would never have forbidden a guest from smoking. He simply expected his guests not to consider smoking in his study.

Frau Hauser returned with the brandy and poured Baier a glass. She gave Adrian a glass of the Château Haut-Brion 2001 he had chosen to go with dinner. Weynfeldt drank good wine even with unwelcome guests.

Bauer dipped the end of the cigar in the brandy. A revolting habit, Weynfeldt thought. They both looked at the two pictures.

"I understand," Baier began, "that you feel betrayed. But whether or not you believe it, I didn't want to betray you."

"No?"

"It just happened."

Adrian waited. He was not going to sit on one of the low cantilever chairs, forced to look up to Baier as he had at their last meeting.

"Doctors and lawyers are bound by professional secrecy. How do you art experts work?"

"We are discreet," was all Weynfeldt said.

"I grew up with this painting. I have spent my entire life with it. It's hard for me now, at the end of my life, to part with it. What am I saying? It's breaking my heart. Got it?"

"Why are you doing it then?"

"Because I have to."

"I understand," Adrian said, although he didn't understand how someone like Baier could have got into this situation. "Why don't you sell one of the other pictures from your collection?"

"You really are discreet, you art experts?"

"Like priests at confession."

"I've already sold them."

Weynfeldt was confused for a moment. "But the Lake Geneva landscape by Hodler was still hanging in your house the other day."

Baier shook his head, saying nothing.

"But I saw it with my own eyes."

"What your eyes saw was a reproduction. Like the Segantini. And the Giacomettis. And the others. So the walls don't look empty."

"You have had your entire collection forged?"

"Not forged. They are facsimile prints on canvas. I'm sure you know about them. I believe Murphy's organizes them for clients who can't bear to part with their artworks."

"But this one is painted by hand." They looked at the

Vallottons through the haze of smoke.

"A print would not have been authentic enough."

"Nor the copy it seems."

Baier interjected. "Oh no, quite the opposite. I'm delighted with it."

"So why didn't you keep it?"

"For that exact reason. Because it's too perfect. Because it's identical. An impulse—I don't know!" Baier drained the brandy snifter. "Wouldn't you like to know which Vallotton you saw that night at my house—the one on the left, or the one on the right?"

"The genuine one."

"There is no genuine one. There is only a left and a right one; an old one and a new one."

At this moment there was a knock and Frau Hauser entered. She asked the gentlemen to come to the Green Salon, dinner would be served in a moment. She waited till they had left the room, Baier limping, then opened one of the plate glass windows, shaking her head in disapproval.

Frau Hauser kept notes on Weynfeldt's guests. She had noted, for instance, that Klaus Baier liked her homemade clear oxtail soup. Weynfeldt and his guest had barely sat down before the new Asian woman served them just such a soup.

Weynfeldt waited till Baier had finished praising Frau Hauser's memory, attentiveness and culinary skills, then returned to the matter in hand. "There may be a left and a right Vallotton, an old one and a new one, but one of them will always be forged. Always."

Baier started his oxtail soup. He had to bend right

over the bowl and his hand was shaking. Weynfeldt didn't watch him, concentrating on his own soup to avoid making his guest feel awkward—at least in this respect.

After a few spoonfuls Baier pushed the bowl aside. "It's the same painting. It is an identical execution of the same idea using the same technique in the same format."

Weynfeldt finished his soup in silence.

"The only difference is that the idea did not originate in two heads but in one. Vallotton came up with the picture in his head and painted it directly from there. My fellow painted it indirectly from the painting. The difference, my dear art expert, is not material, it is ideal."

Frau Hauser and her assistant came in and cleared the table, Frau Hauser making no comment on Baier's half-full bowl. Shortly afterward the two women returned with the next course. Ravioli ricotta with sage butter. Homemade, and so big, only three pieces fit on each plate. Judging by Baier's reaction this had also been noted in Frau Hauser's card index.

Weynfeldt waited till they were alone again. Then he said, "You're challenging one of the basic principles of art, you do realize that? What you're saying is forger's logic. Just say it: *I tried to take you for a ride but it didn't work.*"

"I'm not challenging the basic principles of art. Great artists have thought the same way. Old Masters let their pupils paint indirectly out of their heads and signed their names at the bottom—quite rightly. As my fellow has done here. I'm challenging the basic principles of your profession. If my opinion prevailed, you'd have to close up shop, Murphy's and all the rest."

He put his glass down, noticed it was empty and let Adrian pour him another. "There are people who have better ideas in their heads. And there are others who can execute them better. Have you ever stopped to consider what art could be like if the two were to work together? It wouldn't surprise me if my fellow was actually better technically than Vallotton. Unfortunately he is fated never to create better ideas. Imagine what artworks could be created if forgers were allowed to be better than artists."

Baier ate little of the antipasti either. Weynfeldt was certain that Frau Hauser's coq au vin would follow, skinned and braised with slices of bacon in cabernet sauvignon, another classic for guests of Baier's generation.

And so it did. With all the adulation and alcohol, Baier was a little tired now, and restricted himself to a few exclamations of delight before digging straight into the chicken flesh, which fell from the bone at the merest touch.

"So if it makes no difference," Weynfeldt ventured, "whether the work is by the artist or an imitator, if there is no material difference, only an idealistic one, why didn't you keep the imitation?"

Baier put the piece of meat he had arranged on his fork back on the plate. "It makes no difference to anyone except one person: me."

He wiped his mouth and placed the napkin next to his full plate. "For me—and only for me—the difference is material too. This painting is part of my life. It is this board, this paint. Under this patina there are fingerprints from my parents. Fingerprints from me as a toddler, as a child, an adolescent. It has the same patina as me. It has the same memories as me, if paintings can have memories—and who knows they don't?"

He reached for his wineglass and emptied it down to the finger alcoholics leave. "For the new owner it's not an issue. He can begin a new life with a painting that is new to him. It is not important to anyone whether the painting is original or not. Not to anyone. Except to this old man,"—he pointed wearily to the napkin, now at his chest, one corner shoved roughly under his collar—"who doesn't know how much longer he will live." He coughed, as if to underline his frailty.

Weynfeldt felt a little sorry for him; he was old. Tentatively, he asked, "You do understand, though, don't you, that I must insist on the original."

Baier shook his head. "I can note what you say, but can I understand it? No, I can't."

The Asian lady cleared their plates and Frau Hauser brought the dessert: her homemade *cassata*. This time Weynfeldt heaped on the praise. Baier was too downcast.

When they were on their own again, Baier said, his voice a shade more pathetic, "I need one and a half million to spend my last years in a decent, dignified way. No more. One and a half million. Not much to someone who used to juggle millions. To someone who regularly made and lost much bigger sums. And would make them again if he still had the strength. One and a half million, Adrian! It's too little to sacrifice the one thing you love. The one thing you have left. The consolation of your twilight years. You must see that."

Weynfeldt couldn't work out where Baier was heading here. He put some cassata in his mouth so he wouldn't have to say anything.

"The old Vallotton, I won't call it the genuine one, I'll say the old one, the old Vallotton is priceless. To me it is priceless. Only to me. Are you forcing me to sacrifice it for one and a half million?"

Baier let the question hang in the room. Then he continued. Pleading. "I need the money, though. Otherwise I'll be spending my final years on welfare. Do you want that, Adrian?"

Weynfeldt had eaten his ice cream and had no further excuse not to speak. "Of course I don't want that. But I think, just between the two of us, I wouldn't swear to it, I think *La Salamandre* would fetch more than one and a half. A lot more."

Baier shrugged his shoulders. "Quite possibly. But never the sum it is worth to me." And with a gentle smile, he added, "Would you mind calling me a taxi."

Adrian got up uncertainly. It didn't feel right letting the old man leave like this. But before he had reached the telephone on the dresser Baier spoke again, without a trace of pathos. "I'll make you a proposal: take the new one, and anything over one and a half you make from it, you can keep."

Weynfeldt picked up the receiver and ordered a taxi. Then he asked, "Are you taking both of them or just the forgery?"

Baier got up from the chair, groaning. Adrian passed him his cane. "Jesus, you're square," he grumbled. "I'm leaving them both here. I'm not going to wander around in the middle of the night with two-million-francs' worth of art. Have a good look at them both and give it some thought."

While they waited in the hallway for the taxi to ring the bell, Weynfeldt asked, "Who copied the painting for you?"

"A young artist. A collector I know recommended him to me. He sometimes boosts his income with jobs like this. Lots of collectors have pictures they have come to love copied before they part from them."

"What's his name?"

"I'd rather not drag him into it. He acted in good faith."

Both of them jumped as the doorbell rang. They walked through the hallway into the elevator, which had not been used since Baier's arrival.

Baier broke the silence during the short trip down: "Let's say one point six. Anything over one point six is yours."

Weynfeldt shook his head in disbelief and grinned softly.

The elevator stopped, the chrome doors parted and Weynfeldt opened the glass security door with his magnetic card. Before he opened the heavy wooden door, Baier said, "Think about it."

"You think about it too," Weynfeldt said, and opened the door.

Lorena stood outside.

"Thank God!" she cried. "I thought there was no one home." She took Adrian's hand and kissed him briefly three times on alternate cheeks. He stood stiffly in front of her for a moment, flabbergasted, then remembered Baier. "May I introduce you, Klaus Baier: Lorena ..." He didn't know her surname, and she made no move to assist him.

The two shook hands. Lorena turned back to Adrian. "It's terribly embarrassing, but could you help me out? I've lost my wallet and can't pay the taxi."

Now the two men realized that the waiting taxi was not the one they had ordered. Weynfeldt started walking toward it, but Lorena stopped him. "I'm going to ride on, I'm exhausted. Fifty francs will be enough." Adrian whipped out his wallet.

Baier, who had been staring at Lorena with blatant curiosity, butted in. "I need a taxi too. Could I take yours and drop you off on the way?"

Without a moment's hesitation, Lorena replied, "How kind of you. If it's no bother."

And then they walked straight to the taxi. And then she got in, and blew Adrian a kiss from inside. And Baier's parting words were, "Sleep on it." And then the taxi's red rear lights vanished.

And then the taxi they had ordered came.

And Weynfeldt gave the driver twenty francs for the wasted journey ... instead of getting in and shouting, "Follow that car!" he thought in the elevator, dejected.

17

THE REDHEAD LOOKED FAMILIAR TO BAIER. HE WASN'T sure why.

Weynfeldt had been completely flummoxed, stood there like a stuffed dummy. His face had darkened; by day you'd have seen it was red.

Baier wasn't sure what had made him offer to take her home. Instinct. And when it came to affairs of the heart, his instinct had served him even better than with money.

Weynfeldt certainly hadn't been pleased about it; he'd noticed that. And after his stubborn behavior that night, that was reason enough.

In the taxi he was suddenly certain he had done the right thing. He realized why the woman seemed familiar. She looked like Daphne, Weynfeldt's art student back then. His memory for faces wasn't so good he could identify someone after so many years. But he clearly remembered the image of Weynfeldt standing like a lackey next to a red haired, pale-skinned girl. Weynfeldt too by the look of it.

"Have you known Adrian long?" he asked.

"No. You?"

"Since he was born. Our fathers were friends."

She showed no great interest in this information, staring out of the window as the city center passed.

"When did you last have it?"

"What?"

"Your wallet. When I lose something, I try and reconstruct the scene—when I last had it."

She hesitated, and her answer surprised him:

"I haven't lost it. I just don't have enough money on me."

"And why didn't you tell Adrian that?"

She shrugged her shoulders. "Do you like people to know when you don't have any money?"

"To be honest, it doesn't happen very often."

"Of course. Silly question."

A few youths in summer clothes were sitting on a bench, surrounded by bottles and cans. One of them threw a can at the taxi but missed. They heard his pals booing.

They would reach the address she had given the driver in about five minutes. Too little time to talk, Baier decided. "Would you give an old man the pleasure of joining him for a nightcap?" he asked. "I don't sleep well, and it's still early."

She turned her gaze from the window and examined him with a look which verged on the professional. "Where then?"

"Wherever you want."

"Somewhere I can get a bite to eat. I haven't had dinner."

"What kind of thing?"

"Lobster. That kind of thing."

"You're thinking of the Trafalgar?"

"Maybe I am."

The Trafalgar was a hotel bar in the style of an English pub where classics from the hotel's fish restaurant were served until late at night. Including lobster. Cold lobster, grilled lobster, Lobster Thermidor. It wasn't far off their route.

Baier told the driver the new destination. Shortly afterward Lorena helped him out of the taxi.

The bar was dimly lit and half empty. Hotel guests sat at a few of the tables; at others, traveling businessmen, in the company of the attractive young employees of a local escort agency. Ill-matched pairs like Lorena and himself, Baier thought.

She ordered cold lobster and champagne, Baier an Armagnac, double. "I'm sure you don't mind," he observed, and started lighting a cigar.

"Sure," she said.

"'Sure, go ahead' or 'Sure, I mind?'"

"Sure, I mind but go ahead."

Baier laughed and continued his incendiary ceremony. He knew women like this. But how had Weynfeldt met her?

"Adrian is a fine lad," he noted.

"He's nice."

"Nice like this too," Baier rubbed his thumb and index finger together.

"I know. I've seen his apartment."

"You can lose your wallet as often as you want with him."

"Would you order me another?" She pointed to the empty champagne flute. Baier waved to the motherly, neatly-dressed barwoman.

"He worships you. I can tell."

"Why are you telling me all this?"

"I thought it might interest you."

"Financially?"

"That too."

"I prefer to earn my own money."

Baier nodded thoughtfully. "I believe I can think of a way to combine the two."

The barwoman brought the cold lobster and a fresh glass of champagne. When she had gone Lorena asked, "Combine what?"

"Your influence on Adrian and your desire for financial independence."

She put a piece of the white lobster meat between her lips, without cocktail sauce. "I'm listening," she said, her mouth full.

18

LORENA WOKE WITH A BACKACHE. BUT WITHOUT A HEAD-ache. That might have something to do with the quality of the champagne she had been drinking in the Trafalgar. Perhaps it was true what she had read recently, that people only feel one pain at a time, and that one pain obscures any others. Perhaps she would have a headache if her entire capacity to feel pain wasn't taken up with her backache.

Her clock radio had eased her gently awake. She always set it so she heard the last couple of songs before the news while she was coming to. She hated being woken abruptly by the latest disasters.

The main topic was the weather. Even now, at eight in the morning in late February, it was already 54°F. And there wasn't even a *föhn* wind. Previously unreleased sections of the UN climate report alleged that a climate catastrophe was now unavoidable.

Lorena wondered what she should wear. If she got up at all. She hadn't decided. Another day as a booth babe in the dreary world of motorbike fans wasn't exactly enticing. Never mind seeing the Ducelli asshole again. But she had no intention of letting the agency keep her wages from the day before.

At the end of the news, after a weather forecast fit for a nice day in June, she got up. She touched the sensitive spot and realized the pain wasn't coming from her spine or her back muscles.

She clambered over the suitcases, bags and cardboard boxes to the bathroom and examined the spot with a hand mirror.

Around the kidney area was a dark bruise, almost black, the size of her palm. A bloodshot patch caused by that macho Ducelli idiot's fist. She decided she would go to the motorbike fair after all. The man wasn't going to get away with this.

In the streetcar to the exhibition center she took a free newspaper from the dispenser and sat down cautiously on one of the hard seats.

Her picture was on the cover. Wrapped around the Ducelli in a provocative pose, with a seductive look for the camera. The caption read: "Superbike with ultra-transparent chassis and high-torque motor: the new Ducelli 7312."

She read the article carefully; she wasn't mentioned anywhere in the main text either. Not even as an accessory, not even as something which stopped you from getting a good look at the bike. It was as if she didn't exist.

At the next stop she got out and took another streetcar, to the offices of the agency which had arranged the job for her. She would demand the fee for her work yesterday, and if they were awkward about it, she would show them the bruise on her back, threaten to make a big fuss about it, naming the agency and their client and giving all the details.

A snotty receptionist led Lorena into the waiting

room. She sat down and began leafing through today's newspaper, already tattered.

She came across her photo here too. Now the article was not about the motorbike fair but "The image of women in the world of two-wheeled racing vehicles." It was a critical article, and she read it keenly; here too she wasn't mentioned here at all.

She stood up, told the receptionist where her boss could shove the fee and left.

This was always happening. Lorena liked making big gestures. Throwing in the towel, telling everyone to go to hell, then finding herself faced with the big question: What now?

She tottered along the pavement past the morning crowd, pensioners with shopping carts, mothers with strollers, unemployed people, schoolkids, traveling salesmen, streetcar drivers before or after a shift. The smell of freshly baked bread and melted cheese wafted from the open doors of a supermarket. She went in and looked for a cash machine among the takeaway stands in the foyer. She found one and luckily it wasn't her bank. That meant that the computer might not know she was hopelessly overdrawn, and she might manage to entice a few hundred franc notes out of it.

Lorena put her card in the slot and tapped her code in. She sensed someone standing behind her. She turned around and saw a pudgy young man with bad skin. He stared at her expressionless. "Would you mind standing a few steps back?" She pointed to a line on the ground marked "Please stand behind this line."

He failed to move, simply pointing to the cash

machine with his chin. The display said, "Card retracted."

"Shit!" she yelled. And left. She didn't quite manage to ignore the pimply boy's salacious grin.

She bought a coffee and a croissant at one of the takeaway stands. She didn't have money for more. A tray in her hand, she looked for a free table and finally found one, at a distance from the others. But as soon as she got settled, an old lady came and joined her. She too carried a tray holding a coffee and a croissant. Alongside it was a red wallet, a pair of glasses, and a copy of the free newspaper graced with Lorena's photograph.

Lorena didn't look up. Old women in supermarket food halls can be very chatty.

But this one clearly wasn't. She put her glasses on and started reading the paper. Every so often she dipped her croissant in her milky coffee, bit the dripping, soggy bit off and chewed it, audibly.

All at once she said, "Could you keep a quick eye on my things. I have to pay a visit." Without waiting for Lorena's answer, she stood up and walked off.

She had left the glasses and newspaper behind. And the red wallet.

Lorena looked around discreetly. The next table was several yards away. A group of schoolkids were eating their junk food. A line had formed at a nearby pizza stand. No one was watching Lorena.

She picked up the wallet as if it was hers, opened it, and looked in the section for notes. A few tens and twenties were there. She took forty francs out. Now she saw the small photograph behind the transparent plastic sheath in the wallet. It was of a young Bob Dylan.

The old lady must be over seventy, a normal elderly woman wearing something with big flowers on, dug out of her wardrobe early this year for the muggy summer-like day. She wore glasses that enlarged her eyes slightly; her hair was gray and unkempt.

And she was a Bob Dylan fan. How old was she when Dylan was a young rock star? Around thirty? Younger than Lorena was now.

She imagined the old thing as a young woman. At festivals. With a joint. Topless with a peace sign painted on her forehead. A young woman with dreams and ideals, like she had once had.

Vet. Not in a little veterinary practice for parakeets and Chihuahuas. Big animals. Horses, maybe cows too. A country vet with a Land Rover, who made it to remote farms in the middle of winter. Or even bigger: zoo animals. Elephants, rhinos, giraffes, hippos.

Lorena had pursued this dream as far as university. Just two semesters. A bit of modeling on the side. And a bit of coke. Then she postponed a semester—she was young and had time. That semester became two. And once she forced herself to go back to college after a third, she had gotten used to a lifestyle she couldn't afford as a student.

Perhaps one day she would be like this old woman: her head full of unfulfilled dreams, and a photo of Robbie Williams in her wallet.

She put the forty francs back and put the wallet on the old woman's tray.

She hadn't sunk so far she had to take from people

who had nothing themselves. You took from people who had more than enough.

Like the old man yesterday, for instance. He had offered her fifty thousand, "If you can give our fine upstanding Adrian a shove."

The man had had a valuable painting he owned copied, and wanted Weynfeldt to put the copy up for auction instead of the original. Weynfeldt had refused of course, because he was much too square. She was now supposed to "give him a little shove."

She asked how he envisaged that.

She knew full well, he had answered, how to get a man who fancied her to do something against his principles. He only had to look at her.

She asked what made him think Weynfeldt fancied her.

"Oh he does," he answered. "Trust me, I know him."

The old woman returned.

"Thank you for watching out," she said with a smile.

"Don't think twice, it's alright," Lorena replied, and left.

Back home she called Weynfeldt at his office. He was not at his desk, his assistant informed her.

So could she please give her his cell phone number? Lorena asked.

She was told that Dr. Weynfeldt did not own a cell phone.

In that case please could he get himself one, Lorena told the assistant. She would give him the few francs it cost.

19

IT HAD BEEN A BAD NIGHT FOR ADRIAN. HE HAD FIN-
ished the bottle of wine then started on the brandy,
which the otherwise conscientious Frau Hauser had left
in his study, along with the snifter Baier had used.

He had tried to concentrate on the two pictures and
the question of how he should behave in this situation.
But another image, Lorena's, kept getting in the way.

She had looked tired. Tired and older than he
remembered her. How old was she anyway? Thirty-five?
Or closer to forty?

What incredible bad luck. If she had come just ten
minutes later Baier would have been gone. He could
have taken her home, and however things went after
that, at least he'd have known where she lived.

Even if she'd arrived earlier, things would have
panned out differently. She would have rung, he would
have gone down and might even have been able to persuade her to come up for a moment. Failing that he
still would have had the chance to exchange a few words
with her in private. To find out her address, or her telephone number.

He had sipped at the brandy, taking care all the time
not to drink from the spot Baier's lips had touched, and
with every sip his fury at the man grew. First Baier tried
to hoodwink him, then to buy his complicity and finally

he went off with the first woman Weynfeldt had been interested in for years, right under his nose.

He imagined everything he would do to Baier. The repertoire ranged from reporting him for fraud to the use of violence.

He held long, hard-hitting conversations with him in his head, refilled the glass again and again, and noticed how late it was only after lurching to his bedroom: two in the morning.

He battled with his water pick, with the buttons on his pajamas and the decision whether to call Baier now, despite the time of night. To tell him what he thought of him and—ridiculous as the idea was—to be certain the old man was in fact at home.

By the time Adrian finally made it to bed, unsteadily, it was ten to three. When he woke, thinking he had overslept, it was just twenty minutes later.

He slept in short uneasy bursts, finally appearing for breakfast around nine, with red eyes and three cuts from shaving, annoyed at the double Alka-Seltzer Frau Hauser served him wordlessly alongside his orange juice.

He didn't reach the office till shortly after ten. Véronique also handled him with demonstrative discretion, which he found particularly hard to cope with on this excessively warm morning.

"She called again," was the first thing she said.

"Which she?"

"The one who called you at Agustoni's that time. Lorena: she didn't say her surname."

Adrian was suddenly wide awake. "What did she say?"

"That you should get a cell phone; you can get them for a franc. She'll give you the money. I told her I agree."

"Did she leave a number?"

"No, she'll try again later."

He went into his office, closed the door and attempted to do something constructive.

After a short while he heard Véronique's hint of a knock before she appeared in the door frame. "I'm going out for a minute; would you take the calls?" It wasn't a request. He owed her this for coming late.

She had barely left when the telephone rang. "Good morning. Murphy's, Adrian Weynfeldt speaking," he answered.

"The boss in person." Lorena's voice. "Do you already have plans for tonight?"

"No," he said, although he had intended to pay a visit of condolence to Mereth Widler.

"Would you invite me for dinner again? I'll come this time."

Adrian was unable to answer, he was so surprised.

"Hello? Are you still there?"

"Yes, of course I'm here. Sure. In Châteaubriand again?"

"Your place would be better. Is seven thirty a good time?"

"Seven thirty? Yes, a perfect time. Seven thirty at my apartment."

"Then I'll see you then, ciao."

"Yes, see you then. Wait!"

"Yes?"

"What do you like to eat?"

"I like simple, expensive things."

"Such as?"

"Such as caviar, Kobe steak, that kind of thing." She laughed and hung up.

He got up from his chair, walked to the window and opened it—air-conditioning notwithstanding.

The sky reflected in the lake was a deep, fresh blue of a kind he otherwise knew only from the Engadin. The Alps looked like a painting by Hodler. The traffic and streetcars beneath him glittered in the sun like shiny toys. And the pedestrians wandered down the sidewalk as if it was a major holiday. Weynfeldt inhaled deeply and smiled at the picture-book world beneath him. Then he closed the window, called Frau Hauser and asked her to prepare a few simple things for tonight, giving her the details.

He waited impatiently for Véronique. When she finally arrived, with a black plastic bag bearing one single, neon-green Thai letter, he took his leave again. He wasn't sure when or if he would be back that afternoon, he informed her. Then he joined the happy pedestrians on the street. As the happiest of them all, perhaps.

It was Thursday lunch club today, but he had an appointment beforehand. Kando, Claudio's girlfriend, had called and asked to meet him at eleven thirty in Südflügel, a trendy bar close to Agustoni's. It was a surprise, she said. Weynfeldt assumed it was a surprise relating to *Working Title: Hemingway's Suitcase*.

He still had time till half past eleven and decided to walk the long way. He raced through the town like a man in love. Everything seemed so familiar and yet so new. As if he were showing the city to an outsider, seeing it through their eyes.

As usual Weynfeldt arrived too early for the rendezvous, but when he entered Südflügel, he saw Kando immediately, sitting at a secluded table. She waved him over, and when he got there, he saw there was another glass on it. A Campari, Claudio's aperitif. She greeted him with the auspicious smile of a mother shortly before the Christmas presents are opened. "Claudio had to visit the bathroom; he's terribly excited," she whispered conspiratorially.

Adrian did something he hadn't done for years: he ordered a Pernod. It suited the day and his mood.

Soon after that Claudio returned. Weynfeldt shook his hand, still damp from washing, they sat down, and there was an expectant pause. Mommy Kando couldn't wait for her little boy to recite his verse to the guest.

It clearly felt like this to Claudio too. Sullenly, he said to her, "You're acting as if it's a miracle. In fact it's just a very normal stage in the evolution of a film." Then he said casually to Weynfeldt, "I've brought you the script."

Claudio Hausmann reached to one side and revealed a small, black leather folder. Inside this was a spiral-bound booklet with a transparent cover which read: *(Working Title) Hemingway's Suitcase—A Feature Film by Claudio Hausmann.*

Adrian took it from him like a fragile treasure, stood up formally, and shook hands with Claudio, now red-faced with pride. "Congratulations!"

He sat down again. Weynfeldt's leafed through the document respectfully, with his clean, manicured hands. He had no idea about scripts and was surprised to see that a feature film of over a hundred minutes took up so few pages.

Claudio looked at Adrian's face in anticipation. But Kando seemed to have read his mind. "Claudio doesn't believe you should determine the dialogue in advance," she explained. "He develops it on set with the actors. That makes it much more authentic."

And beneath the title of each scene there was indeed a short description of the events, the names of the characters appearing and a brief outline of the dialogue. For instance: "Dialogue Ernest/Headly/Lost Property Clerk, Montreux Station—dispute over filling out the form for lost property. Ernest gets very angry, Headley tries to mediate, Clerk remains stubborn. No solution to the conflict."

"I've always worked like this," Claudio confirmed. "I don't like to tie up the actors in a dialogue corset. It inhibits them, and you notice it later on the screen."

Adrian agreed. He had always thought that the skill of acting lay precisely in the ability to deliver something prescribed as if it were spontaneous. But today Claudio could say anything he wanted; he would still have agreed with him. He would have agreed on other days too, but perhaps not so cheerfully.

"I see a big film here," Claudio declared. "International coproductions. Swiss executive control, but international. With sexy locations like Lake Geneva and Paris, it'll be easy to free up some Swiss-French cash.

And with one of America's greatest authors, some Hollydollars too. What do you think about Brad Pitt as the young Hemingway? I don't mean as a name necessarily, but as a type? Kando is thinking more Matt Damon."

Weynfeldt found both eminently suitable, but wished to read the script first before making a firm decision.

They talked for a while about casting and setting, the commercial importance of staying under two hundred minutes—Claudio's initial estimate had come to two hundred and twenty—and the idea of a multilingual film—everyone speaking their own language, with subtitles in the other languages. Suddenly Kando said, "You know Talberger, don't you?"

"Gabriel Talberger?" Weynfeldt knew him slightly. They had overlapped at a boarding school in eastern Switzerland. Adrian had only spent a year there before his mother removed him following some disciplinary measure she considered excessive, as had happened with various other such institutions. Talberger had become one of the most important film producers in the country. But so far Weynfeldt had managed to be vague enough about this acquaintance that he hadn't had to make use of it for Hausmann's benefit. Today however, he was in such high spirits he said, "We were together at Rittergut, although he was a year above me."

"Claudio has sent him the script. But experience shows it's better when a personal acquaintance puts a word in too. Would you do that for him?"

Weynfeldt looked at Claudio. He was sitting there as if Adrian had the power in this second to decide whether he would flourish or flounder. Claudio tried to make the

166   MARTIN SUTER

decision easier for Adrian, and explained, "You just have to say, *This guy I know has written a script. Check it out.*"

Weynfeldt assured him he would gladly do just that. And at that moment he meant every word.

If anyone at the Thursday lunch club had paid him any more attention than normal, they might have noticed that Adrian Weynfeldt wasn't making much effort to join in with the conversation. He even failed to notice once that the wine bottle at the other end of the table was empty, and when he stood up to greet Karin Winter, he forgot to do up the top button on his jacket.

But he did not receive any more attention than on any other Thursday. And so it did not go down in the history of Thursdays as the day on which Weynfeldt was a changed man, but as the Thursday when Strasser didn't show up.

"Do you know what four ounces of Kobe meat cost?" Frau Hauser looked as if she had been waiting all day to ask Adrian this question.

"A lot of money, I should think."

"Forty-three francs!" She looked at him in triumph. "For some beef!"

"It comes from Wagyu cattle. They grow very slowly."

"They'll be eaten quickly enough."

"The animals get a daily massage and beer to drink."

"For that kind of money they could drink champagne."

Adrian was forced to laugh.

"Your mother would never have allowed so much money to be spent on a slice of beef."

"The amount of caviar my mother went through cost more money than some people earn their entire lives."

"Caviar! We're talking about cows!"

Frau Hauser had laid the table in the dining room. Weynfeldt's grandfather had had the room redesigned in 1905. On one of the long walls were two windows to the street, opposite them two doors, one opening into the corridor, the other to the kitchen and office. There was a fireplace on both end walls, each the mirror image of the other, clad with green and white marble in a geometric *Jugendstil* design set into the paneling, which took up the quadratic pattern with light and dark woods, and continued it throughout the room.

A table with twenty-four matching chairs in the same style had previously stood in the center of the room. Like many other pieces of the original furnishings, this was now in storage. Weynfeldt had replaced it with two classics of 1950s design: Ulrich P. Wieser's minimalist pull-out table with solid walnut boards and black-lacquered steel supports. And beech chairs by Willy Guhl, black-painted with rattan seats and backs.

The space between the doors was filled entirely by a sideboard of untreated ash, also delineated by a black painted framework. Two additional one-off pieces by Swiss designers stood between the windows.

The walls held nothing but fruit and culinary still lives by nineteenth- and early twentieth-century Swiss artists.

Frau Hauser had laid the table splendidly, decorating it with tulips. And there were vases overflowing with tulips on the mantelpieces and sideboards. Adrian had not revealed who he was expecting for dinner, but judging by the way she had prepared the room, she seemed to know it was a woman.

And the way she had received him—giving him a playful telling off—was a sign that she assumed he was having a lady visitor, and was pleased. He was certain his mother had confided to Frau Hauser her suspicion that he was gay. A suspicion he had maliciously failed to dispel. His mother's hope that Adrian would not be the last Weynfeldt lived on in Frau Hauser.

He got changed for dinner. A dying custom, regrettably. If he had lived in the world of his much-loved Somerset Maugham, he would have been one of those unmarried governors on a far-flung island who put on a tuxedo each evening for his solitary supper.

Weynfeldt wasn't about to don a tuxedo, instead choosing a classic-cut, dark-green, worsted cashmere, summer suit, with a pair of shiny black Derbys his Hungarian shoemaker from Vienna had made him with soft aniline calfskin.

Shortly before half past seven he started to assume Lorena wouldn't turn up. Soon after half past he started persuading himself he didn't care. At quarter to she rang the bell.

She was wearing the stolen Prada with the round neckline and the narrow slit extending below the ribs, and black platform shoes with cross-straps over the ankles—were platforms back in? She had a black silk scarf wound tightly around her head to make her hair fall behind her ears and over her shoulders. Her ears stood out a little, which he found touching, he wasn't sure why.

Lorena greeted him with three kisses, as if they were meeting at a cocktail party. She smelled of an expensive, slightly matronly perfume, and a peppermint she had probably been sucking to hide the smell of a drink.

This was the fifth time they had met, and each time she had seemed different. Lascivious and disenchanted the first time, in La Rivière. Bitter and world-weary the next morning. Urbane and devious after the shoplifting attempt. Desperate and disheveled yesterday at the door. And now? Upbeat? Determined? Affected?

"I'd like to introduce you to my housekeeper in a second; actually, what is your full name?" He had worked this question out while he was changing. It would help him find her again, if she withheld her address or telephone number again this time.

"Lorena is enough. My family name is ghastly."

He led her into the dining room, and when she saw the preparations she broke into raptures, which were interrupted by the appearance of Frau Hauser.

"Lorena, can I introduce you to Frau Hauser. Frau Hauser: Lorena."

Frau Hauser shook her hand, as if she had taken the decision to like Adrian's guest a long time before.

Lorena praised the table decorations and flower arrangements. "And I told Adrian he shouldn't go to any trouble."

Frau Hauser smiled. "Think nothing of it. It'll just be something simple."

She excused herself and Adrian opened the champagne sitting in the silver ice bucket.

"Louis Roederer Cristal is my favorite champagne.

Do you know why? The bubbles are so tiny. The smaller the bubbles, the more of them can fit in your mouth. And the main thing with champagne is the bubbles."

They toasted and took a sip. Lorena closed her eyes. "I bet a bottle like this has more bubbles than ten bottles of cheap champagne."

"At least," Weynfeldt confirmed.

"And what does a bottle cost?"

"No idea."

"Over two-hundred francs, I'm guessing."

"I should think so."

"A fair price for ten times more bubbles."

Frau Hauser had laid the table so they were sitting in the middle of the long side. She brought the caviar. It was placed in a crystal dish embedded in a silver bowl full of ice; an item Adrian's mother had used. The cutlery was also silver, but the parts which touched the caviar were mother of pearl.

Frau Hauser served the classic accompaniments: diced egg yolk and egg white, diced onions, lemon, as well as buckwheat *blini*, potatoes and sour cream.

Lorena was as blasé as a Russian countess tucking into the caviar, but restrained herself when it came to the side dishes.

When Frau Hauser brought the grilled Kobe steaks Lorena laughed. "You didn't have to take it so literally."

With a sideways glance at his housekeeper, he said, "It made Frau Hauser's job easier. The more expensive the ingredients, the simpler the preparation."

They stuck with champagne. With dessert too, where Frau Hauser took the opportunity to demonstrate that she was not afraid of complex preparation: five different kinds of confectionary. Having placed it on the table, she took her leave for the night.

Lorena was animated now. Her freckles weren't standing out as conspicuously as they had when she arrived—the false spring this February had given her a few more. Adrian had already opened a second bottle, and there wasn't more than a glass left in that either.

Throughout the meal she quizzed him about his work. And he described it to her, with growing enthusiasm; his work was probably the one thing which really interested him.

He learned virtually nothing about her.

Adrian went to the kitchen and returned with a fresh bottle of champagne. While he wrestled with the cork, she asked, "Will you show me the apartment?"

"I already did."

"At the time I wasn't very … alert."

Each holding a champagne glass, they wandered through the silent rooms, Weynfeldt's commentary on the pictures and furniture echoing like a museum guide's monologue. Aside from the occasional "Wow" or "Super" Lorena said little.

Until: "What's in here?"

"Nothing. It was my mother's room."

"And it's taboo?"

"Not at all."

"But it's locked."

Adrian took the key from behind the painting, opened the door and turned on the light.

"Wow. Very different."

"Pretty much how she had it herself."

"You left it like that? That's so sweet."

He was silent. No one had found it sweet before.

"But a bit uncanny too. Like in that old film."

"Rebecca."

"Is that her?" She pointed to the portrait.

"Yes. She was seventy."

"Her eyes follow you."

"True."

Lorena gazed at the picture as she walked around the room. "I wouldn't be able to handle that," she decided.

He surprised himself with his answer. "Sometimes I'm not sure I can handle it."

In his study she said, "Wow! The same painting twice."

"Felix Vallotton. 1900."

"Who was the woman?"

"His wife, some say."

"Mighty fine ass."

Adrian smiled. She was the first person who had said—in his presence—what everyone thought when they saw the picture.

"Nice, anyway. Is it worth much?"

"The original, sure."

"So these are copies?"

"Only one of them."

"And the other is the original? Which one? Wait! Don't say anything." She went up to the paintings, studied them, compared them and chose the left hand. "This one!"

"Almost."

"The other one?"

"Congratulations."

"And how can you tell?"

"From the signature, for instance." Adrian explained the question of the second period.

"You can only tell from the signature? Not the painting itself?"

"From the painting too, sure."

"Don't say anything. Don't say anything." She went from one to the other and back again, several times. Finally she turned to him and sighed. "I give up."

Adrian explained the differences, the elasticity of the paint, the primer, the wax varnish.

Lorena listened with increasing astonishment. "But to the eye it's the same picture."

"To the eye, maybe."

"I thought that's what visual art was about—the eye. Did you notice immediately?"

"Not straight off. But on closer examination, yes." She looked at him skeptically. He changed the subject: "Another few thousand bubbles?"

She followed him with her empty glass to the dining room, where he filled it. "And why have you got the original as well as a copy?"

Adrian was getting carried away and became indiscreet. "Someone needs the money, but can't bear to sell the original. He wanted me to put the copy up for auction."

"And?"

Adrian didn't understand.

"And? Are you going to do it?"

"Of course not."

"I thought so."

"Why?"

"Because you're so straight."

"Not agreeing to participate in fraud is not being too straight."

"It's not fraud. You didn't even notice yourself."

"Not straight away."

"Wait a moment." Lorena left the room. He heard her footsteps disappearing down the corridor then returning again. She had fetched her handbag, and opened it now, took her tiny makeup bag out, and from this an eyeliner pencil, which she took the lid off. She walked to the original and Adrian realized what she was doing, although her hand was hidden by her body.

She stepped aside, like a painter admiring her work, put the lid back on the pencil and said, "Voilà. Now they're identical."

Weynfeldt shook his head. "One of them is forged."

"Now they are both forged," she replied.

Weynfeldt laughed. She wasn't completely off the mark.

"What is something like this worth?" she wanted to know.

"With a bit of 'auction luck,' two or three million."

"Wow! Just the fact that someone will pay so much for it makes the painting genuine."

After a short pause Weynfeldt admitted, "I've never thought about it like that."

"See!"

He shook his head slowly, as if he wanted to bar

access to a thought.

"Why don't you do it?" This wasn't a question, it was a dare.

"It just wouldn't be okay," he answered, collected himself quickly, and, without managing not to go a red, delivered the lady-killer sentence he'd been saving up: "The guided tour isn't quite finished yet." Now she had to ask: *What's left?* And he would answer: *The bedroom.*

But she said, "Let's save the bedroom for the next tour."

"Pity."

She tried to imitate his tone, as she added, "It just wouldn't be okay."

In the elevator he asked, "Would you give me your address?"

And again she echoed him: "It just wouldn't be okay."

But she gave him a kiss that was slightly more than a polite, social kiss and gave him hope that there would actually be another tour.

Back in the apartment he refilled the ice bucket and retreated to his study with the remaining champagne. He enjoyed the tingling sensation of the bubbles in his mouth in a new way as he gazed at the Vallottons. The doubled Vallotton. The Vallotton and the Strasser. The same and the similar.

It took him awhile to find it: it was in the cast iron relief on the *salamandre* stove. Not all forgers let their vanity get the better of them. But Rolf Strasser did.

He stood for a long time facing the Vallotton in thought. Finally he walked to the black tool cupboard with its red shiny handles and opened a drawer. Mixed

MARTIN SUTER

up inside lay boxes and tubes of paint, brushes and other painting things from the time when he still secretly tried refreshing what he'd learned at art school, perhaps even developing it.

He found a fine brush and carefully mixed a little tempera in the deep reddish brown of the paneling in the top right-hand corner of the painting.

20

TO THE LEFT—A STORE THAT BOUGHT, SOLD AND repaired old TVs, stereos, radios and cell phones; to the right, a store offering "Bankruptcy Bargains." Between the two, the entrance to number 241, Lorena's building. The door was made of wire mesh glass with a metal frame. In the top half of the pane a transparent plastic patch with the name of a glazing firm had been stuck over a small hole the size of a pickaxe. It had been there when Lorena moved in.

She opened the door and entered the hall. To the left and right were twelve mailboxes and milk-bottle holders, the labels changed many times by hand, with scraps of paper taped on to the metal. To the right were the stairs to the basement; to the left, the stairs to the four floors; in the middle was the elevator shaft, the elevator door a slightly smaller copy of the front door. The hall had an indeterminate smell of filth and the products used to tackle it.

The elevator was dominated by the smell of grease used to lubricate the cables extending down the shaft. Lorena had seen them as she left earlier, through the open door to the elevator, where a sign had hung saying, "Safety check, sorry!"

She took the stairs to the second floor now; the elevator technician had done nothing to inspire her confidence.

Her apartment door led straight into the room that served as both bed and living room. It opened just far enough for Lorena to slip through. If her provisional living arrangements continued much longer, there would be no space for her to move between the boxes, suitcases and clothes.

She switched the light on and sat on the edge of the unmade bed. The effect of the champagne was wearing off and what she saw now sobered her up completely. Why hadn't she stayed? She could have drunk a few more glasses of that champagne, which she'd never be able to afford herself as long as she lived, then sunk into his big, soft, freshly made bed. She wouldn't have had to make out with him; he wouldn't have insisted. But maybe she'd have wanted to?

Sure, it would have been a tactical mistake. But whose tactics were we talking about? Baier's? As if Weynfeldt were the kind of man you could seduce into accepting a forged painting for an auction. No, Weynfeldt was what she'd called him: straight. His world was divided into what was okay, and what *just wasn't okay*. She could just as well have slept with him.

She climbed over her possessions to the kitchenette and looked in the fridge. As she thought: nothing. Nothing except a beer. A two-pint bottle of cheap store-brand beer from a low-cost supermarket. She left it there. She hadn't degenerated to drinking cheapo beer after Roederer Cristal.

The Spotlight purchases hung from coat hangers hooked over the open door of the only built-in closet. There was more to be had from someone who was prepared to pay twelve thousand francs to get her out of an unpleasant situation. There were other unpleasant situations she could get into. Lorena knew about unpleasant situations. She didn't need the old man's help there.

Lorena thought of the various chances she could give Weynfeldt to get her out of a tight spot and soon came up with a great many. Matching each to a sum of money, added up it made a figure which more than equaled Baier's fifty thousand.

Then there was plan C. When would she ever come across a man like Adrian Weynfeldt again? Money and manners were a rare combination. And for someone possessing both to be interested in her—late thirties, her best years clearly behind her, nothing much to hope for in the ones to come—for someone like Weynfeldt to be interested in someone like Lorena … When had that ever happened?

Why not try the most obvious thing and become his girlfriend? Make him her rich boyfriend: like in Spotlight. He didn't seem to object to the role. Quite the opposite. Why shouldn't Lorena Steiner move in with Dr. Adrian Weynfeldt? The apartment was large; the mother dead.

She went into the bathroom and removed the wet towel wrapped around the leaky faucet. She washed her hands and started removing her makeup.

She knew exactly why she wouldn't be moving in with him, even supposing that was what he wanted: because she would never ever, ever again move in with a man. She had sworn it—not for the first time, but certainly for the last—two months or so ago, when she moved out of Günther's.

Günther Walder was the man who was supposed to bring calm into her life. He was a scientist from Berlin. An authority in the field of cell biology. He spent his days trying to reprogram the cells of fruit flies. With the aim, one day, of reprogramming human cells so that they could become skin or muscle or liver or something else useful.

She had met Günther at an after-work party which the organizer sometimes mobilized her to attend for a discreet fee, because of the notorious imbalance of men. Günther was standing with a glass of orange juice in the midst of all the forced good cheer, a head taller than anyone else. Like a fish out of water, as she told him later. He was the only one wearing jeans, along with a baggy tweed jacket and a yellow T-shirt with the words in red: "4th International Sand Sculpture Festival Berlin."

She had asked him what he did with his life, and he had answered, "make fruit flies mate." She found that funny, and let him buy her a couple of glasses of champagne. It turned out he had moved here three months ago from Berlin and hadn't eaten out anywhere except the university canteen. She took him to Mistral, the best fish restaurant in the city, and when they came to order she discovered he didn't eat fish.

"I think they have a few meat dishes," she said.

And he replied, "I don't eat animal cells of any kind. I program them."

Günther didn't drink a drop of alcohol either, which made Lorena moderate her consumption that night.

And the decision to go home with him wasn't taken under the influence of alcohol. He took her to his three-bedroom apartment in a modern block on the edge of town. He owned a bed, a desk with a computer, a sofa and a TV, which sat on the floor. His clothes were hanging from a wheeled clothing rack of the kind found in stores. Half empty boxes of books lay all around, and in every room there were books piled according to a system only he understood. The kitchen contained crockery for just two people, and a huge stock of spaghetti and *pelati*, with a dozen pots of basil growing outside on the balcony. He was very proud of his *spaghetti al pomodoro e basilica* and ate practically nothing else.

Günther wasn't particularly good looking, nor was he an amazing lover. It would remain a mystery to her why she fell so completely in love with him. After barely three weeks, she abandoned all her good intentions and moved in with him, taking everything she owned. She set herself up in one of the rooms with her few pieces of furniture, cooked complicated ovo-lacto-vegetarian recipes from her hitherto unused cookbooks, and got ready to live a normal life from now on. She stopped drinking alcohol and started enjoying life without parties.

She was so smitten, she accepted his foibles with unconditional, blind faith. The telephone foibles in particular should have given her cause for concern. She was forbidden, for instance, from answering the telephone in the apartment. And when she made a call, she had to use her cell phone, for which he paid the bill. He didn't own one himself, and when he was traveling, which was often, as he had another project in the works in Berlin, he never left a contact number and almost never called her.

Till one day Ilsa stood at the door, and showed her the photos of Rebecca, 11, Klaus, 8, and Gabi, 3, and suggested, not entirely without sympathy, that she find herself another place to live as soon as possible.

When Lorena demanded to hear this from Günther's mouth, Ilsa led her to the window with the words, "Unfortunately my husband isn't very good at things like this."

Standing there next to a mustard-yellow Volvo wagon, he looked up at her and raised his shoulders helplessly.

When Ilsa had gone, Lorena emptied Günther's boxes of books and filled them with her things, cleared her room, called a moving van and took the housekeeping money from the kitchen drawer. It would pay for the transport to a storage facility and a few nights in a hotel.

Before she went, she emptied sixteen cans of *pelati* onto the bed and decorated her offering with all the basil she could harvest from the kitchen balcony.

So much for Günther.

Lorena turned off the faucet, wrapped the towel back around it, went to the fridge and took out the beer.

21

THE STORE WAS BIG AND BRIGHT AND FULL OF PEOPLE. At its many counters, salespeople stood serving customers. The walls were lined with cell phones.

Weynfeldt had drawn the number 418, and was waiting to see it light up on the electronic display.

Was he in love? Lightly smitten, certainly. He had never met a woman like Lorena. So direct. So nefarious. And yet so … innocent? Nonsense!

Obviously she was playing games with him. But he was playing along, letting her play her games. It brought back feelings he hadn't known since his youth, his teenage years. Back then the girls played games with the boys. Kept them guessing. Didn't show up to dates. Got their girlfriends to say they didn't love you anymore. Asked for time to think. Denied you kisses, and the few other things you dared to do back then.

He felt like he had back then: soaring between hope and fear; sky-high one minute, despondent the next.

Every so often there was movement among the people waiting, as a salesperson finally finished serving someone. And from time to time the electric ding-dong from the number display forced its way into his daydreams.

The similarity to Daphne faded the more he saw Lorena. It was her hair, her pale skin, and her mouth, above all. Her mouth, which looked almost the same if one looked at a photo of it in reverse.

But otherwise? They behaved so differently the superficial similarities paled into insignificance.

The display went ding-dong again. Another six customers till his number.

"You really should buy a cell phone," Véronique sighed, as Adrian arrived back in the office, two and a half hours late. "Herr Baier called four times; it is extremely urgent. You know what it's about apparently."

"That's why I'm so late," Weynfeldt replied. "Because of this bloody cell phone." He put the carrier bag with the phone on her desk. "Don't ask me how it works."

"By the time you leave this office, you will know," Véronique beamed, and began unpacking the device.

"What does Herr Baier want so urgently?" she asked.

"Do you know Vallotton's *La Salamandre*?"

"The nude from the back, by a stove?"

"He inherited it from his parents and now he's selling it to finance his last years. It's coming in the auction."

"A Vallotton after all. Gauguin was right."

Weynfeldt was saved from responding to this as Véronique squealed, "Jeez! They've sold you a brick!" She held Weynfeldt's new cell phone up.

"It's the most user-friendly model available, according to the salesman," Adrian said in his defense.

"Do you know what this is? It's a granddad phone. You acted so dumb they sold you an old fogey cell. How are you going to schlepp it around? In a man-purse?"

"I'll have Diaco sew a phone pocket in the lining of all my suits."

For the rest of the afternoon he took an intensive course from Véronique on the use of his old fogey cell.

In the evening he stayed in the office to catch up on the day's business. And called Baier to tell him his decision.

First thing Monday morning he would make an appointment with the reproductions photographer. The copy deadline for the catalogue had passed, but it wasn't too late to put *La Salamandre* on the cover.

Weynfeldt had never felt out of place in a morning suit at a funeral before. Gray and black striped trousers, black jacket: it was surely the correct attire for any formal occasion before midday.

But at Dr. Widler's funeral he seemed to be the only one maintaining the tradition.

It was not a fitting funeral congregation for a man who had placed such emphasis on dress.

In the church Weynfeldt sat between Karl Stauber and Paul Schnell, whom he had last seen at the White Turf in St. Moritz. Right in front of him sat Mereth Widler, flanked by daughters, themselves already around sixty.

The widow wore a high-collared black costume she'd undoubtedly had made in advance, solely for the occasion. Once the rest of the congregation was seated, she was led in by her daughters, like a bride by her bridesmaids. Adrian saw her face before she reached the front seat. She was wearing perfect, mask-like makeup, white, without rouge, with heavy eye-shadow and dramatic wine-red lipstick.

He gazed down throughout the service at the old lady's well-groomed, blonde, bouffant hair. She had probably been encouraged to lie down for a few minutes before the funeral by her family. At any rate there was a random parting at the back of her head, revealing her pale scalp. If he had been fighting back tears throughout the ceremony, it was because of this single, touching flaw in her impeccable appearance, visible perhaps only to him.

Guarded by her corpulent daughters, she stood at the edge of the grave during the burial, delicate and vulnerable, but upright, like a member of the Chinese terracotta army. Adrian remembered his father's burial. He had stood at the open grave, his mother's arm in his, and as she threw down roses and her spade-full of earth she said softly, with a smile he had never seen on her face before, "Licorice stick."

He was the only one who heard it, and he didn't mention it ever again during her remaining twenty years. But since that day he first had to banish the image of a licorice stick before he could think about his father.

The priest asked all those present to say the Lord's Prayer. In the midst of the murmuring, a chirpy, silly cell phone melody sounded out. A few people reached into their jackets and handbags, but the melody played on. Several heads turned toward Weynfeldt, who waited indignantly for the disruption to cease, with folded hands and lowered gaze.

Only then did he realize the extent of the catastrophe. He went furnace red, fumbled in his pocket, retrieved the device, stared at it helplessly, pressing various buttons, till someone took it off his hands, silenced it for him and returned it.

Mereth had not turned her head during the whole incident.

Once everyone had dropped their spade-full of earth onto the coffin, the widow led the congregation at an appropriate pace to the cemetery exit. In the bright spring sunshine around eighty mourners walked along the crunchy gravel, making a concerted effort to maintain a serious, composed expression, the graveyard sprouting and budding all around them.

At the exit, Mereth Widler received their condolences. Her daughters whispered the name of the place everyone was meeting afterward: Vue du Lac, an old-fashioned gourmet restaurant serving *ancienne cuisine* in the hills outside town. A row of taxis was waiting for guests who had not come in their own car.

Now and again the widow tried to live up to her reputation as a porcelain doll with a shocking tongue. As she embraced Adrian, she hissed in his ear, "He's kicked the bucket on me." He saw tears in her eyes for the first time.

In a dining hall with a view down to the lake stood a cold buffet of the old school, with hors d'oeuvres, butter and ice sculptures and attentive staff, continually refilling the platters and keeping them appetizing.

As Weynfeldt returned to his place with a full plate, Baier stood in his way. "Yesterday your secretary claimed you didn't have a cell phone. Today you sabotage the whole funeral with it."

"Yesterday I didn't have one."

"And why today?"

"Availability."

"You're really starting to see sense," Baier grinned, and hobbled off.

Back home Weynfeldt remembered the phone which had got him in such trouble. He succeeded in switching it on. But although he spent a good half hour tapping around the menu options, he couldn't figure out who had called him.

He tried to listen to the messages on his answering machine. Also without success. He searched for the instructions, couldn't find them and pressed various bits of the device so many times that eventually a red light started blinking incessantly on the display and couldn't be stilled no matter what he did.

22

ADRIAN WAS WAITING FOR LORENA TO CALL, AND WAIT-
ing was not an activity for him; it was a state, not such
an unpleasant one. Like flying.

As soon as he boarded an airplane, he was placed in
a state of absolute passivity. Of course he ate the food
served him, and read a newspaper, or a book. But he was
passive as far as flying itself was concerned. He knew
there was nothing he could do to influence it and del-
egated it unconditionally to those who could.

He approached Lorena's call in the same way. He was
leaving it entirely up to her and her ability to pick up
the phone and call him whenever it seemed appropriate
to her. She had done it before, so she would do it again.

Véronique, who happened to be in the office that Saturday morning, had taken a call from her. "From the lady
I was definitely to give your new number to if she called."

That meant it was Lorena who had called during the
burial. He handed his phone awkwardly to Véronique.
"Could you look to see if she called?"

His assistant pressed a couple of buttons. "You had
a call from an unknown number on Saturday morning.
And a few missed calls over the weekend, and also 'number unknown.' If I was waiting for a call I would pick up
when my phone rang."

"It didn't ring."

Astonishingly slender compared to her body mass, Véronique's fingers darted over the keypad once more. "Rocket science," she smiled. "You had it on silent mode. Voilà. Now it will ring again."

It had taken longer till the answering machine started working again. It was two days before Frau Hauser realized that not only had there been no new messages on the machine, the telephone itself had stopped ringing. The technician she called informed them that someone had managed to wipe out the outgoing message then program the machine so it answered before the first ring, playing a silent message.

In the same way that Adrian Weynfeldt could read newspapers and eat when he was in the flying state, he could get on with his everyday life during the state of waiting.

The final preparations for the auction took up most of his time. Adrian and Véronique proofread the catalogue and, for the first time since they had begun working together, it was she who took the proofs to Murphy's headquarters in London.

Normally Weynfeldt took the opportunity to make a few purchases in Mayfair and stay at the Connaught— at his own expense; Murphy's travel budget would not nearly have covered it. The discreet establishment had been his father's favorite hotel. Sebastian Weynfeldt never forgot to mention that the hotel butler there even knew what temperature he liked his bathwater.

The Connaught had lost much of its style since then, and now lured guests with the promise of nonslip mats in the bathrooms and two rooms for the price of one for families with children. But Weynfeldt still liked it.

It reminded him of his childhood. He had stayed there sometimes when his parents took him to Royal Ascot.

But now Adrian decided to stay home to wait for the call. He put his mind to organizing the exhibition of selected works from the auction in St. Moritz, only to find that there was nothing left to be organized, thanks to Véronique. He spent a lot of time on the phone to collectors and curators he knew would be interested in certain lots from the auction to add to their collections.

When she returned after three days, Véronique's office was as chaotic as his. He welcomed her with a box of chocolates and a bouquet of lilacs, her favorite flower, and decided it really was time to talk to the director about her salary.

While he was waiting for a sign of life from Lorena, the long awaited cold spell arrived.

Weynfeldt saw the cold front coming. He was at Diaco's for the final fitting of the two suits he'd had made for the unusually warm winter, when it went dark in the fitting room. A dense layer of cloud, like gray felt, slid in front of the sun, which just now had still been shining cheerfully—from an admittedly streaky sky. At the same moment an icy wind billowed through the tulle curtain at the half-open window. Giuliano Diaco shut it.

"I think you can take your time with the suits now," Weynfeldt observed.

As he got into a taxi outside Diaco & Sons, tiny sharp snowflakes bit at his face.

"Fucking winter," the driver snarled.

"Good for business though," Adrian said jovially.

"How's that? Are you a ski instructor?" the driver spat caustically.

"I meant your business."

"I don't own the business. I'm just a badly paid taxi driver who can't afford custom suits."

Neither of them said a word for the rest of journey through the dark snowstorm. Weynfeldt punished the man with a humiliatingly big tip.

It was the same as ever: everyone was expecting it, it was a foregone conclusion and yet the cold snap still unleashed chaos. It overwhelmed the city's street-sweeping teams, blocked the roads with the abandoned vehicles of optimists who had changed to their summer tires, caused delays on public transport, formed the main topic of conversation in offices, businesses and restaurants and pushed global politics out of the headlines.

The waiting Weynfeldt viewed adjusting to the extreme weather as one of the many tasks that would shorten his wait. Others included making an appointment with Gabriel Talberger, the film producer he went to school with years ago. Weynfeldt invited him for lunch at the Bel Étage, the restaurant at the Grand Imperial Hotel. Talberger was a little surprised at the invitation, and it hadn't been easy to find a window in his diary. But he had succeeded on short notice, undoubtedly out of curiosity.

The Bel Étage was not a place you could get reservations on short notice, either, but as Murphy's used the Imperial's ballroom, the impossible was always made possible for Dr. Weynfeldt. He was given one of the tables the hotel kept in reserve for their VIP guests. He waited at it for Talberger, much too early, as usual.

He hadn't seen the producer for several years, and only recognized him as he came close. He had put on weight, and gone bald in an old-fashioned way. His nose, once a landmark of his physiognomy, was less marked now that his face was more rounded; more in proportion, but less distinctive. Only his eyes, ice blue and light-sensitive, still gazed critically and haughtily as ever.

Talberger worked his way through the gourmet menu; Weynfeldt stuck to the business lunch. This meant he had longer pauses between courses than his guest. He felt obliged to dig through his scant reminiscences of their shared school days.

Only after the dessert and cheese could Weynfeldt get to the real point of the invitation.

"A friend of mine, Claudio Hausmann, known throughout the industry, I'm sure"—Talberger's nod didn't look promising—"… has recently finished a script."

"… *Working Title: Hemingway's Suitcase*," Talberger said.

"Ah, you know it?"

"Known throughout the industry."

Weynfeldt had no option but to ask, "And? What do you think of it?"

Talberger pushed the empty plate of cheese aside and leaned back. "Can I be honest?"

"Best not," Weynfeldt said.

"What exactly did he say?" Kando wanted to know. She had called frequently since their drink in Südflügel, and had pressed for the meeting with Talberger. He had barely returned from lunch at Bel Étage when she was on the line again.

They arranged to meet for an aperitif next day, in Südflügel again. Although he was over-punctual as ever, Kando and Claudio were waiting for him, glasses almost empty.

Weynfeldt felt terrible. He was dreading this meeting more than the meal with Talberger.

"How did it go?" Kando asked, as soon as he sat down. Hausmann acted as if the whole business was immaterial to him.

"Not badly," Weynfeldt replied, "in principle."

"He's read the script?"

"He knew it."

"And?"

"He finds the project interesting"

"You see," Kando said to Claudio. "I knew it. Talberger was the one to contact."

"The project," Hausmann muttered. "Obviously the project is interesting. I'd like to know how he found the script."

"How did he find the script?" Kando gave Weynfeldt a severe look.

"As I said, I got the impression he thought it wasn't bad in principle."

To which Kando asked, "What exactly did he say?"

Adrian had an answer prepared for this: "He feels it needs more flesh on the bones in some places."

Hausmann rolled his eyes. "That's what really makes me sick. You add the flesh during shooting. I hope you told him that."

Adrian had an answer here too. "I think it's purely a question of financial tactics. The atmosphere and the dialogue help attract funding. After that you're free again."

Instead of giving an answer Claudio made a dismissive wave with a weary hand and reached for the dregs of his Campari.

Kando, the more pragmatic of the two, asked, "And what does he suggest?"

"A script doctor and a dialogist."

"And a director," Hausmann added sarcastically.

Talberger had indeed suggested this, but Adrian refrained from saying so.

It was Kando again who bit the bullet: "And who will pay for all that?"

Now the conversation had returned to Weynfeldt's home turf.

March, and it was still winter. The uppity foretaste of spring had made it hard for people to cope with the cold, wet and gray again. Adrian Weynfeldt didn't care; he wasn't susceptible to the weather. He participated in conversations about the weather, of course, but in the same way he participated in any conversation he wasn't remotely interested in: with polite interest.

Not only that, the weather's return to normality fitted his preference for regularity. At the Alte Färberei for instance, where, disconcerted by the spring-like weather, they had replaced the Saturday *Berner Platte* with something lighter, everything was back to normal:

the restaurant was overheated, the coat stands hung with overcoats and the mountain of sauerkraut wheeled by on the serving trolley was again crowned with steaming tongue, bacon and sausages.

Adrian Weynfeldt stuck to the tradition of meeting his elderly friends there on Saturday nights. Mereth Widler and Remo Kalt, his family's former asset manager, were the only others present. The old lady was doing her best to switch from her lifelong role of shocking lady to that of disgraceful widow. But she couldn't pull it off. She was as lost as the funny half of a comedy duo whose straight man has died. And she no longer had the energy to put away impressive quantities of the *Berner Platte*. Perhaps, Adrian thought, this had also just been part of her act. Without an audience she would just have eaten the modest portions presumably required to maintain her slender physique.

At Agustoni's too it was cozier with real winter weather. The ceramic coal stove, piled with napkins in summer, was used to boost the central heating in winter. At busy times Agustoni insisted on stoking it with coal briquettes, personally and ceremonially. The windows remained closed, and it was left to the ventilation system, continually damned by the relevant authorities, to extricate the mixture of smoke and kitchen vapors. The waiters had to negotiate the hems of coats dangling on the ground from the backs of chairs. It was louder and people drank more; the guests postponed, again and again, the moment they would have to return to the chilly streets.

Rolf Strasser had skipped the Thursday lunch club

only once; now he was back, surly and drunk and late as ever. Weynfeldt had never challenged him about his commission for Baier. Not only because he preferred to avoid conflict. He had other reasons too.

As Strasser was always one of the last to arrive, and thus sat far away from Weynfeldt, it was easy to avoid talking to him. They waved noncommittally to each other from a distance, and that was that.

Aside from Alice Waldner, no one noticed that their relationship had cooled; she asked, "What's with Rolf? Did he ask you for money and you said no?"

"The other way around is more like it," Adrian said. She thought this was a good joke, and let out one of her childlike laughs.

During one of the Thursday meals Weynfeldt made an appointment with Kaspar Casutt to discuss another activity which would shorten the waiting period.

For various reasons they met in Weynfeldt's apartment, and for reasons relating to these reasons, he asked Frau Hauser simply to prepare a cold buffet with a few Grison specialties—dried meats, cheese, *Salsiz*, *Birnbrot*, *Nusstorte*. They would serve themselves.

As always in winter, Casutt came without a coat, simply wearing a red wool scarf over his black jacket. Adrian was convinced Kaspar felt as cold as he did, the city boy. But Casutt clearly wanted to express his disdain for the pathetic winter down here in the valley.

He was visibly disappointed by the frugal meal—he was used to finer things from Frau Hauser. But given that everything was from his Alpine home, he helped himself and suppressed any objections to what was on offer. And he showed growing enthusiasm for the Velt-liner, an unusual, outstanding example of the genre.

When he then discovered that the reason for the invitation was a job, his mood rose to those rare peaks of warmth which reminded his friends why they were friends with him in the first place.

Each holding a glass, they inspected the future building site, and Kaspar said, "Fitness studio? Why a fitness studio? Having a midlife crisis? Just get more exercise—go jogging, walking, climbing. Or try tennis, golf. Yes, golf, that would suit you. And we'll make a multimedia room here. Or a home movie theater. Yes, a movie theater. Eight seats. Or twelve. Dolby five point one."

"I'd prefer a fitness room, Kaspar," Adrian succeeded in asserting.

Casutt thought for a second. Then he surprised Adrian with the words, "Okay, you're the boss." And switched from movie theater to fitness studio in an instant. "Rubber, black rubber surface, good cushioning. Elastic sports flooring. Perhaps continuing up the walls, ten or twelve inches. Maybe not though. And here perhaps mirrors down the entire wall. At the beginning you can pull a curtain across," he grinned, "but after a few months' training ..."

Casutt was good at that: he could conjure up a space so graphically, with just a few words and gestures, that you saw it in front of you, felt you were in it and viewed the transitional phase from reality to dream as a minor detail.

And this was how Weynfeldt felt now, although really

he knew that a building project with Casutt meant an eternal series of delays, arguments with contractors and suppliers and fundamental discussions about architecture, architectural rigor and the social significance of building to humanity.

In the middle of his enthusiastic explanation, the architect stopped short. "I wouldn't be able to handle that," he said.

"What?" Weynfeldt asked.

Casutt pointed to the painting above the sofa: "She doesn't take her eyes off you for a moment."

23

EVERY RUN OF BAD LUCK COMES TO AN END, LORENA thought, as she finished the conversation with Barbara and threw her cell phone on her unmade bed.

Mallorca! Wow!

Barbara. Of all people. Barbara: last time she'd seen Barbara, Lorena had called her a filthy whore. She had no idea how long ago that was.

They had once been best buddies, as far as it's possible for two catalogue models to be buddies. Barbara was the only one who hadn't sucked up to the photographers and clients, and hadn't obeyed the ban on smoking joints and drinking during working hours. The only one aside from Lorena.

They'd had a lot of fun together. The falling out, like most in that milieu, was bedroom related. Barbara had done exactly what they'd despised their colleagues for; she had slept her way into special treatment. She had started something with the mail order company's head of advertising and had become the star of the troupe overnight. It was no use Barbara pleading that she really had fallen head over heels in love: Lorena called her a filthy whore.

And now she had called to ask, "How do you feel about two weeks on Mallorca? We fly in two days. But you have to decide now. Last minute."

"No cash," Lorena said.

"You don't need any. My husband will pay."

"You're married?"

"Guess who?"

"No!"

Two weeks on Mallorca was exactly what she needed now. Two weeks in the Caribbean would have been better, but Mallorca was fine. She had never been there, but a Mediterranean island at the end of February was always good, particularly just before a cold spell here. Not many tourists, long walks on empty beaches, discos closed, healthy living.

She considered who she could tap for money. Even if the flight and hotel were paid, she couldn't travel with no money at all. The only person who came to mind was the man with the signet ring, Adrian Weynfeldt. She found his card and called his apartment. Answering machine. She hung up.

She tried his office. Without high expectations; it was Saturday.

But her streak of good luck held; his secretary answered. Weynfeldt now had a cell phone, and the woman actually gave her the number.

She called and let it ring for ages. Finally he answered. "Hallo?" she said. Nothing. Just murmuring voices. "It's me, Lorena!"

Still nothing but murmuring. Then the line suddenly went dead. She called again. The person she was trying to call was unavailable, a voice said. Weynfeldt had switched his phone off. He was probably at a meeting.

On a Saturday morning? At a meeting? It had

sounded like some other kind of gathering.

She would try again in an hour; in the meantime she started packing.

An hour later Weynfeldt's phone was still switched off. But now Lorena knew she needed shoes for Mallorca. And a bathing suit, in case it was at all summery there. And other bits and pieces.

If she'd had any money at all, and if there'd been more time till the stores closed, she wouldn't have called Pedroni, and might never have had anything to do with him again in her life.

But she called him now and offered him the Issey Miyake she had never worn, half price, if he could pay her in the next couple of hours.

"In a few weeks it'll only be worth half that price anyway," he said, "but I can lend you some money."

An hour later they met in a *piadini* bar near Spotlight. She told him about the Mallorca plan.

"And why don't you call your boyfriend," he asked.

"Away on business," she replied.

"Bad timing," he said, and handed her a thousand.

"You're not worried I'll never pay it back?" she asked.

Pedroni shook his head. "Business trips don't last forever."

All evening she tried to reach Weynfeldt. His cell phone was clearly back on, but he wasn't answering. No one was in the office, and the phone at his apartment produced white noise as soon as you were connected.

On Sunday morning at eight she tried all three numbers. With the same result. Now she was sure it was deliberate. Dr. Weynfeldt had changed his mind. She had misjudged him: he was just like all the other signet ring men.

She got into the shower, which was so narrow the stained shower curtain kept clinging to you. The clogged shower head shot thin jets of water in all directions. She looked down at her body and wondered if things had gotten so bad the men wanted to shake her off before they'd even had sex with her.

Sunday late morning she tried to get hold of Weynfeldt one last time. Again without success. Then she finally gave up. She would stick with Pedroni. He was the kind of man she was used to.

On Monday morning she met Barbara at the check-in. Barbara's outfit was a shade summery for Lorena's tastes. Although the predicted cold spell hadn't come yet, the temperature at the airport didn't justify a sleeveless, low-cut, belly-free top. She was accompanied by her husband, the advertising manager, already chubbier. He greeted her like a pal, helped with the luggage and accompanied Barbara to passport control; it seemed like the couple could hardly bear to part.

Yet as soon as they were inside the charter plane, Barbara asked her to swap places with a young man she introduced as Mischa. Now Lorena realized what her role was.

After a choppy flight over an ever denser blanket of clouds, they landed on the island. Lorena first caught a glimpse of the sea just before they landed. They were taken in a half-empty bus down a three-lane highway to a six-floor hotel surrounded by other six-floor hotels—

the only one open.

So this is Mallorca, Lorena thought.

She barely saw Barbara, who was sharing a double room with Mischa; Lorena was given a single. It was on the lowest floor, with a view of the single rooms in the neighboring hotel. Damp and so badly heated she had to stay in bed the whole time. There she hid under the synthetic duvet drinking a lukewarm Cuba Libre—at least one Caribbean thing—and watched depressing talk shows on the fuzzy TV via the hotel's German channel.

A few times she pulled herself together and walked down the flotsam- and trash-strewn beach along the restless, grubby, gray sea.

For trips she was reliant on the hotel's shuttles. She couldn't afford taxis; Pedroni's loan wouldn't stretch that far.

Her birthday fell during the second week of the vacation. Her thirty-seventh. Only three more till forty. Thirteen till fifty. Twenty-three till sixty.

Twenty three years; that was nothing, when she thought about how quickly the time from zero to twenty three had gone: a bit of childhood, bit of youth and—all of a sudden—twenty three!

She got up at nine that morning and entered the chilly dining room. At a couple of the uncleared tables sat pensioner couples in tracksuits saying nothing to each other. Two younger couples were discussing their children, who were the same age, now staring aggressively at each other. Lorena ordered an espresso and orange juice from a carton—no matter that the orange trees all over the island were groaning under the weight of their ripe fruit—and sat at a window table.

The wind blew a gust of rain against the glass. A few gulls were showing off their moves in the storm.

Lorena ordered a bottle of *cava*. Brut, and cold, for fuck's sake.

"Happy birthday," she said half to herself, as she began the first glass. The wind tousled the dry palm fronds of the sun shelters and made plastic bottles and chunks of white Styrofoam dance on the one distant bit of beach visible between the better situated hotels.

By the time she had finished the bottle, the staff were setting the tables for lunch. Lorena went to bed and woke up three hours later with a foggy head and a rage against Barbara. She got dressed, stomped up to her room and knocked fiercely.

"Si?" Barbara asked, after the second knock.

"It's me. The friend you took on vacation."

"Not a good time," Barbara said, and Lorena heard them both giggling.

"I just wanted to say that today is my fucking birthday!" Lorena yelled, crying now. "Filthy whore!" she added, and ran off.

In the elevator Lorena pressed the top button. On the sixth floor she ran down the corridor to the door with the red sign: *"Salida."* A stairway took her one floor higher to a door which opened onto the roof. She walked through it.

It was still, as if the storm had never happened. It smelled of cement and tar. A wheelbarrow full of building tools stood in one corner, along with a transistor radio thick with dirt.

MARTIN SUTER

Lorena walked to the balustrade. A long way below was a patch of asphalt holding a couple of overflowing dumpsters, adjoining a playground. She had passed it on the way to the beach: a metal frame with two child's swings, both attached on one side only, a rusty, dented slide and a sandbox serving as a dog toilet. Farther away was a patch of beach, where a couple of stiff-legged gulls were strutting around. Beyond the two neighboring hotels, the same height as this, the sea was still churned up from the storm. It was the same leaden gray as the sky, now letting the late afternoon light glimmer through a threadbare slit.

Lorena swung a leg over the balustrade and looked down. There, between the dumpsters and the broken swings, was where she would split apart. The thought brought tears to her eyes. She stood, crying, one foot on each side of the balustrade. With no one to stop her from jumping.

Weynfeldt came to her now. The way he had stood, helpless, at a safe distance, in white pajamas with a ruffled Kennedy haircut. How he suddenly started crying.

As they had parted, he'd said, "There's always something worth staying alive for."

"Can you guarantee me that?" she had asked.

"Guaranteed," he had replied.

Lorena took her leg off the balustrade. Perhaps it was time to claim something. While the guarantee was still valid.

On the day they left, a summery sky stretched big and blue over the island, as if it wanted to give the departing guests an idea of how things could have been different.

Lorena had spoken to Barbara only once more the entire time. It was not a reconciliation. Barbara wanted Lorena to walk into the arrivals hall with her and act out the rest of the comedy. Lorena refused. She was being picked up herself, she claimed.

And it was true. She had thrown a coin. Heads meant she would call Weynfeldt and ask him; tails meant Pedroni.

She threw the coin three times. Each time tails.

24

The call came late. Weynfeldt had stayed on in the office to work. The auction catalogue had been sent out, and reactions from collectors and curators kept pouring in each day. He found time for the regular work only in the evenings.

He ate alone, in a restaurant with the ridiculous name Esserei—eatery. The proprietor was an ambitious young man who had set out to create a new style of food, which he named *la cuisine simple*.

According to the introduction in the menu, Esserei was derived from the Spanish *comedor*, a word for which, to his great regret, there had been no equivalent in the German language till now.

The restaurant was furnished on the same principle. Simple 1950s-style kitchen tables covered with lino-leum, similar chairs and white stoneware crockery; the walls decorated with large blow-up photos of salt and peppercorns, garlic cloves, onion rings, potato peelings, rice grains or slices of bacon.

The food, however, was excellent. Decent, simple dishes made from top quality ingredients. Aside from salt and pepper, never more than three herbs or spices per dish. And aside from onion and garlic, never more than five main ingredients.

You went to the eatery to eat. The eaters were

required to lower their voices; the main sound heard was the cautious clinking of cutlery on crockery. Adrian doubted whether the owner would succeed in enforcing this strict interpretation of his concept for long. It affected the atmosphere and thus the number of guests. But when he was on his own he liked to eat there. You didn't have to chat with the staff, there was no smoking and no one minded if you asked for the check as soon as you'd taken your last mouthful.

Weynfeldt went straight home once he'd eaten. There were building materials piled in the hallway outside his apartment. The floor leading to the future fitness room was protected with floor liner. Early that morning the contractors had begun ripping out the old parquet. Adrian had sat in his breakfast room trying to ignore the brutal banging, crashing, rasping and splitting.

Frau Hauser, who had been strangely quiet and thoughtful since he had confessed his decision to revamp, came into the room and said, "I've given it some thought: I think it's good what you're doing with the room."

Adrian couldn't believe his ears. "You think it's good that I'm turning my mother's bedroom into a fitness studio?" Frau Hauser was the last person he had expected to support his delayed attempt to achieve distance.

"Yes, because it's for your health. It's what your mother would have wanted."

The dust had a particular smell, generated as the parquet was torn out to reveal the space beneath the floor. The ancient stuffiness was mixed with the aroma of freshly sawn wood. During the big renovation four years ago they had found newspaper pages from 1893 between the joists, and half a tin of snuff.

But now Adrian went straight to his study. He was not curious about the secret recesses of his mother's parquet.

He switched on the light and pressed play on the stereo. J. J. Cale was still in the CD tray. The last time he had listened to the music was when he discovered Baier's Vallotton was forged. Now the two easels, on which the genuine painting and the forgery had stood side by side, indistinguishable, were empty.

He thought about Lorena and her comment, lodged in his memory: "Just the fact that someone will pay so much for it makes the painting genuine."

Weynfeldt put his coat on and went out again. Recently he had begun challenging the passivity of his waiting state with a particular activity: visiting La Rivière, where he had first met Lorena. Less in the hope of meeting her there; more in the knowledge that the barman would tell him if she had shown up. Without Weynfeldt asking; he would never ask.

He walked through the deserted streets, where the *föhn* was clearing away the last dirty vestiges of snow. A streetcar passed. The passengers sitting in the garish light looked tired and serious.

As he approached La Rivière a figure emerged from the shadows of a wall. Weynfeldt jumped, but then he recognized the man. A drug addict who had been begging for a few francs from passersby in the area for years. Adrian had never seen him out so late. He must have had a bad day. Weynfeldt gave him ten francs as always, and they wished each other good night.

La Rivière was not busy. It was Wednesday: no live music. He nodded to the barman, sat at his usual seat and waited for his martini. Recently he hadn't been confining himself to the olive.

He had planned to drink just one tonight, then leave. But he ordered another after all.

Just as the barman was bringing it, his cell phone rang.

Weynfeldt reached into the phone pocket in the lining of his jacket, which Diaco was slowly adding to all his suits. He read "number unknown" on the display, pressed the right button, as he'd been practicing, and answered.

He wasn't surprised that it was Lorena. She asked that cell phone question he'd always made fun of: "Where are you?"

"In La Rivière."

"Can we meet?"

"Sure. Where?" He heard her talking to someone. A man's voice. Then: "I'll just pass you to someone else."

"Is it true, you'll lend her five thousand francs if she asks you?" the man asked.

"Who am I talking to, please?"

"Tell me. Is it true?"

"Please tell me who I'm talking to."

Weynfeldt heard the man say, "He won't say. Forget it."

Then Lorena's voice came on again. She sounded pretty desperate: "Tell him it's true please." Then quietly: "Otherwise he'll freak out."

The man's voice returned, rough: "What's it to be?"

"I'll lend her five thousand francs. But it's not so easy

right now; it's nearly midnight."

"I'm sure you have cards you can use to take five thousand out of an ATM."

Adrian hadn't thought of that. Of course he had such cards. "Yes, I do."

"Corner of Poststeg and City-Strasse there's a cash point, you know it?"

"Yes."

"When can you be there?"

"In ten minutes."

"See you in ten minutes then."

Weynfeldt paid, took his coat from the coat stand and put it on as he walked down the street.

The *föhn* was beating the ropes against the empty flagpoles along the riverbank. The moored excursion boats bashed against the jetties at irregular intervals. Weynfeldt kept his hands deep in his coat pocket and marched on, bowed against the wind. He was concerned and delighted at the same time. What kind of trouble was she in this time? Whatever. At least she had chosen him to get her out of it.

It took him less than five minutes to reach the meeting point. There was no one to be seen. The cash point was brightly lit inside. He slid the magnetic strip on his bank card through the reader slot and walked in.

It smelled of stale cigarette smoke; on the floor stood a Starbucks cup. But the four machines were all working. Using his bank card and his credit card, he took out five thousand francs. In big notes: around here no one dealt in small bills.

He put the money in his coat pocket, left the stuffy

room and waited.

A car approached and stopped at the curb. Weynfeldt walked towards it. A middle-aged man stepped out, regarded Adrian distrustfully, took his card from his wallet and opened the cash center door. Before he had reemerged an aging Audi pulled up. It stopped and blinked its headlights twice. Adrian walked over to the car.

At the wheel was a man of around forty with gray-streaked, receding hair. He had wound the window down. In the half-light of the back seat, Weynfeldt could see a woman. She nodded almost imperceptibly. It was Lorena.

"Have you got the money?" the man asked by way of a greeting.

Weynfeldt ignored him. He went to the back door of the car and tried to open it. It was locked.

The man got out, aggressive, and planted himself in Weynfeldt's way. He was smaller, but clearly violent. "I asked if you've got the money!"

Weynfeldt took the notes out of his coat pocket and handed them over. The man counted them with practiced speed. Adrian watched him as he did it. For a moment he thought he recognized him. But he rejected the idea. He didn't know anyone like that.

The man put the money in his pocket and got into the car. Weynfeldt heard the child safety lock click, and immediately afterward Lorena got out. She had barely slammed the door shut before the car raced off, tires screeching.

There they stood, both disheveled by the *föhn*, both waiting till the other said something. Lorena shrugged her shoulders; Adrian copied her.

"No questions?" She was the first to speak.

"None at all."

"Now I could do with a drink."

"La Rivière?"

"Aren't we closer to your place?"

This wasn't strictly true. But Weynfeldt nodded, and they headed to his. After a few paces she put her arm through his. As she had after the shoplifting incident.

The *föhn* developed into a true windstorm. The lights above the streetcar cables shook, and not so far away came a splitting crash as the wind blew something off a roof terrace or windowsill.

"How have you been since last time?" Weynfeldt inquired.

"I was on Mallorca."

"Isn't it ghastly at this time of year?"

"No, it was quite pleasant. Hardly any tourists. Have you ever been?"

"Years ago. Twenty or so."

"And?"

"We only stayed one night."

"Why?"

"We were travelling on a ship."

"A yacht?"

"No, it was a pretty big ship."

"Yours?"

Weynfeldt laughed. "No, it belonged to friends. Of my parents."

"Pity. A yacht would be cool."

"Too many people in too small a space, if you ask me.

And you can't escape. No, no, yachts are a bit overrated."

Now Lorena laughed too.

They had reached the door to Adrian's building. He carried out the complicated entry procedure with his keys and card.

"Doesn't that drive you crazy sometimes?" she asked.

"Sure, sometimes. But it also gives you a feeling of security. Quite nice, when you live alone."

"Do you get scared?"

The question surprised him. But then he answered. "Yes, a bit."

In the elevator she asked, "Have you got lots of buildings like this?"

"No."

"But a few?"

Weynfeldt had indeed inherited another office building, bigger than this one, also in a top location, not far away. But not many people knew that. None of his younger friends. And Lorena was definitely one of them. "No," he said simply.

As they entered the apartment Lorena asked, "Are you having construction work done?"

"Just renovating one room."

"Which one?"

"Down there," he said vaguely.

Since Lorena's last visit Adrian had been keeping a small supply of Louis Roederer Cristal on ice. For just this eventuality. But when he asked if she fancied a few thousand tiny bubbles, she said, "Tonight is a gin fizz night."

"I don't know how to make gin fizz."

"I do." To get to the kitchen, they had to pass his

mother's bedroom. The door was missing and a transparent plastic dust sheet hung from the frame.

"Ah. You're redoing your mother's room. What's it going to be?"

"A fitness room."

She looked at him sideways in astonishment.

He watched her making the drinks, measuring gin, ice, lemon cordial, soda and syrup in the mixer then shaking it like a professional.

"Where did you learn that?"

"It was my job once."

"Barmaid? Tell me more."

"You don't want to know. Where are we drinking this?"

"Wherever you want. You know the apartment."

"In your study."

The *föhn* had swept the sky clear, and a pale moon shed a sparse light into the room through the tall plate glass windows. "No, no light," she begged, as he reached his hand to the switches.

They sat and sipped their long drinks in silence. "Did you do it?" she asked finally, pointing to the empty easels.

"Yes."

"Which one?"

"As they are one and the same, it doesn't matter," Weynfeldt said.

"True."

They took their time with the drinks. Then she sat on his knee and kissed him. He smelled the gin and a hint of her slightly matronly perfume.

"Maybe we could complete the tour today," she suggested.

25

"Oh!" Frau Hauser exclaimed, and closed the door again. Weynfeldt hadn't heard her knock.

The room was in semidarkness, the curtains drawn, night-lights dimmed. The alarm clock was projecting 08:22 onto the ceiling.

They were lying on top of the quilt. He had his head at the foot; Lorena was the other way around. He could imagine the picture they presented to Frau Hauser.

Once, around forty years ago, she had walked into his parents' bathroom without knocking and surprised his father—who told the tale often and with glee—naked at an untypical time of day. "I'm terribly sorry!" he exclaimed. To which she is said to have replied, "Come now, do you think I've never seen a naked man before?"

This time she had seen a naked man with a naked woman. She had probably been surprised he hadn't appeared for breakfast. Worried even.

Weynfeldt looked at Lorena's feet, next to his head. This time every nail was painted vermilion. Not like the first time, when they had poked through between the balcony and the balustrade, red, yellow, green, indigo, violet.

He looked at her white body—dappled with freckles on the neckline and forearms, more skinny than slender, more vulnerable than sensual—and imagined it painted. By Ferdinand Hodler, sketched with a thick, black outline; by Giovanni Giacometti, sculpted with colors, shades and reflections; by Felix Vallotton, realistic yet graphic, expansive yet detailed.

He got up quietly, slipped into his robe and slippers and left the room. Now he could hear the muffled din of the construction work. He'd forgotten the contractors altogether. For a moment he was tempted to retreat to his bedroom, take a shower and get dressed first. But then he reminded himself it was his apartment after all.

He walked to the telephone, called Véronique and told her he would be taking the morning off.

"What do you mean, *taking the morning off?* Blancpain is coming at quarter past ten, and Chester has already called twice; he's expecting you to call back before half nine when he has to check in with Sydney."

Blancpain was the curator of the Musée d'Orly, and Chester was the secretary of an Australian private collector. They were both top-notch clients, high on Weynfeldt's list. "Stave them off with something convincing," Adrian said, and ended the conversation.

He sauntered into the breakfast room. The table had been cleared. A little cross, he made his way to the kitchen. He was met by a clattering sound. His first thought was that it came from the contractors. But when he turned the corner of the corridor toward the kitchen he almost collided with a serving trolley. Frau Hauser was pushing a breakfast for two. "Ah," she said in surprise. "I thought you were having breakfast in bed today."

She looked at him without the faintest hint of a smile or a wink or any other tacit understanding.

"Good idea," Weynfeldt said, and took the trolley from her.

Lorena was awake. She was lying under the covers, two cushions stuffed behind her back, leafing through the auction catalogue. When she saw breakfast she stretched and put the catalogue aside. "Between 1.2 and 1.5 million. I thought it was 2 to 3."

Adrian knew what she was talking about: the price the Vallotton was valued at. It was gracing the cover, although due to its late inclusion it had been given a high lot number, 136. "That's the estimate. The rest is up to the bidders."

"I'd like to be there, at an auction where people bid millions."

"Then come along."

"Really?"

"Really."

They ate breakfast in bed like a couple just fallen in love. And talked like one too. Lorena asked her disarming questions and Adrian surprised himself by how frankly he answered them.

"How much rent does the bank pay you?"

"Somewhere over a million each year, I think."

"You think?"

"I'm sure."

"Wow! And what do you do with all that money?"

"I spend most of it. The rest adds up slowly."

"Why do you still work then?"

"What else should I do?"

"Travel."

"I'm not really the traveling type."

"Do nothing."

"That was driven out of me as a child."

"Lot 142. Estimate: forty to sixty thousand."

Weynfeldt grinned sheepishly.

Lorena pulled on his earlobe. "Is that done? Putting your mother's portrait up for auction?"

"If no one did it there would be no portraits of older women on the art market."

She fished out another croissant. There had been four in the basket. Normally there were only two. Adrian wondered how Frau Hauser had got hold of the second two so quickly. Perhaps she bought four every day: two for him and two for herself. And this morning she had sacrificed her two.

"Which of the two paintings did you put in the auction?"

"I don't know."

"Come now."

"You made them identical."

"But *you* can still tell them apart."

"Me and the forger."

"And you're both keeping mum?"

"I wouldn't be so sure about the forger. They can be very vain."

"Do you know this one?"

"Yes." And then he said it: "A professional artist, as in professional circus artist, or professional bullshit artist."

Lorena laughed. "Don't you have a girlfriend?"

"No."

"Why not?"

Adrian reflected. "It just hasn't happened that way."

"And friends?"

"Sure I have friends."

"Friends are important."

"True."

"I know. I don't have any."

"None at all?"

"No real ones."

Weynfeldt considered whether he had any real friends himself.

"Why aren't you asking me anything?"

"What should I ask?"

"Don't you want to know if I'm a hooker?"

"No, I don't want to know that."

"Why not? If you liked me, you'd want to know."

"If I liked you, I wouldn't want to know."

In the distance they heard the howling and roaring of an electric drill.

"Why would I think you might be a hooker?"

"Because of yesterday. Didn't you think that guy was a pimp?"

"I wouldn't know."

"Don't you want to know if he was a pimp?"

"If you want to tell me, you will."

"He isn't."

"There you go."

"He's a debt collector."

"Not to be sniffed at either."

Lorena laughed, and so did Adrian. "Not to be sniffed at," she repeated, and laughed so much she spilled coffee on the quilt.

When she'd calmed down, she asked. "Don't you

want to know why I owe a debt collector money?"

"Used to owe."

"If only."

"You still owe him money?"

"A question at last."

"And?"

"A hundred and twenty."

"Not to be sniffed at either."

26

Rolf Strasser got to the Thursday lunch club late as usual. He first noticed Weynfeldt wasn't there when he looked for a bottle of wine and found only a small carafe of house white. "Isn't Adrian coming today?" he asked Luc Neri, who sat mute and exhausted next to him.

Neri raised his shoulders, and released them again as if he'd had to hold them up for hours.

The friends pored over the menu for longer than usual, and several kept one eye on the door. When Weynfeldt finally arrived they had already ordered. This week it seemed no one had felt like the *bistecca alla fiorentina*—at forty-nine francs, normally a favorite at the Thursday lunch club.

Weynfeldt was accompanied by a redhead. Much younger than him and not really his style. Although Strasser had never seen Weynfeldt with a woman before, if he tried to imagine him with a girlfriend she would be more the high society type. This one was not that. She was good looking, for sure. But in a common kind of way. Although she was expensively dressed. Designer dress. But if you were Weynfeldt's girlfriend you could afford designer clothes.

Weynfeldt had never had as much attention at the lunch club as he was getting now, with this woman.

Everyone was watching how he behaved toward her. Strasser's verdict was: head over heels.

Lorena—she had been introduced formally to each of them as Lorena—sat next to him. At one of the two extra places Adrian had long reserved in vain for unexpected guests. Now it had been worth it. She ordered the *bistecca alla fiorentina* and Weynfeldt joined her. The first time he hadn't opted for his *insalata mista* and *scaloppine al limone* with risotto. Clearly head over heels.

She was funny. Unlike Weynfeldt, who tended to be boring. Late thirties. Done a lot. Good figure. Four or five more pounds wouldn't look poorly on her. Seemed a bit affected, but that was understandable meeting Adrian's friends for the first time. He'd presented them to her as "my friends."

"So you're an artist," she observed. Weynfeldt had described him to her as "my friend, the artist Rolf Strasser."

"I'm not so sure about that. I prefer the term 'professional artist.' It implies an occupation rather than an attribute. Like a professional circus artist, or professional bullshit artist."

Lorena exchanged glances with Adrian.

"Rolf is both," Adrian interjected. "Artist and professional artist."

It was the first time he'd described him as an artist. Today was Weynfeldt's day for firsts. No doubt about it: head over heels.

Then she asked the moronic question: "So what kind of things do you paint?" and Strasser started to revise his estimation of her.

"Whatever you want," he replied.

And she saved herself with, "So more of a professional than an artist after all."

The best thing about her was, she didn't care about his chain-smoking, even helping herself to one of his Chesterfields without asking, and she could match his pace when it came to drinking wine.

It was three by the time the last of them left. Weynfeldt stayed till the end, also a first.

Afterward, in Südflügel, where Strasser went with Casutt for a grappa, they both agreed: this Lorena was a great addition to the Thursday lunch club.

27

"Now this bit. That's luuvely," Tereza said for the umpteenth time. The client said nothing, but Lorena heard an audible intake of breath as the beautician tore off another whole strip of wax.

Lorena was lying on a beauty treatment couch which, as Tereza liked to point out, had four motors, castors which could be lowered electrically and a foot pedal to ensure hygienic working conditions. She was wearing a headband to keep her hair out of her face, and the face mask Luxusní, formulated by Tereza herself using a closely guarded secret recipe. The mask alone cost a hundred and forty francs.

But Lorena had a bit of money at the moment, and she needed to come clean with herself. For some reason that always worked best with Tereza at Salon Perfektní.

The beauty salon consisted of one large space partitioned with a system of gold-trimmed brocade curtains to create a waiting room and three treatment cubicles. It smelled of perfume, nail polish remover and warm wax. A stereo system set on repeat played a selection of chill-out CDs which Tereza's daughter replenished regularly.

Despite the background music you could hear every word spoken anywhere in Salon Perfektní. These were often intimate words, spoken by clients expressing themselves as freely as if they were in soundproofed rooms. But when they were silent, like the one in the next cubicle, Tereza entertained them with stories about her daughter, who lived on Fuerteventura with a man who worked in tourism, or about the defects in the three-room apartment they had bought there. At the moment it was the apartment, where she had just spent two rainy weeks. "Now this bit. That's luuvely."

Tereza was somewhere between fifty and sixty. She had lived in Switzerland since 1968, the Prague Spring. Her face was unwrinkled, thanks less to her profession than to her corpulence. Her eyebrows were depilated, and redrawn in a different place in black, arched so highly that her otherwise impassive face gave the impression of astonishment. Lorena had first met her at a catalogue shoot. Tereza had stepped in at short notice to do the makeup, and was the only one who occasionally made her laugh. Since then Lorena had been a regular customer—when she could afford her services.

The fact that she could afford them now was thanks to the two and a half thousand—her share of the five—which Pedroni had screwed poor Adrian out of. They had planned this job as a test. As a test, and to introduce Pedroni as Mr. X. For future, bigger jobs.

It had been fun. She'd come up with the idea, including the location for the handover—the cash point on the corner of Poststeg and City-Strasse, which sounded very professional. She'd been impressed by how hard she'd been—Lorena the ice-cold angel.

And afterward, at his apartment, she'd followed it

through. Had hung up her heart with her coat and slept with him.

Next morning she'd had to remind herself a couple of times that he was just a signet ring man, who would get rid of her now that he'd gotten her into bed. Even if he was nicer than most.

And as if to prove to herself she'd left her heart with her coat, she started improvising. She'd come up with the figure one hundred and twenty thousand at random. Without consulting Pedroni. And Weynfeldt had laughed. What had he said? "Not to be sniffed at." Nothing more. Just, "Not to be sniffed at." And laughed.

Easy money, she thought, and the other project, with the old man, was looking promising too.

But then Weynfeldt had invited her to lunch and introduced her to his friends. That was definitely not signet ring man behavior. And it had been very pleasant. A meal with a group of very nice people. And she had officially been treated as one of them. Not only that: as the one who was his.

Back to plan C then? Certainly, when she'd met Pedroni later to discuss the state of play, told him about the hundred and twenty, and worked out the thing with the promissory note, she'd felt a bit sleazy. She'd have felt better sitting with Adrian, planning how to get one over on Pedroni. At any rate, when they had finished the business and he asked, "Your place or mine?" she had answered, "Whatever."

The mask started to tighten, and the conversation on the other side of the curtain re-entered her consciousness. "... nothing but a little convector. No one thinks about heating on Fuerteventura."

Was it happening again? The heart sabotaging the head?

The curtain behind her moved, and she heard Tereza's voice: "Now the luuvliness is sinking into your pores, darling."

Lorena nodded cautiously beneath the stiffening mask. "And drawing out the stuupidness I hope."

28

THEO L. PEDRONI LAY FULLY CLOTHED ON THE DOUBLE bed in Room 212 of the Belotel waiting for Weynfeldt.

His jacket hung on a hanger in the narrow wardrobe between the imitation wood closet and the door to the ochre- and beige-tiled bathroom. Room 212 was described as a junior suite and therefore included an olive-green sofa bed with a matching armchair, and a mini coffee table strewn with leaflets.

Pedroni had his left hand bent behind his head; with his right he was smoking a cigarette, using the mug as an ashtray, balanced on his chest. Room 212 was a no-smoking room.

The TV was playing quiet Muzak. On the screen it said: "Welcome / Willkommen / Bienvenu Mr. Hans Meier!"

A daytime room, Lorena's idea. To be honest, Pedroni hadn't realized such a thing existed. A room you could rent for half price or cheaper to use during the day. She had come up with the idea while they were considering where he should meet Weynfeldt. Somewhere discreet, with just the two of them, not his apartment or Lorena's. And not Weynfeldt's either. It was swarming with people there, Lorena had told him.

Then she had said suddenly, "Why don't you just rent a day room at the Belotel?" And explained what that was. He could well imagine how she knew.

If Weynfeldt actually showed up—and Pedroni had no reason to doubt that he would—he would congratulate himself yet again on his instinct, which had told him he should hook up with her. The girl was a gold mine.

For a while it had looked like it was going nowhere, but when she showed up to borrow money for Mallorca he knew they'd be doing business again. Although he'd been surprised himself how soon it had worked out.

The test with the five thousand went smoothly. Weynfeldt handed it over like something he'd been trying to get rid of all his life. He was so into the chick he'd pay any amount to score points with her. Well, maybe not any amount, but a hundred and twenty thousand wouldn't be a problem. Perhaps he should have gone higher—a hundred and twenty had been her idea—but this was certainly not the last chance.

He was particularly proud of the promissory note. Not just some vague letter acknowledging a debt of a hundred and twenty francs, but a document with signatures dating back two years, claiming a total debt of a hundred and forty-two thousand, three hundred and forty, and a neat record of repayments in varying sums, each with his signature, using a variety of pens. The last was Weynfeldt's payment of five thousand, also entered correctly and signed for. The balance was a hundred and twenty thousand, which Weynfeldt would hand him in a few minutes. He was pretty certain of that.

He had done some research about the man, which had not been at all easy. He lived a very inconspicuous life, the final descendant of an old family of industrialists, once incredibly rich, who had still left him enough that he had more income than he could spend. According to Lorena, he made over a million a year simply from the building he lived in.

The man worked—this information also came from Lorena—because he enjoyed it. Something Pedroni found very hard to grasp.

But it was fine by him. That way he used up less of his fortune. Because if everything went as smoothly as he expected with the hundred and twenty, there was no reason not to use him again. He wasn't sure how, but together with Lorena he'd think of something. Weynfeldt felt responsible for her, she'd told him. They would make sure that was interpreted financially.

The telephone rang. Reception informed him a Dr. Weynfeldt had arrived. "Send him on up." He got up, went into the bathroom, washed his hands and ran his wet palms over the short hair he'd been growing again for a while.

A coincidence. Even if his head had still been shaved, Weynfeldt wouldn't have recognized him. Before the meeting in front of the ATM Pedroni had said to Lorena, "I'm sure he's never seen me, not even that day at Spotlight. People like him treat sales staff as if they're invisible. Bet you anything you like he doesn't recognize me."

A knock. Pedroni took his jacket from the hanger and put it on. Then he opened the door and invited Weynfeldt in.

The man was wearing a rain-soaked, camel-hair overcoat, holding a wet felt hat in his hand. Pedroni hadn't noticed it had started raining again.

While Weynfeldt was unbuttoning his coat, Pedroni took one of the two hangers from the wardrobe and held his hand out toward Weynfeldt's coat. The man shook his head. "I'll keep it on. I don't have much time. Could I ask you to give me the promissory note, please?"

"Could I ask you to give me the money first, please?" Pedroni responded.

It was too good to be true. The man made no attempt to argue about the procedure. He reached into the inside pocket of his coat—he was carrying a hundred and twenty big ones in his coat pocket!—and took the money out. He placed it on the coffee table among the leaflets.

Pedroni sat on the sofa bed. They were fresh notes in the original wrappers. A hundred-pack of thousands and two hundred-packs of hundreds. Pedroni broke open the wrappers and counted the notes unhurriedly. Weynfeldt didn't sit down. He stood in his overcoat at the window looking out at the gray rainy afternoon. Only when Pedroni said, out loud, "Correct," did he turn around.

"Could I have the promissory note now please?"

If the asshole hadn't looked at him so arrogantly while he'd said it, he would have gone to his briefcase and taken out the document. But now he said, "You'll receive it by post in a few days."

Weynfeldt went bright red. Didn't say a word, just stood there in his five-thousand-franc coat and went red.

Pedroni shook his head, stood up and walked over to his briefcase. "My little joke," he grinned, and handed him the document.

MARTIN SUTER

The best bit was what came next: Weynfeldt reached into his trouser pocket, took out a small leather case, extracted a magnifying glass from it, went to the window and examined the piece of paper.

"Do you think it's a fake?" Pedroni asked incredulously.

Weynfeldt gave no answer.

"I'm sure she was able to confirm that she owed me the money."

Weynfeldt put the magnifying glass away, nodded, folded the paper and secreted it in the inside pocket—of his jacket this time. "In order," he said.

"What do you mean, *in order*?"

"It's the original."

"Right. You know about things like that?"

"Yes." He walked past him towards the door. Before he opened it, he turned around once more. "From now on you will leave Frau—he hesitated—Steiner in peace, I hope that's clear."

"Or what?"

"Then you'll find out what."

"Or you'll go red?"

Weynfeldt searched for a response. Then he said, quietly, but loud enough for Pedroni to hear, "Or you will."

29

It wasn't the first time Lorena had been in the Grand Imperial Hotel, but she preferred not to think about that time.

She was ushered in by a doorman in discreet livery, and went straight to the bar. She had arranged to meet Adrian's friend, the painter Rolf Strasser, on the pretext that as a professional he would be a good person to guide her around the exhibition; Adrian didn't have time.

That was not entirely true: she hadn't asked Adrian, she had just told him she wanted to visit the preview with Rolf, because he was probably very busy, wasn't he? Adrian had approved of the idea and given her Rolf's number.

The real reason she wanted to go to the preview with Strasser was of course the Vallotton. Adrian had given her a heavy hint that he was the one who painted the copy. And therefore the only one aside from Adrian who knew if the painting on show to the public here was the authentic one or not.

Strasser was not in the bar. She ordered a glass of champagne and waited precisely fifteen minutes—the maximum she ever waited for a man.

Then she walked to the grand ballroom, following the signs attached to the auction posters, and passing through the lobby.

It was four in the afternoon, hotel guests and art enthusiasts were sitting in the easy chairs drinking coffee and eating cake; a pianist was playing tea music.

The auction poster showed the nude kneeling by the stove, now so familiar to her.

At the entrance to the ballroom, at a table full of catalogues, sat a fat young woman with a blonde bob in a loose black dress. Opposite her stood a scary man in the uniform of a private security firm. At first Lorena thought she would have to pay admission, and reached into her handbag. But the fat girl gave her a friendly nod and wished her a good day.

Lorena walked into the ballroom. The curtains had been closed. Temporary exhibition panels had been placed in front and between them, and the large dance floor was also partitioned with panels, forming a labyrinth of art.

A few visitors were walking from lot to lot, talking in an international museum whisper.

The first picture to grab Lorena's attention was the portrait of Weynfeldt's mother. It was ascribed to "Varlin (Willy Guggenheim, 1900-1977)." Beneath this was written, "*Luise W.*, mixed media (oil and charcoal) on canvas, 1974, private collection, Switzerland, CHF 80,000 to 120,000."

She paused in front of it, nodded to the old lady as if to an old acquaintance, and, under her watchful eye, set off in search of the Vallotton.

She soon found it. It was hanging alone on one of the exhibition panels in the center of the ballroom. Two men stood in front of it, both armed with notebooks, writing things down.

"Félix Vallotton, (1865-1925), *Femme nue devant une salamandre*, tempera on card, 1900, private collection, CHF 1,200,000 to 1,500,000."

The two men were standing close to the painting, and Lorena waited till they had moved away. No sooner had they done so, than a middle-aged couple arrived, the man clearly an art expert. "It was sold by Vallotton's heirs two years after his death, and it's remained in that family ever since."

"So why are they selling it now?" the woman wondered.

"Perhaps there are too many beneficiaries. You can split money. You can't slice up a painting."

"I don't know," the woman snorted. "In this case it wouldn't be such a pity!"

"What do you mean?" the man said aghast.

Lorena was forced to sit out a long argument involving allegations of faulty perspective and the female torso as a phallic symbol, before she was finally left alone and could examine the signature close up.

There'd been no need to meet Strasser; it was easy enough to identify the original. Weynfeldt had removed the period she'd added with her lipstick after the surname.

Weynfeldt, that little mama's boy, hadn't had the nerve to put the copy up for auction, and now he'd robbed Lorena of Baier's fifty thousand. Along with her share of the two other recent jobs, she would have made a total of one hundred and twelve thousand, five hundred francs. For the first time in her life she would have had a degree of independence.

She turned in fury, and nearly collided with Strasser.

"Sorry, I was held up." There was a red wine mark on his lower lip.

"Doesn't matter. I've seen all I need to see."

Strasser glanced past her at the Vallotton, took a few steps toward the painting, looked at it quickly and came back to Lorena. A strange smile on his lips.

Lorena had to vent her anger. "Someone wanted to hoodwink Adrian with a forgery of the painting, but it didn't work. It was very clumsy."

If there'd been any uncertainty whether Strasser was in fact the author of the copy, his reaction to this banished all doubt. "Oh yes?" he snapped haughtily. "Too clumsy for the expert eyes of Dr. Weynfeldt. Is that so?"

She could see it was eating him up, and announced, "I'm going to the bar now."

"It's very expensive."

"It's on me."

They crossed the lobby, full of tea guests, and entered the bar, all gleaming polished wood, where the first cocktail guests were already sitting. They commandeered a niche upholstered in green leather and ordered: Lorena a glass of champagne; Strasser a Black Label on the rocks.

"Very clumsy," he said, when the drinks arrived. "Is that so?" And repeated this a few times, till, after the third whisky, he asked, "Can you keep a secret?" He put his fingers to his lips, or tried—he had to have several goes at it.

Even if Lorena hadn't nodded, he would still have

told her: "The Vallotton in the exhibition—it's not by Vallotton."

"No?" she said, trying to sound disinterested.

"The *Salamandre* in the grand ballroom is a blatant forgery."

"How do you know that?"

"I'm the only person who can know."

Lorena pretended not to understand.

Strasser succeeded first in pointing to his chest with his index finger, then placing it to his lips conspiratorially.

"You mean … You mean—you? You forged it?"

He waved dismissively. "Not forged. Let's say, doubled."

Lorena laughed, with a similar gesture. "Doubled!" She drained her glass.

Strasser placed the catalogue in front of him, took out a mechanical pencil and pointed to an area of the painting on the cover. "See here, in the right hand corner of the *salamandre*, the cast-iron relief?"

"It looks like a bud or something."

"To me it looks like a little ass."

"True, could be a little ass," Lorena admitted.

"A little ass seen from the left," Strasser pointed out. "That's Vallotton's Vallotton. Now I'll show you Strasser's Vallotton." He called the barman, Lorena paid and they returned to the exhibition.

"We close in five minutes," the fat girl at the entrance said.

"We only need four," Strasser replied.

The hall was empty now, except for an elderly woman holding a catalogue full of yellow sticky notes. She was standing in front of the Hodler with the telegraph posts, and took no notice of them.

Strasser led Lorena up close to the Vallotton. "Can you see it, the little ass?"

Lorena could.

"And do you notice anything?"

"Something's different." She peered intently, but couldn't say what. Strasser gave her the catalogue to compare.

"Now I've got it: the perspective."

Strasser nodded proudly. "They are both little asses, but this one is seen from the right, like the big lady here."

No shit: the cast-iron relief on the *salamandre* looked like twin buttocks here too. But unlike on the catalogue cover, here you could see more of the right buttock than the left. Like the kneeling model.

"Pretty clumsy, right?" Strasser said, "Of Adrian. Not to notice."

"Maybe he did."

She looked at the signature again carefully. The period after the Vallotton's surname was missing, like the original she'd seen in Weynfeldt's study.

Then she compared it with the cover photo on the catalogue. The resolution and the print quality were good enough for her to read the signature here too.

Here too the second period was missing.

As soon as she got rid of Strasser, she met Pedroni in the Old Scotsman, an old-fashioned pub in the area of the old town once popular among revelers, now out of favor. Various Scottish tartans were stretched across the panels lining the interior. The advantage of this form of decoration was it absorbed noise; the disadvantage, it retained odors. Now early evening, it stank of stale smoke and the legendary goulash which had made it a favorite last port of call for the party crowd.

Pedroni was the only guest. He was sitting a long way from the bar, at a corner table, and waved her over, somewhat impatiently. Lorena was over half an hour late.

He was accordingly grumpy toward her, but Lorena wasn't going to let her good—almost euphoric—mood be spoiled.

And it was heightened when Pedroni pushed an envelope across the table toward her containing, as she confirmed in the ladies bathroom immediately, sixty thousand francs.

When Lorena was in a good mood she couldn't handle people who didn't feel the same way. She either had to look for new company or cheer up her current company, at any cost.

In Pedroni's case, the cost was several hugs and kisses. And the story of the doubled Vallotton.

When he dropped her off at Weynfeldt's building, he was almost euphoric too.

30

"Now!" He heard Lorena's voice through the closed door to the dining room.

She had turned up at his place, highly buoyant; they had thrown together a cold supper from the contents of the fridges and eaten it in style, with Lorena's favorite champagne, by candlelight and firelight—Lorena had insisted on lighting one of the stoves, and had got it going herself. She told him about her visit to the auction preview, and her meeting with Strasser. Suddenly she said, "Go outside for a minute, and don't come back till I say so."

"Is this a game?" he asked, and she nodded.

He left, smiling, and she called after him: "Only when I say, *Now!*"

He had been standing quite awhile outside the door before he realized he still had the smile on his lips he'd left the room with. The realization made it broaden.

I think I'm something along the lines of happy, he thought. Not that till now he'd been unhappy. But he had to say, standing outside the door like a naughty schoolboy, that there was a huge difference between not unhappy, and happy.

"Now!" she called, and Weynfeldt entered.

The room was darker. The only light-source was one of the spotlights, normally pointing at the art on the walls. Now it was pointing at Lorena. She was kneeling in front of the stove, her hair tied up, naked.

Adrian didn't dare move. He hardly dared breathe for fear of destroying the image.

She was the one who broke the spell, observing, "I'm afraid I can't compete ass-wise."

They made love right there and then. With a passion Weynfeldt had not thought he was capable of.

"You surprised me," she said, as he returned with pillows and quilts from the bedroom. "With the Vallotton, and just now."

"What about the Vallotton?" he asked, lit one of her cigarettes, took a drag and passed it over, before snuggling up to her.

"I didn't think you had it in you, to put the, erm ... the newer one in."

"I didn't."

"You so did. Your friend Strasser showed me the subtle difference."

"The second period?"

"You painted that out, admit it." She told him about the thing with the little cast-iron ass. Weynfeldt went to his study and fetched the catalogue.

Lorena looked at it and said knowledgeably: "The original. Ass seen from the left. Take a look at the copy in the Imperial tomorrow. There you see it from the right."

Lorena laughed like an excited child.

Adrian congratulated her silently, and had a sudden desire to kiss her again. But she turned her head away and evaded him. "Only if you admit it," she laughed.

In the end Weynfeldt admitted it, and surprised both of them a second time.

31

ADRIAN WAS STANDING IN THE LOBBY CHATTING TO A group of auction guests. He was looking good, in a lightweight wool suit the color of cigarette ash. His left hand was in his pocket, his gaze continually wandering from the people around him to search the lobby.

Now he saw Lorena, excused himself and walked over with a smile. They greeted like a couple still getting to know each other. "I'll take you in. It's starting in a minute," he said. She put her arm through his and he led her to the grand ballroom.

The fat girl with the bob was standing at the entrance. "May I introduce you: Véronique Graf, my assistant; Lorena Steiner, a good friend."

The two women shook hands. "We met briefly at the preview, right?" Véronique said. So this was his assistant.

The center of the room was filled with rows of chairs now, like a concert hall. The exhibition panels had been pushed to the edges. In front of the audience, a podium had been set up, a lectern placed in the middle with "Murphy's" written on it. Paintings were leaned against the foot of the podium, lots with low numbers.

The hall was filled with a sea of voices. At least a hundred people were there, and more kept entering.

Weynfeldt took Lorena to an aisle seat on the second row. He removed a sign saying "Murphy's—Reserved."

"What about you?" Lorena asked.

"I'll be sitting over there," he pointed to a table to one side of the podium, where his assistant had just sat down, "on the telephone."

"To who?"

"To bidders. Several regular clients bid by telephone. If you'll excuse me, I'll see you in the break."

She watched as he wandered around, greeting guests, then made his way to the table where, alongside Véronique, a young man was also now sitting. Six white telephones were lined up in front of them. Weynfeldt sat down and smiled at her. Lorena saw Véronique give him a searching sideways glance.

A stocky, gray-haired man was now standing at the lectern, talking to a group of assistants, without exception men in suits and ties. All at once he turned to the audience and banged on the lectern with a small hammer.

The sea of voices fell silent, but the ballroom lights were not dimmed as for a concert or a play. The auctioneer greeted the audience, reminded them briefly of the most important rules and announced the first lot. A drawing by Hodler, study of a female figure in a long dress, oil and charcoal on paper. Lorena saw hands holding numbers shoot up here and there, the auctioneer raised the price in small increments, soon hit disinterest and let an elderly man in the front row with dandruff on his shoulders have the picture.

Lorena prepared herself for a boring afternoon. There was only one lot she was interested in, and that was not up till toward the end. Well, perhaps there was one more: the portrait of Adrian's mother, but that also had a high number.

Weynfeldt had clearly meant well, giving her a seat in the second row. But from here she couldn't really watch the people. She wanted to be farther back.

The Hodler study wasn't a good start. It went at just over the reserve. To Riedel. Anything which goes to Riedel has gone for a song, you can rely on that.

Weynfeldt sat in front of his two telephones watching how the auction was going. Judging by the way it had begun, it would take nearly three hours, he reckoned. At least two till Lot 136, *La Salamandre*, which most people here were waiting for. His two lines were still silent. He wouldn't set up the calls to his two collectors till a half an hour before the sale started.

He couldn't stop looking at Lorena. She was sitting there like a child, in a mixture of impatience, curiosity and boredom, less interested in the lots than the bidders. She kept turning her head in the direction the auctioneer was pointing to see who had made each bid and who the lot went to.

He was confident about the Vallotton. Alongside his two telephone bidders, Blancpain and Chester were sitting in the audience in person. It would likely play out between these four. He saw Lorena stand up between two lots, smile over at him and sit herself a few rows back.

What kind of a crowd was this? Lots of art world people, you could tell by looking at them. Some of the others might be people with a connection to a particular picture: the current owners, or their relatives. Then there were students and people with nothing better to do. And then there were the people Lorena was really interested in: the people who could afford to spend an afternoon getting rid of a few tens or hundreds of thousands of francs. These were the people she wanted to watch. That was why she had moved a few rows back.

She was fascinated by the way they held their numbers up with nonchalance, won lots with composure and left the field free with grace. Throughout the entire auction the hall had been full of the sound of people coming and going. Now more people were leaving; only a few stayed seated. Only when she saw Adrian standing next to her, holding his hand out in invitation, did she realize it was the intermission.

"How are you finding it?" They stood in the lobby. She held a glass of champagne; he held a mineral water.

"Crazy," she confessed. "What about you? Are you excited?"

"Not excited. Intrigued, sure. To see if our estimates were right, whether we reach our targets, exceed them, by how much, whether the magic moment happens."

"The magic moment?"

"When a lot ignites. When several bidders goad each other on, get into something they shouldn't, lose all sense of restraint and reason. That's the magic moment."

And *La Salamandre* wasn't deprived of its magic moment. The hall was already full to bursting by the time there were twenty lots to go. All the seats were taken and the people standing in the side aisles were crammed together.

Two TV crews had set up their cameras in the central aisle and in front of the podium; the security team was busy preventing them from filming the audience.

Weynfeldt, Véronique and the young man had their phone lines connected now, and had begun speaking into the mouthpieces occasionally.

Even two lots before *La Salamandre* people were still coming in. The auctioneer had to ask the audience to be quiet several times so he could deal with these last two lots properly.

As two of the smart assistants finally brought the picture in and held it up in front of the podium, the sea of voices surged. But as soon as the auctioneer's hammer was heard the room went silent.

The auctioneer opened bidding at 1.25 million. Several hands went up, and in a few minutes the price had reached 1.7, 1.8, 1.9… Lorena saw that there were eight people in the race, including the bidders represented by Weynfeldt and his colleagues on the telephones.

At two million there was a moment's hesitation, then the bids soared rapidly up again, two bidders having dropped out at the two-million threshold.

Lorena realized she was holding her breath. Now she inhaled deeply. The bids had risen over the two point five million mark. Now there were just five bidders left. The young man had ostentatiously replaced both his receivers and folded his arms. Véronique was only bidding for one telephone client, Number 17, and raised the card time to time. Weynfeldt was still handling two bidders, but both seemed to be biding their time for the moment.

At 3 million, two of the bidders in the hall dropped out, leaving just one, an English-looking gentlemen, one of those Weynfeldt had been talking to when Lorena arrived.

The next to drop out was Number 17. Véronique replaced her receiver and folded her arms like her colleague.

Around three point two million a strange situation ensued whereby Weynfeldt's telephone bidder Number 28 was bidding against Weynfeldt's Number 33, while the Englishman kept out of it.

Following a brief spat in the run-up to three-and-a-half million, Weynfeldt's Number 28 dropped out.

The "Englishman" reentered the race. Offered 3.6, 3.8 and held up his hand at 4 too.

A murmur broke through the room.

All eyes were on Weynfeldt, talking swiftly and intently into the mouthpiece.

He nodded, and held Number 33 up in the air.

The auctioneer gave the Englishman an inquiring look.

He shook his head.

As Lot 136 was awarded to Number 33 for 4.1 million Swiss francs, awe-inspired applause burst out. Lorena joined in enthusiastically.

The majority of the audience left the ballroom. Lorena stayed for Adrian's mother. She went for a hundred and eighty thousand.

32

In defiance of all the forecasts it had snowed once more, only a little, falling in big soggy flakes. But here in the villa district it had stuck, a pale gray veil over the front gardens and hedges.

On the walkway leading up to the front door he saw small stiletto footprints coming the other way. Someone had left in the previous hour; no one had arrived.

Weynfeldt asked the taxi driver to wait. He was a young man who made a trustworthy impression, with a new, clean Mercedes. Adrian knew him from previous rides and had asked for him specifically when he'd booked. He wanted to know whose hands he was putting himself and his valuable cargo into. On both the outward and return journeys.

The painting was well packed, in a thick layer of Bubble Wrap, tied up with packing string, to which Weynfeldt had attached an old-fashioned wooden handle.

He reached the door and rang the bell; he still couldn't believe he was doing what he was just about to do.

Baier must have heard the taxi. As soon as Weynfeldt rang, he was buzzed in, and entered.

In the hallway stood a few packed, taped-up moving boxes, and a pile of them still folded up.

"Here!" Baier's voice called out.

Adrian followed the direction the music was coming from. Count Basie, as ever. The door to the living room was half-open, and the light pouring through lit a fine curtain of cigar smoke.

"Here!" Baier's voice called again.

He was sitting in his favorite chair: on one arm the glass of port, on the other the ashtray, from which a bluish thread of smoke curled up to the ceiling.

There were a few moving boxes in the salon too, but the furniture was all still in place. The easel was also still in the same position as last time.

"You can start by unpacking it," Baier said.

"Delivery against payment, we agreed. You get the money out and I'll unpack the painting."

"Don't you trust me?"

"No. Would you?"

"No." Baier pointed to the bureau, above which the Vallotton had previously hung. "In there, top drawer."

Adrian opened the drawer. It was empty except for three piles of thousand notes, sorted and bound with wrappers.

"And now the painting!" Baier demanded.

It took Weynfeldt awhile to tear the tape off the Bubble Wrap. When he'd finished he asked, "On the easel or in its old place?"

"Bring it here!" Baier ordered him. Adrian handed him the painting. The old man held it, took a look, then kissed the woman's bottom. "Welcome home, darling!"

He gave it back to Adrian. "Now you can hang her back in her old spot. We have a few days before we head south together."

Weynfeldt hung the painting above the bureau and began counting the packs of notes in the drawer.

"I'll tell you right now, there's only twenty."

Weynfeldt stopped short. "It should be twenty-six."

"Oh come off it, Adrian, be reasonable. No one could seriously have guessed it would fetch over three and a half million."

"Everything over one and a half, was the agreement." He went red, and his helplessness toward any kind of insolence was visible yet again. "It should be twenty-six," he repeated.

"Be reasonable, Adrian. You're rich: Are you really going to argue with an old man about the money he needs for his final years? Two million is very generous."

Weynfeldt took a small, folded nylon bag from his coat pocket, unfolded it and began filling it with the packs of notes. "It just isn't okay," he murmured as he did it, "just not okay."

The wrapper around the second to last pack was torn through. Weynfeldt looked at Baier.

"An unforeseen expenditure," Baier said. "Fifty."

Adrian grappled for words. "You're just not an honest man, Klaus," he said finally.

"Neither are you any more, Adrian."

It had started snowing again, in smaller, denser flakes now. It seemed as if the temperature had dropped during the short time he'd been with Baier.

The light in the waiting taxi was on, and fumes rose from the exhaust, lit by the red rear lights. The driver was reading the newspaper, and only heard Weynfeldt as he opened the passenger door. Inside it was overheated.

"Ready to go?" the young man asked.

Weynfeldt nodded and gave his address as the destination. The snowstorm surrounded the streetlights with swirling halos.

"Don't think I don't care about carbon emissions," the driver said.

"Why would I think that?" Adrian asked.

"Because I left the motor running while I was waiting for you."

"I assumed you didn't want to freeze."

"Basically there's no point anymore," the driver explained. "Even if we radically reduce our carbon emissions, the temperatures will still rise. It says so in the second world climate conference report." He pointed to the newspaper he had just stuffed beside his seat. "I'm not going to freeze my ass off for nothing."

Weynfeldt concurred with him. For the rest of the journey they remained silent, the driver concentrating on the slippery streets, Weynfeldt on his nylon bag with 2 million francs in it. Or with 1 million, nine hundred and fifty thousand, to be precise.

As soon as he got home he went to his study. There, in a fairly unoriginal hiding place, behind a still life by Cuno Amiet he was fond of, was his safe. He used it to store a few valuables, which would have been equally secure anywhere else in his high-security apartment, and made sure it was always stocked with cash in all the main currencies. He opened it with the fairly unoriginal combination, his mother's birthday, and stowed the packs of notes away.

Then he listened to the messages on his answering machine—yes, as part of his communications-technology emancipation, he had not only learned to use a cell phone, he had also gotten Frau Hauser to explain how to use the answering machine, and was getting on pretty well with it.

Lorena still insisted on remaining unavailable by telephone. He now knew her surname, but there was no Lorena Steiner in the phone book. And she had given him neither her address nor her cell number. "Don't call us, we'll call you," she had once told him; this was the standard sentence she'd heard after every casting. And to her, he was still at the casting stage for his role as her constant companion.

For Adrian this meant that on days like today, when she hadn't called him at the office or on his cell phone, the only remaining hope was the answering machine.

The first two messages were about the construction work, the third caller hung up, and the fourth was a man asking, "Just wanted to know if you've received my letter yet." Finally Adrian heard a drunken Rolf Strasser saying, "Well now, I think we'll start at around 1 teeny-weeny million, and stop at around 4.1 teeny-weeny millions."

Nothing from Lorena.

What had the caller meant about the letter? Weynfeldt went to the ensemble of chairs by the apartment door and took his mail from the glass table at their center. It was the usual mixture of circulars and bills. There was only one letter which stood out. It was addressed to him using a typewriter, and the postage was neither prepaid nor franked; a traditional stamp was stuck to it.

He opened the envelope and took out a folded flyer from the auction.

Someone had written their cell phone number on the woman's back. And in the top right-hand corner of the *salamandre* the same ballpoint had been used to circle the cast-iron relief.

33

THE DROP OF WATER HAD COME FROM SOMEWHERE UP above; Weynfeldt had no desire to lift his gaze. Now at any rate, it was just above the level of his eyes. Water must be flowing into its trail, because the drop swelled, till it got so heavy it sped down a few inches, then stopped again. Each time it did this, it left a trail of water behind, which took its time, as if it knew the drop couldn't get away. As soon as the drop halted, it filled up with what it had left behind again, till it had enough ballast to speed down a few more inches.

His pupils were focused on the drops in front of him on the plate glass window in his study. The office windows beyond were blurred. During the time he'd been standing here most of them had gone dark. He hadn't seen this, just deduced it from the minute changes to the illumination of his water drops.

This way he managed to keep steering his thoughts away from the letter. And above all from wondering if Lorena had betrayed him. A very good question. Because she was the only one who knew.

The only one apart from Rolf Strasser. A better question: Was it Rolf, playing a joke, reminding him he was also in on this job. When Adrian failed to steer his thoughts from the Lorena question back to the raindrops, the Strasser question saved him. And when that didn't work there was also the third scenario.

Scenario three was that a third party, independent of the other two, had worked it out for themselves. Not a layperson, a specialist. A great many had spent time in front of the painting. If he had noticed, why shouldn't another expert have noticed?

The drop left his narrow field of vision. Adrian focused on another.

He could have called the number, then he would know more now. He could still call it. It wasn't very late. Eleven perhaps. He had no desire to look at the time.

If he called, he'd have certainty. But did he want that? Who wants certainty when it's a question of love or betrayal?

The drop became fuller and heavier. It didn't stop long, and when it finally broke away, plummeting, not slipping, it left a trail of tiny droplets, which soon smoothed out into a thin film.

The voice on the answering machine had sounded familiar. If he listened again he might be able to identify it. But he refused to listen to the messages again.

Tomorrow, perhaps. Tomorrow.

Weynfeldt didn't call the number the next day either. He resisted waking up, because his subconscious told him a bad memory was waiting for him. When he finally got under the shower, and allowed his thoughts free reign, he decided not to call.

If the letter wasn't simply a joke, its author would be in touch again. He clearly had Weynfeldt's number. Till then the principle of innocent till proven guilty applied to all suspects. Especially to Lorena.

Nothing unusual happened in the office. No calls from journalists, experts or police. No call from the man with the familiar voice. But no call from Lorena either.

Actually, there was one unusual thing worthy of note: Véronique didn't leave the office once all morning for her usual refreshment breaks. When he left for lunch, she wished him "*bon appétit*" in the recriminating tone he recognized from her diet phases. He didn't react; he had other concerns.

One of them was already sitting at the Thursday lunch club table in Agustoni's and greeted him with a kiss which caused a stir among the staff and brought Adrian a huge relief. If Lorena had anything to do with this business, she wouldn't be here. Or if so, she certainly wouldn't be as carefree and exuberant.

Her exuberance infected the other guests, who arrived one by one now. The Thursday lunch club celebrated the Vallotton record—*La Salamandre* had achieved the highest price for a Vallotton to date—as if they were all profiting from it personally. And when Lorena had the idea of ordering a glass of champagne to toast *La Salamandre*, everyone else switched to champagne too, till Agustoni's modest reserves were exhausted and he tried to persuade the indignant group to drink his Prosecco.

Strasser joined in along with the others. He seemed so genuinely pleased about the price, Weynfeldt suspected Rolf might have made a percentage-based deal with Baier, the fee for his work greater according to the result of the auction.

The thing with the letter and the message was now

just a tiny irritant at the back of Weynfeldt's mind. He couldn't remember ever having experienced such a pleasant, easy-going Thursday lunch. He arranged to meet Lorena that evening at his place—discreetly, but not discreetly enough that Alice Waldner didn't notice, acknowledging it with an equally discreet smile.

There was nothing to suggest how disastrously the day would later unfold.

He returned to the office late, with a spring in his step. Véronique greeted him in the mood of a fat woman with an empty stomach. She had put all the pending documents on his desk: four neatly stacked piles. One consisting of printed e-mails, one of opened letters clipped to their envelopes, one of internal memos and one of messages, sorted according to their urgency.

The most urgent was the request for a return call from Hartmann, the branch director of the bank which rented Weynfeldt's building.

He called back and was put straight through. Could he come by quickly after closing time? There was an, erm, unfortunate matter, which in their mutual interests should be concluded as swiftly as possible. Hartmann always talked like this. Weynfeldt promised to come by at half past five.

The second most urgent message went: "Not calling back is not the solution. Greetings from the man from the answering machine and from the Belotel, room 212." Alongside it was a cell phone number and Véronique's note: "The exact words he asked me to write down and read back to him. You know some interesting people!"

Weynfeldt pushed his right hand through his hair and massaged his scalp with his five fingers. As if he could speed up his thought processes like this.

What did this mean, what did this mean, what did this mean? It was Lorena's shady debt collector. But how had he found out about the painting? Lorena had told him. But why? She still hadn't got him off her back. She still owed him money. She was still under his thumb. He had put pressure on her. And she had given him the tip about the painting. That wasn't nice. Was it forgivable? It was understandable; he had met the man twice. He could scare you. So it was understandable. And everything understandable was forgivable. Right? That's the way it is: if it's understandable it's forgivable.

"Are you alright?" Véronique's voice called from the door.

"Why?"

"You've gone white as a sheet."

"I feel a bit sick."

"Try eating and drinking more at lunchtime," she bitched. "Go home and have a rest," she added more gently. "The last few days have been very stressful."

Weynfeldt did indeed get up from his desk and go home.

Perhaps a bad idea. The apartment was full of construction workers behind schedule and suppliers ahead of schedule. Frau Hauser was in the midst of preparing a *dîner tête-à-tête* as she had called it, somewhat salaciously, after he ordered "a little something for myself and Frau Steiner."

As he stood with her in the corridor, still protected

with plastic sheeting, getting in the workers' way, and said, "I'd prefer not to be disturbed for a while," she remarked scathingly: "Who wouldn't prefer that around here?"

He withdrew to his study and tried to think clearly. But the same series of unanswered questions kept returning:

How had he found out about the painting? Had she still not gotten rid of him? Did she still owe him money? Was it forgivable? Was it understandable? Was everything understandable forgivable?

Suddenly he had the phone in his hand, and heard it ring at the other end, his heart beating.

"Yes?" the familiar voice said.

"Weynfeldt," he said.

"At last."

"What do you want?"

"The same as last time."

"Okay."

"Times ten."

Adrian fell silent. Then he said, "That's 1.2 million."

"Well done."

"That's absurd."

"It's reasonable."

"How?"

"Considering the risk."

"What risk?"

"Yours. If you don't pay."

"I think you're overestimating it. A glitch. It's happened at all major auction houses."

"A scandal. First a record price, then a forgery."

Weynfeldt asked the one question which really interested him. "How did you discover?"

"Three guesses."

"What have you got on Frau Steiner?"

The man hesitated. Then he laughed. "Enough. Since you ask."

Weynfeldt asked for time. The man gave him twenty-four hours.

After he hung up, Adrian was hit by a leaden exhaustion. He recognized it from earlier catastrophes in his life. His father's death, his fox terrier's death, the split with Daphne, Daphne's death, his mother's death. He had spent most of his time during these crises in bed. It was that time again.

He dragged himself down the corridor, still hectic at the other end, walked into his bedroom, took his shoes and jacket off, fell onto his bed and sank, or rather plunged, into a bottomless sleep.

Frau Hauser woke him. She was standing next to his bed holding the cordless telephone, her hand enclosing the microphone tightly. "Herr Hartmann—he believes you had an appointment."

Weynfeldt took the phone. "Excuse my impertinence," Hartmann said, sounding less apologetic than impatient, "but our security observed you returning home two hours ago, and I'm therefore taking the liberty of inquiring if you had perhaps forgotten ..."

"I had to lie down briefly, must have fallen asleep. I'll be right with you."

Hartmann's office was furnished with the kind of

pseudo-modernist corporate design which would have wounded Weynfeldt's aesthetic sensibilities sorely on any other day. Today he didn't care about the greenish, matte glass tabletops and cabinet doors, the excess of chrome, and the hi-tech boss's chair. He sat down at the conference table after the usual formulaic greetings and apologies were over, and waited.

Alongside Hartmann, another man was present, in an ill-fitting suit with an oversized necktie-knot. He appeared nervous, and was introduced as Herr Schwartz, head of security.

On the table stood a small monitor, which Herr Schwartz now started fiddling with.

Hartmann was squirming slightly, making his language all the more convoluted. "I must ask you first and foremost not to misunderstand us; nothing could be further from our intention than to interfere with your private liaisons; you can rest assured we are concerned solely with our responsibility to provide security, and you have been able to rely on our comprehensive discretion so far, am I not right, and will in the future too. Discretion is, as it were," he smiled, "the core of our business."

Weynfeldt did not help him out.

"During his routine examination of the SC material, that is to say, the recordings from our surveillance cameras, Herr Schwartz made an observation which we feel obliged to bring to your attention."

Herr Hartmann, the director, hesitated now and rescued himself with the sentence, "Perhaps you should show us the material, Herr Schwartz."

Schwartz took over: "The camera in question is E4, mounted above the entrance you use, Herr Weynfeldt. The material concerns your guest Samba." At this he grinned sheepishly. "We give regular visitors code names; so the material shows Samba in the company of a ..." He looked for assistance to Hartmann, who chimed in again.

"I hope you will not form the impression that we are spying on you here; all of this is carried out using the strictest discretion solely for the purpose of the security of all concerned; the material is destroyed after two months. However ... we were of the opinion ... we felt ourselves obliged to make you aware of the situation, the aforementioned visitor is clearly involved with a person known to Herr Schwartz from his previous work with the city's police force. Herr Schwartz, if you would."

Schwartz pressed a button, and a black and white image of impressive quality appeared. It showed the hood and trunk of two cars, and the sidewalk in front of Weynfeldt's heavy front door. Everything still as in a photo.

Suddenly Lorena appeared in the frame. She was shortened due to the angle of the camera mounted above the door, but there was no doubt this was Lorena. She was wearing the coat he had taken from her the last night she had visited him, when she had reconstructed the Vallotton.

She seemed to be talking, to be looking back at someone, calling him over.

A man came into the picture.

"Theo L. Pedroni, previous convictions for fraudulent bankruptcy, falsifying documents, drug dealing ..."

Adrian no longer heard what the security man was saying. In the picture he could clearly see the man from the car outside the cash point and the room at the Belotel.

Lorena took his hand, pulled him toward her, grabbed his tie and kissed him on the lips. Not for long, but long enough that both Herr Hartmann, the director, and Herr Schwartz, head of security, had time to clear their throats.

Pedroni gave Lorena a slap on the bottom and vanished from the picture. Lorena shouted something after him, laughing.

Then she pressed the doorbell.

34

STRANGE: NORMALLY HIS LIMBS WOULD HAVE BECOME heavy, his brain fogged. But as soon as he was inside the elevator he noticed his body was wide awake; his mind clear as crystal. Even before the elevator stopped at his floor, he knew what he had to do.

Outside his apartment there were mountains of packaging from the fitness machines, and in the corridor the workers were busy rolling up the floor liner. Behind them, a team with professional cleaning machines was waiting to get to work.

Frau Hauser stood at the entrance, sighing. "The dust they're stirring up—I'll never get rid of it."

Adrian patted her supportively on the back. "In a few days no one will see it."

"You might not; I will." She scrutinized him. "Everything okay?"

"Right as rain," he confirmed.

She looked at him distrustfully. Then she said, "I need to check that everything is in order, otherwise this gang won't be gone by the time Frau Steiner arrives." She walked off down the corridor. Adrian watched her. She had become a little fragile, despite her energetic gait.

Adrian went into the bathroom. He shaved, showered, moisturized, blow-dried his hair, manicured his toe- and fingernails, freshened up with *eau de toilette* and slipped on his lightweight cashmere tuxedo.

Thus attired, he entered his study, opened the safe behind the Amiet, counted out 1.2 million francs from the packets of money there, and stashed the remainder in the Paul Artaria dresser. He put the 1.2 back in the safe, then left his study and walked to the kitchen.

The cleaning team had gone, and the corridor was freshly polished. The door to the fitness room stood open. Weynfeldt took a look inside. The machines were positioned somewhat ad hoc, the rubber gym flooring was still strewn with the remains of the packaging material, and the mirror was missing. But Casutt had still come astonishingly close to meeting the deadline they'd agreed upon.

In the kitchen Frau Hauser was talking to two people wearing long waiter's aprons embroidered with the logo of Langoberti, the city's leading catering firm. She noted Weynfeldt's tuxedo with surprise before introducing the pair: "Carla will be helping to serve; Alfredo will open the oysters."

Adrian welcomed them both, then asked Frau Hauser, "Could we take our aperitif in my study?"

"I've already prepared it in the Green Salon, but if it's important ..." She sounded slightly cross.

"Yes, it is important, excuse me. And a few light canapés, perhaps? Your legendary pastries."

Now she appraised him blatantly from head to toe: "Are you going to ask for her hand in marriage?"

"Something like that," he replied, and went back to his study.

He felt both sad and excited, as if heading on a long

journey: parting and anticipation. And the mania which had taken hold of him reminded him of the feelings you distract yourself with before big farewells.

Frau Hauser knocked and rolled the home bar in. One of his favorite pieces. The architect Alfred Roth had designed it in 1932. A wonderfully simple piece of furniture made of steel tubes, perforated aluminum sheets and spray-painted beech. You lifted it on one side like a wheelbarrow, and pushed it on two spoked wheels with solid white tires.

He knew Frau Hauser found it impractical, preferring the chrome serving trolley she had rescued from his mother's things. So he appreciated her decision to serve the aperitif now on the *Kleinbar*, as Roth had named the piece.

Several small plates were arranged on the serving tray's red linoleum, holding variously twisted and sliced sticks of puff pastry, carefully piled in a range of formations. Alongside that, on silver saucers, were two champagne flutes, flanked by tiny napkins. The ice bucket with the champagne was protruding from the bottle holder.

Adrian thanked her and adjusted the dimmers till he found the appropriate balance between festive and intimate lighting. Then he put *Nabucco* in the CD player, paused it, positioned the remote control close to the bar and stood at the plate glass window.

Across the way a classic end-of-the-day office scene was on display: somewhere a meeting was still taking place, the participants increasingly restless; cleaning crews were emptying wastepaper baskets, wiping tabletops and negotiating table legs with vacuum cleaner nozzles; here and there sat the odd solitary figure in the pallid light of a screen. And a curtain of mist and rain was billowing in the space between the two buildings.

The doorbell startled Weynfeldt out of his thoughts. He left the room, returned again, took the napkins off the home bar, took a look around and then stuffed them in a bundle into his pants pocket.

Lorena looked stunning. She was wearing the steel blue Issey Miyake getup with the high collar and the zipper. Adrian remembered he had liked it that day in Spotlight, as Lorena had modeled it for him in front of the speechless boutique owner.

It had an artificial sheen, and the cut was reminiscent of the crew's uniforms on the Starship Enterprise. This gave Lorena an alien, unfamiliar appearance. Perfect for the role he had planned for her tonight.

She greeted him without commenting on his outfit, as if she was received by men in tuxedos every night. Frau Hauser shook her hand like a daughter-in-law she had become fond of. Adrian took her to his study and pressed play on the remote. The sound system filled the room with the theatrical overture from *Nabucco*.

"What have you got planned?" Lorena asked, as Adrian uncorked the champagne and filled the glasses.

He made no reply, passing her a glass and raising his to toast her. He took a sip; Lorena drained her glass and gave him a frenzied kiss with her cold champagne mouth. The kiss was as alienating as the dress. "What are we drinking to?" she asked.

"To the millions," he suggested.

"Which ones?"

"Any of them. No, actually: to the Vallotton millions."

Lorena held her empty glass toward him, he filled it and they toasted again. "To the Vallotton millions." She gave him another damp champagne kiss. Then she fished a pastry from one of the little plates, careful not to destroy the arrangement. "Who were Number twenty eight and Number thirty three?

"Collectors," Weynfeldt replied, "collectors who wanted to remain anonymous. Happens quite often. Increasingly often."

"Four point one million francs," she munched, "a tidy sum to be paying anonymously."

"That's just the hammer price," Weynfeldt explained. "On top of that there's the commission. Twenty percent on the first six hundred thousand—makes a hundred and twenty. Twelve percent on the rest—makes four hundred and twenty. Number thirty three has shelled out four million, six hundred and forty thousand."

"Wow! Have you ever seen that much money in a pile? Okay, sure you have, silly question."

"It's smaller than you imagine."

Lorena fished another pastry from Frau Hauser's fragile construction. "Like Mikado," she observed. "Have you ever played Mikado?"

"I hated Mikado. I was all fingers and thumbs. Still am." To illustrate this claim he took a pastry from one of the plates. But the rest of the artistic pile remained intact.

"See," she said, "you're not anymore." She took one too. The tiny pastry pyramid on her plate collapsed. She laughed. "But now I am."

It was left to him to steer the conversation back to the topic in question. He did it fairly crudely: "I certainly have seen a million in one pile a few times. It's nothing." He demonstrated a small quantity with his hands.

"In thousands?"

"Well not in tens, obviously."

She laughed, held out her glass and grabbed another pastry.

"Do you want to see one?"

"One what?"

"Million."

With an incredulous smile, she asked, "Why? Have you got one lying around?"

"Not lying around. But in the safe, yes. By chance. Do you want to see it?"

"Other men want to show girls their stamp collection. With you it's your million."

"It's not mine." He pointed to the Cuno Amiet: "In there."

Lorena walked over. "You've got a safe behind a painting? In the first place burglars would look?" She sounded amused, but excited too. Now she was standing directly in front of the painting, holding it by its frame and pulling at it gently. It opened like a casement window, with a barely audible click. Behind it was the gray safe door with its numerical keypad.

"Zero nine zero eight zero seven."

"You're telling me the combination?" she said in amazement.

"Indeed."

"One more time. Zero seven—then what?"

He dictated the combination again. "Now the green button."

There was a short beep then the safe door unlocked. Lorena's hand disappeared inside and emerged with a packet of notes. "No shit. You're crazy."

"You see. That's just a tenth," he replied, unperturbed. "Carry on."

She took another packet out, and another. When she had five she walked to his desk, deposited them there, then fetched the rest from the safe. "But there are twelve here," she realized, and put two back.

Weynfeldt filled her glass again and offered her another buttery pastry.

She helped herself, and started arranging the packets in various ways, till she had found the constellation that looked smallest. "That's nothing. A million, sounds so crazy. But then this. Nothing." Lorena sounded genuinely disappointed. "Who does it belong to?"

"A client. We do sometimes handle cash in our business," he lied. He offered her more of the aperitif snacks, which she took, absently.

"Pretty crazy, the way something loses its value once you've got piles of it sitting in front of you. Never knew that happened with money too." She took a packet, waved it about in the air and said, "Hundred thousand? Huh!" She dropped it on the table and took another. She took a note and tugged it out of the currency bundle. It took some effort, but eventually she had a brand-new thousand-franc note between her thumb and forefinger.

"A thousand! That's a load of money! But a million? That's like having too much ice cream as a child. You get sick. Talking of ice cream, when's supper?"

She piled the ten packets of notes on her bent left forearm and pressed them against her body. Carrying the money like this, she walked to the safe, waving her right hand with the loose thousand-franc note above her head, and said, "A million. One-handed. It's a joke!"

She replaced the money in the safe, locked it, hid it behind the hinged picture again, stood in front of Adrian and asked, "Is it far to wherever we're eating?"

Frau Hauser had staged the *dîner tête-à-tête* using candlelight and a fire. She was serving oysters for the hors d'oeuvre, followed by a selection of seafood—lobster, shrimps and mussels. For dessert she brought in a selection of homemade sorbets and petit fours, also her own work. She withdrew discreetly before ten.

Once they were alone, an embarrassed silence descended. Like a couple in an arranged marriage meeting for the first time. Till this moment they had both been playing their roles: Lorena—a society gentleman's simple but cute *mésalliance*; Adrian—a benevolent, amused man-about-town having an affair beneath his social stratum.

But now the official part was over, and they were sitting together in private.

Lorena, quite drunk now, spoke first. "I got you wrong."

He didn't say: *I sure got you wrong.* He said, "How?"

"I never would have thought you'd do it. Never!"

Adrian twitched his shoulders and filled her glass.

"Can I ask you a megalomaniac question?"

He nodded, and handed her the glass.

"Did you do it because of me? Because I said you were too straight?"

"Maybe."

"And how do you feel now? Now you've done it?"

"Totally okay." Adrian realized he was already imagining how he would open her zipper. Without any buildup. Just take hold of the chrome eyelet and pull it, dividing the two halves of the top to reveal whatever they had to offer.

"A pity really," she said.

"What's a pity?"

"I'd rather you hadn't done it."

"It has no significance." He was excited by the thought of sleeping with her like a stranger. He would use her, the way she had used him, the way she thought she was still using him. And then he would throw her aside. He would abandon her to her own undoing without wasting another thought on her.

She nibbled at her glass and looked up at him. "Pity. I think I'd prefer it if you were still straight."

Weynfeldt reached out his hand and tugged at the zipper.

35

PUT IT ALL AWAY OR GET IT ALL OUT? HER STUDIO reminded her of a story she had once read. About an old woman who died at home. When they opened the door to her apartment they entered a system of tunnels made from trash and accumulated objects going back decades. Not only had the woman never thrown anything away, she had collected and retained things other people had discarded.

Lorena didn't collect strangers' trash, but she didn't take her own out as often as she should have. Bottles, for instance. The Veuve Clicquot that Theo Pedroni had brought around that time was still standing there. Pizza boxes too. Various empty boxes, from various delivery services, were piled in various places around the tiny studio.

She wasn't really an untidy person. But to maintain order, you first needed underlying order. A system new things could fit into. And in this room there was simply a varying number of things, useful and useless; there was no system for differentiating them from each other. There was no difference between them at first glance at all. You could only tell the difference between the pizza boxes and the Prada handbag, the soggy dish towel and the Donna Karan blouse, on the second or third glance.

That meant that tidying up was pointless. She needed

to get down to the basis, the underlying order. Which is why she was wondering whether to put everything away or get it all out.

She'd had a bewildering, wonderful, strange, erotic night. She wasn't sure what had happened, but Adrian—Adrian, how it sounded suddenly—had changed somehow. She couldn't see him anymore as just her signet-ring-man with his Kennedy haircut; he had gotten to her. Yes, that was it: the distance which till now she'd maintained, carefully, deliberately, but effortlessly, was gone.

Two things he'd done: He'd sacrificed his integrity for her. No one had ever done that. And not just because she'd not known anyone who'd ever had any. And: he had fucked her like no one had in years.

Take out? Put away?

To put anything away, she first had had to empty something. The things in her boxes and cases were all churned up, she couldn't pack things on top of them. She would have to remove everything, increase the chaos and establish order from this basis.

She began emptying a cardboard box.

He had thrown her out of bed at quarter past seven. He had whipped off the quilt, standing scrubbed and groomed in one of his tailored suits by the bed and inspected her with a look which now, two hours later, she felt could best be described as professional. As if he were writing an expert's report on some nude of his. Then he said, "I've got a terrible day ahead. I'll wait till you're ready and order you a taxi."

And he really had just waited in the breakfast room

for her to appear, had sat with barely concealed impatience till she had drunk her orange juice and espresso, eaten her croissant, then packed her off in a taxi.

Lorena had tried to give him her cell phone number. He had said, "You call us; we don't call you."

The morning with Adrian had been like a morning with any other man. Had she destroyed everything that was special about him?

And fallen for him at the same time?

Could she only fall in love with men who treated her badly?

Bullshit.

Lorena tackled the next box. And the next. And the next. Soon she was standing, hot and bothered, red-eyed and tearstained, surrounded by clothes and books and CDs and kitchen things and the clutter of her entire worldly goods.

And then, knee-deep in the chaos from which her new order was meant to arise, she knew how to go on. She would travel. Get all this crap picked up and put in storage. And go traveling. After she'd paid rent and other expenses, she'd still have over ninety thousand. There were places where that was a lot of money. Asia, Africa, South America. There you could start a new life. Brazil. She knew a Brazilian woman, Iracema or something. She had her address somewhere.

There was nothing to keep her here. She'd ruined Adrian. And Pedroni? She didn't need any more Pedronis in her life. Yes: Pedroni should also be included in the tidying up operation.

She looked for her phone, found it under the clothes

on the bed, dialed his number and arranged to meet in the *piadini* bar where he spent his breaks.

The bar was virtually empty. There were just a few sales-girls dotted around at the little tables; like Pedroni, they couldn't take their lunch breaks at lunchtime. Pedroni was eating a *piadino* with cheese and *Parma* ham, and apologized that he'd already ordered; he had to go back to the boutique in a minute.

"It won't take long. I just wanted to say good-bye," Lorena said casually.

Pedroni swallowed a mouthful. "Where are you going?"

"Brazil."

"And Weynfeldt?"

"I expect he's staying here."

"I thought you wanted to do a bit more ..." He rubbed his thumb and forefinger together.

"That's dried up," she imitated the gesture.

"Why?" Pedroni put the *piadino* he had just raised to his mouth back down.

"It's over. We've split up. He's got no reason to get me out of trouble anymore."

Pedroni grinned. "He's still going to need to get him-self out of trouble."

"What kind of trouble is that?"

"The thing with the forged painting."

"Oh that. Forget it. They were kidding me, Weyn-feldt and the painter. The picture was genuine."

"I see," Pedroni said, raising an eyebrow. "Strange sense of humor. For a senior employee of a renowned auction house, I mean."

"That's what I thought," Lorena said.

"And I was hoping we could make some serious money there."

"Me too. Bad luck, huh?"

"Shame."

"A crying shame."

A few moments later they said good-bye—a parting of the ways which clearly came easily to both of them. Pedroni returned to Spotlight; Lorena returned home, to continue establishing order in her life.

But when she got back to her half-tidied studio, she had an uncertain feeling. Something wasn't right. Pedroni had swallowed the story too quickly. Hadn't asked questions, hadn't doubted her at all. It had all gone far too easily.

36

A BUS WITH A CZECH LICENSE PLATE WAS WAITING OUT-
side the Belotel. The tour group, mostly middle-aged
couples, was standing at the side of the bus, by the
open door to the luggage hold, trying to retrieve their
bags. No one was helping them; the Belotel was only a
three-star hotel, and the driver was exhausted from the
journey.

The weather had taken a turn for the better around
midday. It had stopped drizzling, and the sooty blanket
of cloud had developed holes. Stretches of streets and
buildings were singled out by blinding sunshine, then
submerged again in the afternoon's egalitarian gray.

Weynfeldt pushed his way through the tour group to
the reception desk, murmuring apologies. He was wearing a raglan coat and carried a cheap attaché case he had
bought that morning in a discount store near his office.

In front of him, surrounded by several Czechs, the
tour guide was arguing in broken German with the only
receptionist on duty. It seemed not all the rooms were
ready, although it was already half an hour after check-
in time.

Adrian waited.

This morning he had had his first serious quarrel
with Véronique. He had to admit he had left her in the
lurch a lot recently, arriving late and leaving early with-

out warning her. But that had happened before, with no consequences other than a few pointed remarks—even in phases like this, when she was starving herself.

But this time, not in the best of moods himself, he had become so spiteful he immediately regretted it. Responding to her embittered, "Nice of you to come by," he had said, "Why don't you just start eating again!"

At this she had raised the mouse she held in her hand as high as the cable allowed and smashed it down on the desk with all the strength she possessed. Its components split in all directions, leaving something small and metallic dangling from the arm of her chair for a few seconds, swinging, till it became inert.

"Well, that was that," she said drily, and Adrian wasn't sure if she was referring to the mouse or their working relationship.

He parried it with a dry, "Quite," likewise leaving her to interpret his comment.

The argument about the rooms hadn't been resolved. Weynfeldt butted in front, ignoring the Czech protests. "Please tell Room 412 I've arrived." Pedroni had given him only the room number, and officially Weynfeldt didn't know his name.

The receptionist gave him an angry sideways glance. "Just a moment." She turned back to the tour guide.

"No, now," Adrian said, with his new resolve.

The receptionist refused to look at him. But she did pick up the receiver, dial a number and say, "Your visitor is here."

She put the receiver down, looked briefly toward him and muttered, "Fourth floor," turning straight back to the new arrivals.

In the elevator it smelled of sweat and aftershave. Adrian regarded himself in the mirror. Like a contract killer, he thought. The weapon in his case might not be deadly, but it would certainly cost its victim a few years of his life.

In the corridor was a musty smell of floor surfaces and vacuum cleaner bags. The thin veneer beneath the lock on door number 412 had been worn in a semicircle by the clunky key tag.

Weynfeldt knocked.

Pedroni opened and invited him in with an ironic bow. Perfumed Marlboro smoke hung in the air, the butts filling half the ashtray. Pedroni was nervous— Weynfeldt was pleased to see.

"Do you want to take your coat off?"

Weynfeldt shook his head.

"Is it in there?" He pointed to the attaché case.

Weynfeldt handed it to him.

Pedroni took it and placed it on the table which served as a desk. He flipped open the catches and opened the lid.

There it was, one million, two hundred thousand francs. Slightly askew from the transport, as they nowhere near filled the case. But there they lay.

Weynfeldt observed Pedroni from the corner of his eye: he looked disappointed, like a small boy who hadn't got what he wanted for Christmas. He said nothing for a long while. Then he looked over at Weynfeldt and surprised him with an embarrassed, almost apologetic smile.

"You have to count it now," Adrian told him, almost patronizing.

"I'm sure it's correct."

"I insist."

Pedroni counted the packets, then took one and counted the notes it contained. He checked the others simply with his thumbs, like a cardplayer.

Then Pedroni offered Adrian his hand. "It's a pleasure doing business with you, Dr. Weynfeldt."

Adrian actually condescended to shake hands. "The feeling is not mutual," he said, and headed for the door. They parted like conspirators.

The Czech tour group was still being checked in as Weynfeldt walked back through the lobby, so swift was the handover.

He made a brief attempt to get the stressed-out receptionist to book him a taxi, gave up and made for the exit.

The sky was now virtually cloudless, a false blue, as if painted by Lugardon. Adrian decided to set out on foot. He had time; Pedroni could be given a head start; he wouldn't get away.

He was unfamiliar with the area where the Belotel was situated, and walked now through unknown residential districts, saw bus routes he never knew existed, hit four-lane streets he was unable to cross and passed restaurants, noting their names, then forgetting them a few streets later.

He felt unfamiliar to himself too. Like a man with orders. An automaton executing a task rehearsed a thousand times with practiced ease. Someone who, once dispatched, nothing could halt.

Even as he approached the city center, beginning to recognize his surroundings, finally feeling at home, his distance from himself remained; he observed himself with polite indifference: the way he turned onto his street, mechanically fished the keys from his pants pocket, opened the heavy front door and, slipping the keys back into his pocket with his left hand, took his wallet out with his right, took his magnetic card out with the freed left hand, then slid the card through the reader on the security door and replaced it as he walked through the opening glass doors toward the elevator.

The apartment had also become an unfamiliar, impersonal place. His steps on the parquet sounded like someone else's. The furniture seemed exhibited, just like the paintings, and the smell of newness from the renovated room had spread throughout the space.

He checked the time. Another hour.

He went to the main sitting room and sat in one of the creaking leather chairs, too low for his long legs, which his father had bought in 1936 from their designer Fritz Lobeck. The "Island Chairs" had later been placed in Adrian's playroom, probably because of their size. He had put one on top of another, climbed the lookout tower thus created, and used it to conquer the seven seas.

He picked up an art magazine lying on the cherry wood coffee table, began browsing through it and killed the hour like a forgotten patient in the waiting room of a doctor's office that had closed.

The yellow light of the unexpected afternoon sun gradually changed color and drenched the room in a warm red. Weynfeldt watched as the light became weaker, duller, went gray, then went out entirely. He roused himself, put down the magazine and went to his study. There he picked up the telephone, called the police and reported a case of blackmail. When he was finally transferred to the person responsible, and stated the sum demanded and paid, the officer promised to send someone over.

Only ten minutes later the doorbell rang. Weynfeldt pressed the intercom and said he'd be straight down, then took the elevator.

Outside the door stood Lorena. "I have to talk to you," she said, and pushed past him.

This was enough to knock the automaton Weynfeldt out of kilter. Instead of sending her away, he led her through the security doors and up into his apartment, even asking if she wanted a drink. She declined, but he still had enough presence of mind to take her to the Von der Mühll room, the place with the least comfortable seats.

She didn't notice, she wanted to say what she had to say so urgently.

She opened her handbag, the unbranded number he remembered from their first encounter, took a pile of thousand-franc notes out and threw them on the table. "There are six missing," was her only comment.

"What's this?"

"It's yours. My share of the five, my share of the hundred and twenty. My share of the four point one."

Adrian didn't understand.

"Actually I would quite like something to drink," she asked. "Perhaps a vodka and tonic? Would that be okay?"

"No," he said. "Explain."

"It's very simple: I've been collaborating with Pedroni."

"Pedroni?"

"The debt collector. Only he isn't. He's a salesman. And a little crook. Like me: a filthy little crook."

Weynfeldt was knocked off guard by this confession. "Just a minute," he said, stood up and left the room. He went into the kitchen, found tonic in a fridge, vodka in a freezer. Then he spent several brainless minutes looking for something—he couldn't remember what. No, not this, he thought. I don't want to hear it, no confessions please. Anything but confessions now.

It was only as he opened the drawer of one of the climate-controlled cupboards that he remembered what he was looking for. Lemon! Somewhere he found a plate for the lemon slices, and a knife to cut them, a glass, ice cubes. As he finally returned to the room with a tray holding all the ingredients, he paused outside the door and played for time.

When he entered she was standing with her back to the room, looking out the window. As soon as she heard him, she turned around and continued her confession where she had left off.

"He's a salesman at Spotlight. He saw how generously you rescued me from that situation, and had the idea of inventing a few other situations you could rescue me from."

Weynfeldt had now mixed the drink and handed it to her. She took a thirsty gulp. "Wrong. It wasn't his idea. It was mine. You see, I lie as soon as I open my mouth. That's what I'm like."

Please stop, he wanted to say. But once again he couldn't utter a word. He reached out a hand and held on to her shoulder, in a comforting, reassuring gesture.

She shook his hand off. "You shouldn't have any sympathy with people who have betrayed you and lied to you and ripped you off." She was virtually screaming it. "Do you know Baier offered me fifty-thousand if I could persuade you to put the forged Vallotton in the auction?" She picked the pile of notes up and let it drop again.

Adrian felt himself go red. No, he hadn't known that.

"You shouldn't be going red. I'm the one who should be ashamed. But I can't even manage that anymore—go red."

Adrian sensed the indifference creeping over his face.

Lorena emptied her glass. The annoying tears she had been wiping away like irritating insects now fell hard and fast. "Shit," she gasped. And again: "Shit."

Weynfeldt shook himself out of his paralysis. He mixed another vodka and tonic, took a drink of some of it himself, then handed her the glass.

"Thank you," she spluttered, and then: "You were always such a gentleman."

At this she lost all remaining composure and was shaken by uncontrollable sobbing.

"I thought that was what bothered you about me."

This made her laugh. He waited till the laughing and crying had subsided. Then he handed her his handkerchief. White, ironed, monogrammed.

She blew her nose and took a deep breath. "Pedroni knows."

"What?"

"About the Vallotton. I told him. I'm such a rat."

Adrian acknowledged this with a twitch of his shoulders.

"Sure. You're hardly surprised. That's what you'd expect of me. You'd be quite right."

He made no reply.

"But I retracted it," she said in her defense. "I said you and Strasser were playing a joke." And when he still said nothing, she added meekly, "But I'm not sure he believed me."

"No, he didn't," Weynfeldt said now.

She looked at him, startled.

"He's demanding 1.2 million."

It took her a moment to calm down again. "The bastard! You can't pay. Leave him to me."

Adrian smiled. "Too late."

As if on cue the doorbell rang. "Don't move from this spot till I come and get you," Weynfeldt ordered.

It took over an hour for Adrian Weynfeldt to explain the situation to the two police officers, somewhat intimidated by the size of the blackmail sum and the apartment. They agreed to meet next day at the station to sign the statement and take fingerprints for reference purposes.

Before they left, Weynfeldt fetched Lorena from the Von der Mühll room and introduced her with the words, "This is Frau Steiner. Perhaps she should come with me to the station tomorrow. You will find a lot of her fingerprints on the notes as she helped me count them."

37

IT WAS THE WARMEST MARCH DAY SINCE RECORDS BEGAN, a hundred and fifty years ago. The temperature had officially been measured at 79.3°F. In the taxi Strasser had taken, the air-conditioning was on. As soon as he got out he started sweating in his black suit.

Baier's house looked abandoned. A few of the windows had their shutters closed, the rest were missing their curtains. He rang the bell. The house remained still. He rang again, impatient this time. He still heard nothing.

Baier had been stringing him along with the payment. He hadn't received the money himself yet, he had claimed. And Strasser had been stupid enough to believe this. It was only today, leafing through the catalogue by chance, that he happened upon the terms and conditions. There he read that the buyer was obliged to pay the full sum immediately following the auction.

The old man was trying to take him for a ride. Which is why he was here; Strasser would not be sidetracked any longer.

He pressed the button once more, keeping his thumb on it a long time. As he released it he heard sounds from inside. A door squeaked, then he heard footsteps on wooden stairs.

Frau Almeida opened the door. She was pale and

furious. "What do you want?" she asked, without greeting him.

"Herr Baier owes me something and I would like to
collect it." Before she could make any reply he walked
past her up the stairs. He knew how to get to the salon
where the old man sat.

The house was empty. On the walls were the bleached
rectangles Baier's collection of pictures had left. The
stair carpets were missing; only the brass rods which had
held them in place remained.

The door to the salon stood open. The room was
stuffed with furniture. A disheveled bed stood there,
and a pile of packing cases.

Frau Almeida had now entered the room. "The
things he wanted to take to Lake Como. He would only
have had two rooms there."

"What's going on? Where is he?"

"When I got here today he was lying in bed. First
I thought he was sleeping; he'd been complaining he
felt tired a lot recently. This crazy weather was playing
havoc with his circulation. Then I realized he wasn't
breathing any more. They took him away an hour ago."
She paused. "The move was to have been tomorrow."

The most respectful response Rolf Strasser could find
to this was: "Shit!"

He looked round the room. The canvas reproductions of Baier's collection were standing all around. The
Vallotton hung in its usual spot above the bureau, as if
nothing had happened. "Who will get everything?" he
asked the housekeeper.

"There are two heirs. But there isn't much left. And

the pictures are all as fake as that one you copied for him there."

Strasser squeezed between the furniture and boxes to get closer to the picture.

No second period, after Vallotton's surname. Cast-iron relief like a little ass. A little ass seen from the right. Strasser's Vallotton.

38

It was all terribly banal.

Pedroni was lying in bed in his apartment, Schraubenstrasse 22b, third floor. He wasn't alone. To his right lay Svetlana, a Russian girl he had met the previous night at Megaherz, a strip club. To his left lay Salo, a Filipina, who couldn't be much older than the Russian girl, although he could never tell with Asian women. He had met her in the same way.

It was six in the morning. He wasn't sure how long he'd slept. They had come home pretty early. He'd extracted the two women from the proprietor before two, along with an extra bottle of champagne each, but of course they hadn't gone to sleep as soon as they arrived at the apartment.

Anyway, when the doorbell rang it was six in the morning. Pedroni didn't respond. He wasn't expecting anyone. Certainly not at this time of the morning.

The bell rang again. He ignored it again. He might not have been home. He might have stayed the night with Svetlana or Salo. Then he wouldn't have heard the bell anyway. So he decided not to move, which was an easy decision.

Now there was a knock on the apartment door.

Till this point he had assumed that whoever it was, was standing at the door to the building, on the street.

Now he knew that wasn't the case. So it must be one of the neighbors. Even less reason to clamber over Svetlana or Salo at six in the morning.

There was a louder knock. And now he heard a muffled male voice. It was saying his name. Saying something about "no point" and "know you're in there." And something about "police."

Police?

Police.

He decide to get up after all. Climbed over Svetlana, treading on her hair, to which she said something loud in Russian, found his trousers and slipped into them.

The knocking had gotten louder now, and the voice blunter.

The police? This could only be a mistake of some kind. Or it was about his two visitors. It couldn't be about the 1.2 million. Weynfeldt had too much to lose to report him.

"Wait a minute!" he was forced to shout, as the voice was now saying something about "gain entry using force."

He turned the key and was confronted with the superior strength of a great many police officers. In two seconds he was wearing handcuffs, in ten they had found Svetlana and Salo, and after around fifty, the 1.2. It was still in Weynfeldt's little case. And this was placed at the bottom of his wardrobe. Minus six thousand for the last twelve hours' expenditure.

He took this all in vaguely, through the pulsating haze of his hangover. And distantly he heard himself repeating, "I want to report a serious case of art fraud."

39

ADRIAN WEYNFELDT ALREADY SAW REGULARITY AS LIFE-prolonging; all the more so when it came to the repetition of healthy activity. So of course once the fitness room was finished he spent half an hour there every morning before breakfast.

He had tried each of the muscle-training, body-building machines only once, and decided to continue leaving it to his tailor to improve his figure.

But he had taken a liking to one of the machines: The cross-trainer. A black monster with a huge flywheel you set in motion using two coupling rods, like the wheels of a steam train. The rods were equipped with two platforms, one for each foot, and two poles, one for each hand. Rowing with the arms and stepping with the feet, you turned the wheel and soon fell into a rounded, harmonic rhythm.

Obviously the machine was equipped with electronic devices and displays; it could be programmed for various training schedules, various degrees of difficulty and resistance. But that overstretched Adrian's technical abilities, and he confined himself to binding the heart rate monitor round his chest, pressing the quick start button and walking for fifteen minutes without letting his pulse go under 85 or over 140, the heart rate training zone recommended by his doctor.

While Adrian Weynfeldt exercised on this cross-trainer, the little speakers mounted on the ceiling played a compilation of what Luc Neri claimed was the best classical music to jog to. At the moment it was the overture to Rossini's *William Tell*. It was around seven in the morning, a rainy day in June. The eccentric spring, seesawing between wintry and tropical weather, had given way to a summer of nonstop rain.

It was barely three months since those events, but to Adrian Weynfeldt it felt like a small eternity. However much they had stirred him up at the time, now he saw them as a tiny bump on the smooth asphalt of his life's road. Although a lot had changed since then, these were changes which, however strangely they stuck out, had not altered the larger contours.

The Thursday lunch club was still meeting regularly. Kando was still militant and unshakable in her belief in the cinematic genius of her Claudio. He in turn seemed somewhat philosophical, which made him nicer to talk to, and a better listener. *Working Title: Hemingway's Suitcase* was now undergoing treatment from a second script doctor and, as Talberger the producer put it, the prognosis was not good.

Karin Winter had plans for a new store in a better location which, as the tacit shareholder without voting rights, Adrian Weynfeldt approved of. Luc Neri saw the possible move as the opportunity for the long overdue relaunch of the bookstore's Internet presence, and had already designed some trial versions. At the moment he and Karin weren't together—or perhaps they were. Adrian couldn't keep up any more.

Kaspar Casutt had put his fee for designing Weynfeldt's fitness room into entering an architectural competition way out of his league, and was reliant again on occasional donations to meet his everyday costs.

Alice Waldner had achieved unexpected fame. Her steel sculpture *Toto and Something Yellow,* which had stood for many years without causing offense, high and mighty, in the forecourt of one of the city's administrative buildings, was ruined overnight by graffiti. Or improved. That was the crux of the argument which began on local radio and TV but eventually made it to the most important arts broadcasting program on public television. Alice had appeared for over two minutes and, as Adrian had continually assured her, looked gorgeous.

Rolf Strasser was in Venice, California. He had only survived two weeks in the Marquesas—island rage. On the way back he had gotten waylaid in Los Angeles, where he made contact with a group of artists, in particular a Chinese performer called Syun, as he told Weynfeldt enthusiastically in his e-mails.

Before his departure he had been able to unequivocally identify the Vallotton from Klaus Baier's estate as his own work, executed as a commission. This and the statement, attested by a notary, from the anonymous collector Number 33 saying he had no doubts that his purchase was genuine, led Theo L. Pedroni to drop the false accusations against both Dr. Adrian Weynfeldt and Frau Lorena Steiner on the advice of his lawyer.

In light of his previous convictions and the severity of the sentence anticipated, Pedroni himself was still in custody awaiting trial.

Weynfeldt had indeed succeeded in getting Véronique a salary increase. She was investing it mainly in her A-wardrobe, as she called the clothes she wore in her slender phases. For interpersonal reasons Adrian silently wished for the return of the B-wardrobe.

The cross-trainer announced that the fifteen minutes were up and the cool-down stage had begun. Adrian reduced his speed.

Within his older circle of friends there were few changes to be noted. Luckily, as for people their age, things seldom changed for the better.

Except for Mereth Widler. Having tried in vain throughout her life to shock her friends, she finally succeeded, just two months after her husband's death, when a man fifteen years younger than her moved in, with whom she freely admitted she had been having a liaison for over a decade.

Adrian's cardio training was over. He toweled the sweat from his face and switched the music off. Now came the best part of his morning workout: the contemplative part.

He sat in the comfortable easy chair by Max Werner Moser, an original from 1931, the only item from his furniture collection he kept in this room, and devoted himself to contemplation.

The yellow and brown patterned carpet, lit by a low light source somewhere to the rear right, outside the picture. The strong shadows in the yellow and mauve turmoil of the carelessly flung dress and petticoat. The piece of lilac clothing from which, very naked in the glare of this sole light source, the woman's torso rose.

MARTIN SUTER

The warm red of the glowing fire behind the glazed doors of the *salamandre*.

And in the right-hand top corner of the stove, the cast-iron relief, a tiny bud—or a tiny behind.

A small ass seen from the left.

A very intimate scene. A very private painting.

Adrian Weynfeldt sat for a good while immersed in this vision, and felt happy.

And like every morning, the happiness of the art enthusiast and collector contemplating the work was mixed with the happiness of the businessman at its price: 4.64 million, take away the 1.95 from Baier and the fifty-thousand from Lorena.

He heard the door handle move. Then there was a knock. "Just a second!" he called, stood up and slid the middle section of the floor-to-ceiling mirrors back in front of the painting, till it closed with a soft click and formed a smooth wall, flush to the other two. Then he unlocked the door and opened it.

Lorena was standing outside. She was wearing Lycra pants, one of his blue tailor-made shirts, sleeves rolled up, and a black hairband holding her unkempt hair back. She was clearly carrying out the threat she had been making for weeks, to start training in the mornings herself.

She looked sleepy, her eyes were swollen, her black mascara faded, allowing her russet lashes to glow through. There was a heavy sleep mark on her left cheek, which had undoubtedly annoyed her when she'd looked in the mirror. The tiny creases around her eyes were more numerous and visible now, without makeup. She looked so beautiful he had to kiss her.

"Why do you always lock yourself in?" she asked. "Are you keeping secrets from me?"

"Yes," he smiled.

"And you find that okay?"

"Yes."

I would like to thank Dr. Hans-Peter Keller, Swiss art specialist at Christie's Zürich, for his insights into the world of auctions and art experts and for patiently checking the plausibility of the fictional. And Marina Ducrey for her stunning catalogue raisonné (*Felix Vallotton, 1865-1925: L'oeuvre peint*). And my editor, Ursula Baumhauer, for the pleasant mixture of friendliness and professionalism she brought to our work together. And my wife, Margrith Nay Suter, for her detailed criticism, and for being willing and able to relieve me of a few fatherly duties while this novel was being written.

MARTIN SUTER

THE 6:41 TO PARIS BY JEAN-PHILIPPE BLONDEL
Cécile, a stylish 47-year-old, has spent the weekend visiting her parents outside Paris. By Monday morning, she's exhausted. These trips back home are stressful and she settles into a train compartment with an empty seat beside her. But it's soon occupied by a man she recognizes as Philippe Leduc, with whom she had a passionate affair that ended in her brutal humiliation 30 years ago. In the fraught hour and a half that ensues, Cécile and Philippe hurtle towards the French capital in a psychological thriller about the pain and promise of past romance.

ON THE RUN WITH MARY BY JONATHAN BARROW
Shining moments of tender beauty punctuate this story of a youth on the run after escaping from an elite English boarding school. At London's Euston Station, the narrator meets a talking dachshund named Mary and together they're off on escapades through posh Mayfair streets and jaunts in a Rolls-Royce. But the youth soon realizes that the seemingly sweet dog is a handful; an alcoholic, nymphomaniac, drug-addicted mess who can't stay out of pubs or off the dance floor. *On the Run with Mary* mirrors the horrors and the joys of the terrible 20th century.

OBLIVION BY SERGEI LEBEDEV
In one of the first 21st century Russian novels to probe the legacy of the Soviet prison camp system, a young man travels to the vast wastelands of the Far North to uncover the truth about a shadowy neighbor who saved his life, and whom he knows only as Grandfather II. Emerging from today's Russia, where the ills of the past are being forcefully erased from public memory, this masterful novel represents an epic literary attempt to rescue history from the brink of oblivion.

ANIMAL INTERNET BY ALEXANDER PSCHERA

Some 50,000 creatures around the globe—including whales, leopards, flamingoes, bats and snails—are being equipped with digital tracking devices. The data gathered and studied by major scientific institutes about their behavior will warn us about tsunamis, earthquakes and volcanic eruptions, but also radically transform our relationship to the natural world. Contrary to pessimistic fears, author Alexander Pschera sees the Internet as creating a historic opportunity for a new dialogue between man and nature.

THE LAST SUPPER BY KLAUS WIVEL

Alarmed by the oppression of 7.5 million Christians in the Middle East, journalist Klaus Wivel traveled to Iraq, Lebanon, Egypt, and the Palestinian territories to learn about their fate. He found a minority under threat of death and humiliation, desperate in the face of rising Islamic extremism and without hope their situation will improve. An unsettling account of a severely beleaguered religious group living, so it seems, on borrowed time. Wivel asks, Why have we not done more to protect these people?

GUYS LIKE ME BY DOMINIQUE FABRE

Dominique Fabre, born in Paris and a life-long resident of the city, exposes the shadowy, anonymous lives of many who inhabit the French capital. In this quiet, subdued tale, a middle-aged office worker, divorced and alienated from his only son, meets up with two childhood friends who are similarly adrift. He's looking for a second act to his mournful life, seeking the harbor of love and a true connection with his son. Set in palpably real Paris streets that feel miles away from the City of Light, a stirring novel of regret and absence, yet not without a glimmer of hope.

KILLING AUNTIE BY **ANDRZEJ BURSA**

A young university student named Jurek, with no particular ambitions or talents, finds himself with nothing to do. After his doting aunt asks the young man to perform a small chore, he decides to kill her for no good reason other than, perhaps, boredom. This short comedic masterpiece combines elements of Dostoevsky, Sartre, Kafka, and Heller, coming together to produce an unforgettable tale of murder and— just maybe—redemption.

I CALLED HIM NECKTIE BY **MILENA MICHIKO FLAŠAR**

Twenty-year-old Taguchi Hiro has spent the last two years of his life living as a hikikomori—a shut-in who never leaves his room and has no human interaction—in his parents' home in Tokyo. As Hiro tentatively decides to reenter the world, he spends his days observing life from a park bench. Gradually he makes friends with Ohara Tetsu, a salaryman who has lost his job. The two discover in their sadness a common bond. This beautiful novel is moving, unforgettable, and full of surprises.

WHO IS MARTHA? BY **MARJANA GAPONENKO**

In this rollicking novel, 96-year-old ornithologist Luka Levadski foregoes treatment for lung cancer and moves from Ukraine to Vienna to make a grand exit in a luxury suite at the Hotel Imperial. He reflects on his past while indulging in Viennese cakes and savoring music in a gilded concert hall. Levadski was born in 1914, the same year that Martha—the last of the now-extinct passenger pigeons—died. Levadski himself has an acute sense of being the last of a species. This gloriously written tale mixes piquant wit with lofty musings about life, friendship, aging and death.

ALL BACKS WERE TURNED BY MAREK HLASKO

Two desperate friends—on the edge of the law—travel to the southern Israeli city of Eilat to find work. There, Dov Ben Dov, the handsome native Israeli with a reputation for causing trouble, and Israel, his sidekick, stay with Ben Dov's younger brother, Little Dov, who has enough trouble of his own. Local toughs are encroaching on Little Dov's business, and he enlists his older brother to drive them away. It doesn't help that a beautiful German widow is rooming next door. A story of passion, deception, violence, and betrayal, conveyed in hard-boiled prose reminiscent of Hammett and Chandler.

ALEXANDRIAN SUMMER BY YITZHAK GORMEZANO GOREN

This is the story of two Jewish families living their frenzied last days in the doomed cosmopolitan social whirl of Alexandria just before fleeing Egypt for Israel in 1951. The conventions of the Egyptian upper-middle class are laid bare in this dazzling novel, which exposes sexual hypocrisies and portrays a vanished polyglot world of horse racing, seaside promenades and nightclubs.

COCAINE BY PITIGRILLI

Paris in the 1920s—dizzy and decadent. Where a young man can make a fortune with his wits ... unless he is led into temptation. Cocaine's dandified hero Tito Arnaudi invents lurid scandals and gruesome deaths, and sells these stories to the newspapers. But his own life becomes even more outrageous when he acquires three demanding mistresses. Elegant, witty and wicked, Pitigrilli's classic novel was first published in Italian in 1921 and retains its venom even today.

Killing the Second Dog by Marek Hlasko

Two down-and-out Polish con men living in Israel in the 1950s scam an American widow visiting the country. Robert, who masterminds the scheme, and Jacob, who acts it out, are tough, desperate men, exiled from their native land and adrift in the hot, nasty underworld of Tel Aviv. Robert arranges for Jacob to run into the widow who has enough trouble with her young son to keep her occupied all day. What follows is a story of romance, deception, cruelty and shame. Hlasko's writing combines brutal realism with smoky, hard-boiled dialogue, in a bleak world where violence is the norm and love is often only an act.

The Missing Year of Juan Salvatierra by Pedro Mairal

At the age of nine, Juan Salvatierra became mute following a horse riding accident. At twenty, he began secretly painting a series of canvases on which he detailed six decades of life in his village on Argentina's frontier with Uruguay. After his death, his sons return to deal with their inheritance: a shed packed with rolls over two miles long. But an essential roll is missing. A search ensues that illuminates links between art and life, with past family secrets casting their shadows on the present.

Fanny von Arnstein: Daughter of the Enlightenment by Hilde Spiel

In 1776 Fanny von Arnstein, the daughter of the Jewish master of the royal mint in Berlin, came to Vienna as an 18-year-old bride. She married a financier to the Austro-Hungarian imperial court, and hosted an ever more splendid salon which attracted luminaries of the day. Spiel's elegantly written and carefully researched biography provides a vivid portrait of a passionate woman who advocated for the rights of Jews, and illuminates a central era in European cultural and social history.

THE GOOD LIFE ELSEWHERE BY VLADIMIR LORCHENKOV

The very funny—and very sad—story of a group of villagers and their tragicomic efforts to emigrate from Europe's most impoverished nation to Italy for work. An Orthodox priest is deserted by his wife for an art-dealing atheist; a mechanic redesigns his tractor for travel by air and sea; and thousands of villagers take to the road on a modern-day religious crusade to make it to the Italian Promised Land. A country where 25 percent of its population works abroad, remittances make up nearly 40 percent of GDP, and alcohol consumption per capita is the world's highest – Moldova surely has its problems. But, as Lorchenkov vividly shows, it's also a country whose residents don't give up easily.

SOME DAY BY SHEMI ZARHIN

On the shores of Israel's Sea of Galilee lies the city of Tiberias, a place bursting with sexuality and longing for love. The air is saturated with smells of cooking and passion. *Some Day* is a gripping family saga, a sensual and emotional feast that plays out over decades. This is an enchanting tale about tragic fates that disrupt families and break our hearts. Zarhin's hypnotic writing renders a painfully delicious vision of individual lives behind Israel's larger national story.

New Vessel Press

To purchase these titles and for more information please visit newvesselpress.com.